EMERALD
GREENE

firecroft bay books

EMERALD GREENE

Instruments of Darkness

Daniel Blythe

EMERALD GREENE: INSTRUMENTS OF DARKNESS

ISBN 978-0-9957761-0-4

First published worldwide by Firecroft Bay Books, UK, in 2017

For my wife, Rachel...
who always believed in Emerald.

And oftentimes, to win us to our harm,
The instruments of darkness tell us truths,
Win us with honest trifles, to betray us
In deepest consequence.

Shakespeare, *Macbeth*, Act I: Scene 3

1
Big Trouble in Little Brockwell

The afternoon sun was warm as Tyler Uttley, aged ten-and-three-quarters, strode down the gentle hill from his parents' farmhouse to the village.

There was a cricket match on the Meadows today. White figures flitted on the sunlit grass, their movements graceful as they fought a very English battle. Tyler, swishing a stick through the hedge as he walked, wondered if he would meet up with his friends later. They might watch the game, he thought, as they ate ice-creams bought from the van which parked by the Green.

In the Post Office, he smiled shyly at Miss Trippett, the young woman behind the counter.

'One of these, please,' Tyler said, holding out a packet of prawn cocktail crisps and not quite looking Miss Trippett in the eye.

The till beeped as she scanned the crisps.

Behind her, the door to the back room was ajar, and Tyler could hear piano music. He knew Miss Trippett's Gran, who was almost blind, would be sitting there, listening to the radio. She'd be smiling calmly as always, maybe tapping a finger. He had to admit that Grandma Trippett made him feel odd, as if she knew stuff about you that she ought not to know, and he was glad he wouldn't have to see her today.

'How's school, Tyler?' Miss Trippett asked. Tyler felt his face glowing. He wondered if she knew – if she could possibly have seen him out by the river last Wednesday, making a fire and building his secret camp, when he was supposed to be in classes.

'Fine, thanks,' Tyler muttered, taking his change from her and avoiding her gaze.

'Off to Westmeadow after the summer, aren't you? Catching the bus with the big boys and girls.'

Tyler shifted from one foot to another. He was not at all sure what to say.

'You're quiet today! Better run along, then.'

'Yes. All right.'

Outside on the pavement, Tyler stopped. He stared down at the packet of prawn cocktail crisps and frowned. Was there something he had forgotten? Something else he was supposed to ask Miss Trippett?

For a second, he had the oddest feeling – a prickling on the back of his neck and the brief sense of a shadow passing over him, as if a bird or a plane had passed between him and the sun.

Squinting, Tyler whirled around, but there was nobody to be seen. The street, unusually, was empty, and only the muffled sounds of the cricket game from the Meadows gave an indication that anyone else was around.

And then – astonishingly, on such a warm and sunny day – Tyler felt himself *shivering*.

A breeze ruffled his hair, now, and he was sure he heard a faint sound, as if something just within the range of his hearing had passed him on the street. The swinging OPEN sign with its ice-cream advert creaked as if lightly pushed.

Tyler looked up and down the street and walked away from the Post Office. He headed down the hill, towards the Meadows, passing the weatherboarded cottages and the small, cluttered window of Mr Bidmead's Antiques Emporium. He shivered a little as he passed that dark, gloomy window, with its ancient photographs and vases and creepy-looking dolls staring out at you. Mr Bidmead scared Tyler a little.

Once or twice, he glanced over his shoulder, up the street towards the edge of the village. Without realising it, he had now quickened his pace.

He wasn't sure why, but when he got to the junction just before the village green, he started to break into a run.

Jessica Mathieson tilted her head, frowned at herself in the hall mirror as she turned from one side to the other. Yeah, not bad, she told herself, watching the unaccustomed glint as her new addition caught the light – not bad at all. The needle had hurt, and she remembered crying out, but Aunt Gabi had been there to hold her hand. There was still the discomfort in her nostril, but she'd been told that it would stop within a few days, and she could live with that.

'I just hope you don't regret this,' said Aunt Gabi, passing behind her in the hall and placing her hands on Jess's shoulders for a second. 'Actually, scrub that – I hope it's *me* that doesn't regret it…' She leaned forward, inspected the adornment. 'You know, I still think it'll be messy when you get a cold.'

'Aunt Gabi!' Jessica folded her arms and pouted in mock disgust. 'Will you please chill out? You said I could have one, and so I've got it. I tell you what – I bet Richie will hate it.'

'Hmmm, well… your young friend's the unfashionable sort.' Gabi twiddled her earring, the single gold hoop she wore to remember her sister Chrissie, Jess's mother, who had died when Jess was just a baby. 'Not that there's anything wrong with that, I hasten to add. Steady, safe young man. Very reliable.'

'Yeah, and just a friend, right?' Jessica reminded her.

Gabi lifted her hands up. 'Darling, I never suggested anything else!' she said, bustling through into the kitchen. 'Anyway,' she added with a wag of her finger, 'at your age you

11

should be concentrating on your studies.'

Jess followed Aunt Gabi into the kitchen. The percolator was hissing away to itself, filling the kitchen with an aroma of organic Kenyan coffee. 'Yeah, yeah. Look, I'm not exactly a slacker, Aunt Gabi.'

'Mmm... do a bit of peeling for us, there's a love!' Gabi threw Jess three large cooking apples in rapid succession. Jess, momentarily off guard, fumbled with them but managed to catch them all. Gabi disappeared behind a cupboard door, but a moment later her tousled blonde head reappeared, her face wearing a frown. Gabi pulled a chair up to the table.

'Jess, love,' she said, her tone softer. 'Actually, would you... sit down for a minute?'

'I'm doing the...' She gestured towards the apples.

'They can wait. Sit down.' Gabi held up the coffee-jug. 'Want some?'

'Please.' Gabi poured out two giant cups. Jess adopted her attentive pose – hair tucked behind one ear and legs folded under her on the dining chair. 'So, what is it, Aunt Gabi?'

'I'm... I just wanted to say that I... well I'm really pleased you came through... you know, all that upset you had.' Gabi carefully placed the cups on the table. 'I'd thought for a while that... well, that you were going to be having problems.'

Jess narrowed her eyes. 'Hang on,' she said, wrapping both hands around her mug. 'Is this one of those adult conversations where I have to work out what you're talking about and you hope I've guessed right? Because we don't do those, right? We agreed.'

'I'm sorry.' Gabi let her arms flop down by her sides and started absently patting her pockets.

Jess knew what she was after. 'And no cigs! We can have a conversation without nicotine. Look, this is about Emerald going away, right?'

'Um...' Gabi started chewing on a pencil. 'Yes.'

'And me getting… well, getting weird?'

'Yes, I suppose so.' Gabi put the pencil down.

'Aunt Gabi, I keep telling you. It's been nearly a year. I'm fine now.'

Lying, she told herself sternly. I'm fine apart from the coldness in my hand, and the strange dreams where I see Emerald Greene, of course.

Jessica opened her eyes wide and met Gabi's gaze firmly. It was a complicit look which acknowledged, unspoken, the odd events which had taken place in Meresbury the previous year, many of were still officially unexplained. It also said that they both remembered Emerald Greene, and that they missed her.

'Listen,' said Gabi hesitantly. 'I was… keeping this as a surprise, but I think I'll tell you now.' She showed her a photo on the tablet. 'What do you think of this?' she asked.

Jess, intrigued, peered at the picture on the website. It showed a sturdy, detached house with a big drive and a lush green lawn. The walls of the house were festooned with red creeper, while climbing roses framed the wooden front door. 'Yes, very nice,' she said.

'It's Rhiannon's house,' Gabi explained. 'You know, my postgrad friend from college?' Gabi, in between shifts at a local supermarket, was completing a part-time MA in Women's Studies at Meresbury College. 'She's going to a summer school in America and, well, she wants someone to house-sit for a few weeks. So I… kind of volunteered.'

'You did?' Jess was surprised.

'Well, yes. It's a beautiful place, out in the sticks. She rents it out, usually, but she's letting me have it free. I can write up my dissertation without any distractions. And what with your sister being off on the hippy trail with her Uni mates… I wondered how you felt about spending a bit of the holidays there?'

'Out in the sticks?' Jess repeated. She wasn't sure about that.

'You can ask a friend, if you like. Bring your bikes, do lots of exploring. What do you think?'

'Um…' Jess felt herself torn. She took a deep gulp of the hot, invigorating coffee to help her think.

She wished Gabi wasn't making her decide about this right now. A village miles from anywhere would be a bit of a culture-shock. She was used to the bustle of the city. She had been looking forward to a summer of watching street entertainers, hanging out in cafés, bowling, skating, gigs. Then again, Jess knew she wasn't going to get a holiday until the French exchange, and that was months off – so this might be the next best thing. And, as Gabi said, with her sister Kat in the Far East for three months, 38 Chadwick Road was going to be a bit quiet anyway.

'It wouldn't necessarily be for all seven weeks,' Gabi pointed out. 'You'd still have some time back here.'

'Okay,' she said. 'Why not?' She frowned, peered at the photograph again. 'It's a big house,' she said.

'Yes, Rhiannon's husband was a banker. Paid her off nicely when he ran off with his floozy.'

Jess giggled. 'So what's the place called?'

Gabi scrolled down the page, pointed. 'Rose Cottage.'

'Oh, great. It says it's *quiet*. And picture-skew.'

'And what?'

'Picture-skew – look, here.'

'I think you mean pictur*esque*, darling. Rhymes with *desk*.'

'Gabi, I know. I was joking… Well, I s'pose I could give it a go.'

'Oh, good. Thanks, Jess. You'll enjoy it, I know you will… I'll tell Rhiannon when I go into college this afternoon. She'll be thrilled.'

Jess didn't hear, though, as she was still gazing absently

at the photo. '*Little Brockwell*,' she murmured. 'I just ⬛
not as dull as it looks...'

'Don't forget to ask a friend!' Gabi added, as she bust⬛
out with an armful of washing.

Little Brockwell lay sixty miles north of the city of Meresbury. To the west, the village was bounded by an escarpment with a giant figure of a horse carved into its chalk surface, while to the east lay gentler slopes, leading down to the marshes and the sea. There was a church in honey-gold stone, a cluster of shops, a war memorial and a small school. A red phone-box stood next to the Green, while across the road from the church was the pub, the Dark Horse, famed for its real ales. The properties, meanwhile, were an English dream: timbered cottages, Victorian mansions and modern homes with double garages.

Little Brockwell had won the National Village Contest three times in a row and was the holder of the British Gardens Cup. Its gardens – so well-tended that they almost shone – were adorned with perfect roses, the colours of claret, ivory and gold.

And yet not everything in Little Brockwell was so beautiful.

In the centre of the Green stood an old oak tree, about six metres high. It had a thick, knotted trunk and impossibly twisted branches. Impossibly gnarled and ancient, the tree seemed to squat on the green, an unsettling presence.

It was called the Whispering Tree, and it was the last remnant of a great forest which had covered the Mere Valley some three thousand years ago. Its bark was a deep brown, almost black. Even in the brightest sunshine, the Tree repelled light, casting a clean-cut shadow of itself on the Green – a shadow almost as solid and dark as the Tree itself.

It was said that you could lean in and hear the tree whispering – with the voices of those who had lived in the

...g past.

...be another story going around, a ridiculous ...ich gets told in the corners of pubs by old ...d a pint or five. People said that on some ...er's Eve, for one – the Whispering Tree ...when it moved, lumbering through the streets, it wheezed like an old man, dragging its roots behind it like ancient limbs. Nobody knew exactly what it was said to be looking for, and yet some muttered their suspicions…

There was a time, in earlier centuries, when such superstitious rumblings would have been taken seriously. But in the twenty-first century, Little Brockwell, despite the trappings of heritage, liked to think of itself as a modern, active place. The residents debated broadband speed, traveller camps, road-building and housing schemes. Little Brockwell had a dynamic Rector, too, getting more young people involved in the church, nudging the attendance figures up, and being very persuasive with those who were half-willing to help with activities. It was a thriving community – a very English backwater, somewhere to belong and contribute to.

But it was still an ancient place. And ancient places, especially in the green and shady heart of England, guarded secrets…

Kate Trippett was happy.

She had been running the Post Office and General Stores for a year, now, ever since she'd come here to Little Brockwell to look after her Gran.

Kate had believed that she would be stuck with the grind of her London job for ever – earning money which she never had time to spend, stuck in a soulless city, returning alone each day to her small bare flat. Her parents' decision to give up the Village Stores and Post Office had been a blessing in disguise. Kate never regretted her decision to retreat here, to live the rural life in the spacious flat above the shop – for now, Kate was her own boss. And there had been a man in London, an unhappy romance she was glad to see the back of.

She mostly ran the place single-handed, although her teenage cousin, Ben, manned the counter in the holidays and Zoe Parks, a young mum from the village, helped out at busy times.

Her new life had its hardships. There was the early start to catch the first delivery of newspapers, and burning the midnight oil to work out the accounts. And in the winter, she had discovered, the village became a crisis centre. Kate recalled dark mornings of struggling to light the gas-stove with her gloves on while customers queued outside in the snow, ready to strip the shelves of her meagre stocks of tinned fruit, toilet roll and matches.

But she was happy here. 'It's a good place,' she had told her mum on the phone. 'Everyone's pleased there's still a Trippett at the Post Office. They've all been really welcoming.'

Yes, it was a good place. Or so it seemed.

Kate didn't listen to gossip. She liked the odd glass of white wine in the Dark Horse, but she always laughed at the tales told by the old guys at the bar. The old legends surrounding the Whispering Tree, that strange, dark oak in the centre of the Green. The ongoing gossip about the hasty departure of the schoolmistress, Miss Davisham. And the new stories, like the ones which had started in the last few weeks, ever since that band of travellers had passed through the village.

'Ignore the old fools, Kate,' Harry at the bar would say, winking as he poured her Chardonnay – but then he'd be back there at the other end of the bar, pulling the pints and laughing and telling tales along with them.

Kate was made of strong stuff. All the same, something unnerved her as she locked up the Post Office that afternoon, having left Gran with a cup of tea at her side and the radio tuned to the racing.

Kate paused, and her instincts made her look up beyond the gabled roofs of Little Brockwell, up past the Norman church tower and into the sky. But no – all she could see was a pair of ravens, circling above the trees. The birds headed westwards, heading towards the chalk horse on the escarpment.

'Letting it get to you...' she muttered. She buttoned her handbag and set off down the hill.

She waved to Mr Bidmead, who was polishing the windows of his antique shop. The old man peered through half-moon glasses and waved back. As she passed the Meadows, she saw the cricketers retiring for tea and gave them a friendly wave too. She saw the Reverend Fenella Parsloe scuttling round the Green, her robes billowing behind her as she headed from the Rectory to the church. Kate recalled the tales from the pub of how the village had been in uproar when they were first given a woman Rector... Not that anyone minded these days, now that the Reverend Parsloe had proved her worth. Decades on, women were being Bishops, and Fenella Parsloe was tipped for future greatness.

Something crunched under Kate's feet. She reached down to pick up the discarded crisp-packet. Honestly! She expected litter-louts in the city, but that sort of thing was never tolerated in Little Brockwell. Especially as the bin (engraved to mark the most recent National Village title) was only a few steps away.

The packet felt heavier than she expected. Kate frowned, peered at it, smoothed it out in her hand. Now she saw that it was not an empty packet at all, but an unopened one – prawn cocktail crisps, the same brand she sold every day in the shop. The crisps, still sealed inside, had been mashed – crushed almost to a powder.

An odd, prickling sensation crept up Kate's spine as she

stood there in the afternoon sunlight, her own long shadow falling like a question-mark across the path. She paused for a moment, as if deciding what to do – then, she slipped the crushed crisps into her handbag and hurried on her way to the glass of chilled Chardonnay which she knew Harry would have waiting for her.

In Jessica's dream, she was running through the London Underground.

The ground beneath her feet was squelchy, though, like a swamp. She found herself down on all fours, crawling through sticky mud to the platform, hearing the train slowly approaching. There were no other people on the platform.

Then, one of the advertising hoardings on the far side of the platform came to life, swirling into a shapeless vortex. The shape took on features. Bright red hair, streaming in an invisible wind. Blue glasses perched on a beaky nose above a high-cheekboned, intelligent face. A slim figure, encased in a flowing dress made of –

'Emerald Greene!' she gasped.

'*Please*,' said the watery figure, '*I have not much time. Some-something has gone wrong, Jessica Mathieson. You have to help-help-help me.*'

Something odd was happening when the figure spoke – its voice started to jump, like a badly buffering YouTube video.

'Emerald?' Jess wasn't sure if she spoke her friend's name or if she just allowed it to resonate in her head, like an idea becoming an image. The name was spinning on her retina, bright green letters in a sphere. *Emerald!*

'*Yes, yes. We do not have time-time-time for this. There has been a mal-mal-malfunction.*' The image was stuttering visually as well as in words – its gestures became jerky, as if it was somehow sticking. '*You are in grave danger. I sense a great dar-dar-dar-dar-dar-*'

The image of Emerald Greene was opening and closing its mouth in an endless loop, the word stuck there.

'Dar-dar-dar-dar-'

The figure was flickering, like a TV picture with poor reception. It fizzed and crackled at the edges.

'What are you trying to say, Emerald?' Jess shouted. 'Dart? Dartmouth? What?'

'Dar-dar-dark! Darkness!'

The resolution of the image suddenly fizzed into a shower of droplets, scattering across the surface of the squelchy platform with an almighty splash as if a huge object had hit the surface of the water.

The noise of the splash grew and grew, filling the Tube station, echoing off the roof and hissing in Jess's ears. Emerald's voice, above it, was there – distant, but there.

I will need – your help –

Jess was sure that she had hit the bed, thudding as if she had fallen from a great height.

She heard herself gasp, and then she was sitting up in a too-hot duvet, perspiration soaking her face and her heart going *thump thump*. She was safe in her attic bedroom.

Jess took a moment, held her breath. There was an odd, blue glow in the bedroom, which wasn't coming from the street-lamps outside – and the hissing sound was still there. Suddenly frightened, she twisted round and saw the swirling dots of the TV screen over on her bureau. Of course! The old-fashioned, 1990s portable television in the room. She had started watching DVDs late at night and falling asleep before they finished. She found it more reassuring than Netflix on the phone or tablet, more friendly and personal. The DVD had popped out of its tray and the old screen had defaulted to hissing, swirling static.

She blinked, looked at her clock: 4:52am. Jess staggered to the washbasin, glowered at herself in the mirror as she turned on the tap and splashed tepid water on her face. Droplets spattered the mirror, distorting her reflection. Her stomach lurched as her mind flashed back to the dream. Or vision. Whatever it had been.

'Write down your dreams, they say,' she muttered. 'Fifteen seconds, that's all you've got before they're gone for ever.' She shivered. 'Well, I've not forgotten it yet.' Jess wiped the mirror clean and scowled at herself. 'You're talking to yourself again. Sign of madness, you know.'

She dried her face, tied her hair back and got back into bed. She knew she wouldn't be able to get back to sleep, so she put the television on in the background, then grabbed her phone and scrolled through her favourite sites. On the TV, local news jabbered: a pig farmer in the Mere Valley was being investigated for a major tax fraud, while a pale, distressed-looking couple were talking about how their son had been traumatised by a dark, spectral figure on the road. Jess, her mind still on her dream, didn't really take it all in, and at just after five-thirty in the morning, she got up and made herself some breakfast.

It had definitely been her, Jess thought excitedly as she buttered her toast. *Emerald Greene*. The strange, otherworldly girl she and her friend Richie had met last year. A girl with no past and no future, who drove a green Dormobile camper-van. A girl who had seen the mysterious ways the Universe hung together and had mended the broken fabric of Time. She and her mysterious black cat, Anoushka, who wore an emerald in his collar, had been fugitives from... where?...

After Emerald left – and Jess still hadn't told anyone, except Richie, about exactly *how* she had gone, blinking into thin air as she walked through a magic, invisible barrier back to her secret mansion hidden in a fold in time – odd things had happened to Jessica Mathieson.

During the course of the strange events which she and

Emerald Greene had investigated, Jess's right hand had momentarily felt the cold, unearthly hand of a witch-wraith, a creature halfway between life and death.

She couldn't tell Aunt Gabi, of course, because Aunt Gabi would never have believed half of what had happened, even though she'd seen some of it with her own eyes. Adults were – well, they were just like that. But her hand had started to tingle again since Christmas and New Year – not continually, but at certain times, almost as if it was trying to tell her something.

And now, this was a third. Emerald Greene, like a satellite TV picture on a bad day. *In her head*. Things were getting weirder.

She ran into Gabi on the landing. Jess's aunt looked like a partied-out rock star this morning, her blonde hair all over the place and her mascara still on from the night before.

'You're an early bird,' Gabi croaked, staggering towards the bathroom.

'Revision,' Jess said, sounding perky.

Gabi ran a hand through her dishevelled hair. 'Crikey,' she muttered to the world in general as she pushed open the bathroom door. 'At this time of year? I always said that school of yours was too competitive...'

The Reverend Fenella Parsloe, Rector of Little Brockwell, poured Earl Grey tea into two bone-china cups. 'Now, then,' she said. 'What can I do for you, Kate?'

'I hope you don't mind my just dropping in like this. It's... not the sort of thing I normally do.'

'Please, please,' said the Rector, a plump woman with a steel-grey cap of hair. 'Like I said, it's what I'm here for.' She wore a baggy old cardigan over her clerical collar, with a woollen skirt and flat shoes. Chunky glasses sat on her round, comical face, but a fierce intelligence burned in her eyes.

'Thank you,' Kate said. 'I do appreciate it.'

It was nine-thirty in the morning, and the sunlight was streaming in through the windows of the Rector's study. After serving the morning rush of commuters and schoolchildren, Kate had left Zoe in charge of the shop and set off to see the Rector. She was troubled, and she needed to talk.

'Do sit down,' the Rector added, gesturing with the teapot.

Kate looked for somewhere to sit. Every chair seemed to be piled with folders, documents and books.

'Oh, just move those,' the Rector said, and shoved a pile of papers off the nearest swivel-chair. Her eyes crinkled mischievously. 'Ironic, really. Jesus liked to keep things simple, but some of his followers do seem in love with paperwork. Not me. I like getting out and meeting people.'

'You must have a lot to do,' Kate said, sipping her tea.

Most clergy these days had more than one parish, and the Reverend Parsloe had three to look after. Little Brockwell was the largest, then there was the tiny hamlet of Northmarsh, about six miles away over the chalk ridge, and finally the medium-sized village of Burton Cobbleigh to the west.

'Thank goodness for my car,' said the Rector, perching herself on the edge of her desk. Beside her, the laptop was displaying a screen-saver, a purple vortex of flying doves. 'So… business good in the shop?'

'Yes… yes, it's good. People are very loyal.'

'They remember your mother and father. Fine people… You must find Little Brockwell very quiet, after the bustle of the big city?'

'Well, yes – but that's why I like it.' Kate hesitated, unsure how to proceed. 'Reverend Parsloe, I'm so worried about Tyler.'

The Rector frowned. 'We are all very, very concerned. He's not been the same since the incident. And I have said prayers… many prayers.'

'Tyler won't say what he saw. To anyone.' Kate had more faith in the police than in prayers, but she wisely didn't say so. 'But he was in the Post Office that afternoon, and he was fine. I told the policeman all about that and I gave them the crisp packet I'd found.'

Tyler Uttley had twenty-four hours in his life which could not be accounted for. He had gone missing one afternoon last week – shortly after speaking to Kate in the shop – and then had returned, walking into his house with no explanation, a blank expression on his face. He had spent a day in bed, fussed over by his exhausted, relieved but still worried parents and by several doctors. Nobody had been able to find anything wrong.

He just seemed… different, somehow.

Withdrawn, cold. Not himself.

The Rector sat down heavily on her chair. 'That boy,' she said. 'He hasn't always been easy to deal with.'

'So… you know he's been bunking off school?' Kate asked, sipping her tea.

'Oh, he's done it again and again. You've seen him?'

'Several times.'

'Thing is, it's difficult to get the parents to monitor him. Dad works shifts, mum's an office cleaner in Westmeadow…' The Rector folded her hands in her lap. 'The boy's always had to get his own breakfast and get himself to school.'

'No brothers or sisters?' Kate asked.

'No… But if he did run away, and come back for some reason, then none of his friends had an inkling. They all seem as baffled by it as we are.' The Rector folded her hands in her lap, sat back in her chair. 'One thing did bother me slightly, though,' she added, nodding to herself and gazing thoughtfully into the dappled sun-pattern on her carpet.

'What's that?' asked Kate.

'Tyler's mother mentioned that he used to have…

nightmares.'

'Nightmares?' echoed Kate. 'Well, okay… But surely lots of kids…'

'Yes. But these were quite bad ones. He regularly used to wake up, screaming, for no apparent reason. I believe the technical term is actually "night terrors"… They were quite concerned about it for a while. In fact, in the Whitsun half-term, they took him to a clinic specialising in sleep disorders – night terrors in particular.'

'Could they… do anything for him?'

'Yes and no… Mrs Uttley – Jen – said they were able to reassure her that Tyler wasn't abnormal, that the nightmares were a sign of a healthy imagination and nothing to worry about. They couldn't find a cause, though. Anyway, I understood he'd been getting better.' The Rector smiled. 'So it was probably nothing to do with that.'

'Probably,' Kate said, smiling gratefully, and took a sip of her tea.

Kate's mind was buzzing as she left the Rectory, and she felt wide awake thanks to the tea.

Her red Metro was parked, as usual, in the street outside Orchard Cottages, round the corner from the shop. This morning she needed to go to the shops in Westmeadow, the market-town about fifteen miles away. As she got into her car and checked her shopping list, she kept thinking about Tyler and that crushed packet of crisps.

Something shone slightly in the rear-view mirror. Kate frowned. The glint of light had come from one of the distant hills – up beyond the copse, by Corlett's Farm.

There it was again - sunlight reflecting, as if on a telescope or a pair of binoculars. Kate slid her sunroof open, poked her head up and turned towards the hills, steadying herself on the warm car roof. Slipping her sunglasses on, she watched the gleam of light carefully, trying to pinpoint its position. She felt a creeping unease as she realised the person with the binoculars could be looking directly at her.

After a few seconds the glint faded, although Kate was sure it had come from near Corlett's Farm. She slid back down into the car and started the engine.

Half an hour later, when she was lugging her shopping through the busy centre of Westmeadow, she remembered something odd. Mr Corlett had died the previous year - and his farm was now empty and abandoned.

Casey Burgess had never felt so alone.

At twelve, she imagined she should feel big, able to protect her younger brother and sister when her mum had a go at them. She didn't, though. She felt small, helpless, no more able to stand up to her mum than when she was ten or eleven.

It was usually by the third or fourth whisky that the sneering tone entered her mum's voice, and the slurred insults started coming. *Worthless. You waste of space. Get out of my sight.* Well, tonight, Casey had taken her at her word. Here she was, now, out of her mum's sight – in fact, out of the sight of just about everyone.

She was shivering on Lovers' Seat, the old, mossy wooden bench high above Little Brockwell with its view across the valley.

It was strangely cold for a July night – something to do with it being cloudless, Casey remembered? That had stuck from Geography, anyway. She zipped her fleece right up to the neck and hugged herself as she watched the lights of the village twinkling below her. One of those lights would be her mum's bedroom, she thought, where the TV would be blasting out some American film and her mum would be snoring away, probably with a glass rolling round on the floor. The odd sound washed up towards her – a shout, a laugh, a slammed car door. Somewhere down there, people were getting on with their normal lives.

Across the valley, the chalk horse shone in the moonlight. It made Casey shiver slightly and she averted her eyes.

She took out her phone, toying with the idea of calling her mum and saying she was up here. But there was no signal in this part of Little Brockwell. So instead, Casey stared up at the moon, which was low and orange in the sky tonight. Ragged clouds raced across it, like ships racing on the sea at sunset. She decided she wanted to be on the move, too – not stuck here doing nothing.

She hurried back to the road, hopped into the lane and wondered where she should head for. Change jangled in her pocket. How much? Three or four pounds at most, she thought. Maybe just enough to get to her dad's place in Westmeadow – but she'd missed the last bus tonight, she knew that much.

Casey stopped, rummaged through her pockets for anything vaguely useful, anything that might give her a sign of what to do.

Some chewing-gum. Some tissues. A handful of coins – yes, about four pounds. Her lucky silver bracelet. And her mum's gold cigarette-lighter, embossed with 'S.B.' – Shona Burgess – which Casey had pinched, having a vague idea in her head about needing to light a fire.

A chill wind swept down the lane, ruffling Casey's hair and cutting through her fleece. What was up? This wasn't July weather. Then, her keen ears picked out a sound, coming from some way behind her on the dark road.

The sound of – *hoofbeats*?

Surely not. She listened harder. Yes, hooves drumming, drumming on the tarmac, as if the horse was galloping very fast indeed. Casey, who had lived in the country all her life, knew what horses sounded like, and this one sounded *odd*. As Casey listened, she became aware of an echoing, metallic edge to the hoofbeats.

She did not have time to dwell on this, though, as a sensation of terror had started to creep through her whole body.

Casey took a millisecond to make the decision. She turned and ran. Back down the hill, down towards the glittering lights of Little Brockwell.

She heard her own feet pounding the tarmac, felt the thudding shocks pounding through her trainers and into her calves as she sprinted. She didn't know why she was running. She just had to. Because whatever was coming down the lane behind her was utterly terrifying.

The galloping horse's hooves grew louder and louder. Casey, hearing her breath echoing raggedly in her head and feeling it burn like liquid fire in her lungs, risked a glance over her shoulder – but saw nothing.

Her mind was racing like her feet. Casey Burgess was a fighter, a survivor. She stood up to girls at school who picked on her, who called her *skank*, called her *alkie's girl*. She gave as good as she got, which had led her into trouble. But she could think on the move.

The thundering hooves were right behind her. She could hear something else, now – *breathing*. Heavy, regular, like an animal, but colder and more evil-sounding than any horse she had ever heard.

There was a patch of grass with a signpost creaking in the wind. Through the trees, she could see the lights of a farmhouse set back from the road. Casey caught hold of the signpost and spun herself into the ditch – she felt soft, cold mud beneath her body, gripped the thorny plants and felt her palms prickle with pain.

From her cover, Casey watched and listened.

The galloping hoofbeats slowed. They became a canter, slowed as if the rider was bringing the horse to a stop. She heard the whinnying of the animal, but, even in the coppery moonlight, she could see nothing at all. Casey hardly dared breathe.

And then, looking closely, she made out… *something*.

It was like an optical illusion, Casey thought, her heart pounding so hard she was sure the rider could hear her. It was there, and yet it wasn't there – a horse-shaped outline in the darkness, almost invisible. The animal's eyes were glowing crimson and the jets of its white breath steamed into the night air. It was tossing its head this way and that, pawing the tarmac as if anxious to be off. Sparks flew from its iron-shod feet.

Casey, attuned to the odours of the countryside, couldn't smell the horse, which she found strange. And then there was something odd about the creature's face, too. She couldn't focus on it properly, couldn't quite see. The shape was – *not right…*

Licking her dry lips, Casey now sneaked a look at the rider. She could hardly make him out – he seemed to blend into the night even more effectively than the horse itself. She was sure he wore some kind of armour, shimmering with just the odd shard of moonlight, as if the rest was absorbed and eaten up by its blackness. He had a cape and hood on, covering a helmeted face, and he was swinging his head this way and that. He appeared to be brandishing a long staff, fluttering with dark crimson pennants like the lance of a medieval jouster.

She could hear him. He was sniffing the air.

Of course. Like the foxhounds, sniffing her out.

Oh, no.

In that instant, Casey decided to break cover. She scrambled from the ditch, trying to cover the few metres between there and the farmhouse gates.

The horse and rider reared up above her, the rider's lance with its fluttering pennants held aloft in the moonlight.

She heard the beast whinnying in triumph, heard a hiss

from the rider, and slammed herself hard against the gates, her numbed fingers scrambling to undo the catch.

It was stiff. It wouldn't budge.

Casey Burgess whirled around. In the split second when she saw the animal bearing down on her, she took in the face of the horse and rider.

And realised, with a sickening lurch of her stomach, what was *wrong* about them.

The horse and its rider were –

Something dazzled her eyes, and she put her arm up to shield her face.

A fox, which had been cowering in the hedgerow, waited until everything had gone quiet in the lane and then trotted out across the moonlit tarmac, still on the alert.

It was hunting chickens in the farm, and so it slipped easily through the bars of the gate. Its brush tail disturbed a shiny object lying in the mud but the fox paid it no heed – it had no interest in the trinkets of humans, and it had the scent of the chickens.

The gold lighter, adorned with the letters S.B., caught the reflection of the moonlight.

Somewhere, an owl hooted.

Otherwise, all was still.

'I've seen her. In a dream.'

Richie Fanshawe had been lost in thought at his table in the dining-hall, and now he looked up as Jess plonked her tray down opposite his and made her announcement.

He glared at her suspiciously. 'Seriously?' he said. 'You've seen her?'

Richie hadn't failed to notice that his friend looked different. Her hair, straight and glossy, was shorter these days, and set off by a thin, hippyish braid. And she'd had her nose pierced.

'Yes. I have.'

She wasn't winding him up, he could tell.

'Look,' he said awkwardly, 'I'm meant to be going to Astronomy Club in five minutes. They're expecting me.'

Three Year 7 girls, Richie noticed, were watching them with interest, trying to cover their giggles beneath pink hands.

'Okay, Rich,' Jess said, leaning forward, 'is there somewhere else we can go and talk? Where we won't be disturbed by *children*?' she added pointedly.

'Fine, fine.' Richie held his hands up in defeat. 'Just let me get rid of this tray.' He pointed at her untouched Coke. 'You know, it annoys me on telly when people buy a drink, then get up and leave two seconds later without taking a sip...'

Jess waggled the cup. 'Don't worry, it's coming with me.'

Five minutes later, they found themselves in the darkest corner of the playground – behind the giant bins in the shadow of the Science block. There were two others there already, a blonde girl and a lanky boy. They were leaning against a bin, gazing into each other's eyes and murmuring urgently. The girl caught sight of Jess and Richie and scowled.

'Get lost, Daisy Hopgood,' said Jess. 'We're having a meeting.' She threw her empty beaker into the nearest bin with more force than necessary, just to underline her point.

Richie hung back nervously. Although he was slight and intellectual-looking, he usually managed to avoid being picked on, as even the hardest kids considered him useful. He wasn't going to chance his arm, though.

The girl looked Jess up and down before deciding she wasn't worth arguing with. She said something to her boyfriend and they moved round the corner.

'That Daisy,' Jess muttered, narrowing her eyes. 'Thinks she's really someone...'

Richie leaned cautiously against the nearest bin, re-adjusting his glasses. 'You know, if I didn't know you better, I'd be scared of you,' he said. 'Actually, I think I'm a bit scared of you anyway.'

'Why? I'm still me.'

'Yeah, but ever since… she left, you've been a bit weird. Going all distant and looking past people all the time, like you can still… see things.' Richie shivered, remembering the apparitions which had stalked the playground just a few months ago. It seemed like years.

'That's what I'm trying to tell you!' Hands clasped behind her back, she squared up to him. Eye-to-eye. 'Hey, you've got taller,' she said, almost accusingly.

'I'm allowed to, aren't I? My mum says it's a growth spurt. Come on, then, what's it all about?'

Richie listened as Jess told him everything she could remember about her dream of the previous night. It all sounded extraordinarily detailed to him. He found it hard to recall anything of his dreams, except the ones about being in the exam hall and rapidly running out of time. They were a killer - he imagined everyone had them, though.

'…and the hissing sound was my TV, because I'd fallen asleep with it on. I was watching *Jurassic World*.'

Richie blinked, and became aware that Jess was looking at him with her head on one side.

'Well?' she said.

'Ummm… Well, there could be nothing in it. Dreams are… They don't always mean something. She's still on your mind, that's all.'

'Oh, right.' Jess scowled. 'That's it, be cynical again. You never completely trusted her anyway, did you? Even after she sent the witches back, you were still wary of her… What is your problem, Richie?'

'Nothing! Look - I just think you're reading too much into it.'

'Rich, it was more than a dream. I'm sure it was her, trying to speak to me! What about the way she appeared? All jerky and flickering, as if the transmission wasn't quite getting through?'

'Princess Leia,' said Richie.

'What?' Jess looked confused.

'Princess Leia, from *Star Wars*, remember?... Jess, you have seen *Star Wars*, right?'

She tutted, folded her arms. Of course she had. It was the one old film everyone had seen. 'Go on.'

He took his glasses off and started polishing them on his sleeve. 'The scene where her hologram message pops out of R2-D2... It's just your subconscious replaying that. Sorry.'

The corners of Jessica's mouth turned down, and for a second her urgent, wide-eyed gaze broke from him and wandered across the playground. 'You think?' she said, sounding disappointed.

'Yeah,' said Richie. He suddenly felt guilty but wasn't sure why. He patted her on the arm, a little awkwardly. 'And did she say "Help me, Jessica Mathieson, you are my only hope"?'

Jess folded her arms, narrowed her eyes. 'Not those words, no.'

'But something like that?'

'Possibly,' she muttered.

'There you are, then. *Star Wars* on the brain,' he said.

'You're not taking me seriously, are you?' The crushing disappointment flowed through her. This was what she needed Richie for – grounding her, making her realise when something was really nothing. But she still didn't have to be pleased about it.

'Jess, I'm sorry. I miss her too, but... life goes on, right? I'd like to think she was going to come back, but I don't really think about her much. I've got other things going on. There's exams, and then I'm going to be secretary of the Astronomy Club next year when Robby Holmes leaves…' Richie adjusted his glasses. 'Sorry,' he said again.

Jess scowled and folded her arms. She leaned back, taking in the riot of colour and activity in the playground. 'I just get the feeling I'm… missing something,' she said absently, rubbing the back of her right hand as if it itched.

'Oh, that's just universal paranoia. Quite normal.'

'Yeah, I expect so.'

The bell echoed out across the playground, bringing an end to the various activities. Footballs were stowed in bags, phones and trading cards pocketed, ties straightened. A chattering, lively throng began to make its way towards the school buildings.

'Time to go,' Richie said.

'Bowling tonight,' she said, as they went their separate ways. 'I need to ask you something.'

'Now,' said Kate, sticking labels on the boxes to be delivered to her housebound customers, 'that's Mrs Gregory, and that's Mrs Yewland. Don't get them mixed up, will you?'

Her young cousin, Ben Hemingway, was leaning against the counter, not looking up from his phone. He was a tall boy of seventeen, with jet-black hair which fell in a floppy fringe over his chestnut eyes.

Ben was in the languid, listless weeks between exam retakes and his sixth-form life – he'd re-sat Year 11, for reasons Kate didn't ask too much about. He had been helping Kate out in the shop for a few weeks now. Ben had a motorbike, now, since his seventeenth birthday, and so he sometimes made home deliveries for Kate on it. This was an old tradition which the owner of the village shop was expected to keep going.

He turned to give Kate his best winning smile, showing off firm, white teeth. 'Relax,' he said. 'Have I ever got it wrong?'

'Not yet,' said Kate with a wry grin, 'but there's a first time for everything.'

'You know, if they taught these oldies to use the internet... Whatever happened to the Silver Surfers club?'

'Look, it's a service and we're proud of it. They like it. Reminds them of how it used to be.'

'I know, I know.' Ben pocketed his phone.

'Go on, get off with you.'

'And shall I watch out for ghosts?' he said mischievously.

'Ben. Don't be like that. Those poor kids, they were scared.'

'Okay, I know.'

Ben hefted the boxes in one hand and his crash-helmet in the other – but before he got out of the door, they both heard a commotion on the Green.

Peering over the newspaper rack, Kate saw the cause of the noise – a woman with wild, bleached hair, who was brandishing a bottle and screaming. She was swinging on the door of the old, disused telephone kiosk, seemingly with enough force to snap it off. A group of lads had gathered around and were, it seemed, trading insults with her.

Kate narrowed her eyes. 'Oh, no,' she muttered.

'Who's that?' asked Ben.

'Shona Burgess,' Kate muttered. 'Not again.' Kate rolled up her sleeves and tied her hair back. 'Stay with Gran for a minute,' she told him, and strode out into the sunlight.

'Don't you gimme that!' Mrs Burgess was yelling at the boys, who had stopped laughing and were starting to look very uneasy now. Kate could see now that she was hanging on to the door of the phone-box for a good reason, as she appeared unable to stand up without support. 'Don't you give me... that... you little...' She hiccupped loudly, pulled her bottle from the pocket of her denim jacket, swigged from it and spat at them. 'Jus' get out of my sight. Outta my *sight*!'

'Mrs Burgess?' said Kate gently. 'Shona?'

The woman spun to face her, tried to straighten up and to focus. Kate saw that her pale face was streaked with smeared mascara. Shona Burgess was only about thirty-five, Kate knew, and yet her crumbling make-up couldn't quite hide the lines which aged her prematurely.

'Miss Tripp,' said Mrs Burgess, and covered her mouth for a second. 'Misstripp. K-K- Katie. Ver' kind of you. You're a kind woman, Miss Tripp. Katie. Not like these... *evil* little boys.'

The lads nudged each other and one of them called out, 'You mad old cow!' His mates sniggered.

Kate glowered at the boy who had spoken. 'Either help, Dalton Williams, or get lost,' she snapped.

Dalton physically recoiled, turning bright red and stepping back as if he had been shoved.

'Sorry, Miss Trippett,' he mumbled.

Kate went over to Shona Burgess, who had fallen on her knees. She appeared to be hugging the telephone box and was shaking quietly, making small whimpering noises. Beside her, the cheap red wine flowed from the overturned bottle, staining the grass.

Kate placed her hands on the woman's shoulders. Holding her breath against the overpowering odours of alcohol and tobacco, she squatted down beside her and murmured to her. 'What's up?' she asked gently. 'What is it?'

Shona Burgess looked up, but she was looking through Kate, her eyes somewhere else entirely.

'My Case,' she whispered. 'Them evil boys. They know where she is.'

Kate felt a heavy, sickening feeling in her stomach, as if someone had punched her. 'Casey is missing?' Mrs Burgess opened her mouth but didn't answer. 'Shona, please!' said

Kate, her tone urgent. 'This is important. Has your Casey gone *missing*?'

For a moment, Mrs Burgess looked as if she hadn't understood the question. Then hot tears flooded from her bloodshot eyes and cut paths through her make-up.

'All right.' Kate rounded on the boys. 'Well, do any of you know where she is? Dalton? Kyle? Mason?'

They looked at each other, shook their heads shamefacedly.

'She jus' went mad,' said Dalton Williams, the boy who had spoken before. 'Started accusin' us.'

'So you do know Casey Burgess?'

'Yeah.'

'But you don't know where she is?' Kate persisted, eyeing them carefully. The boys shook their heads. 'Right,' said Kate, 'Run and get Dr Baker.' They looked at one another uncomfortably. '*Well*?' Kate barked. The boys turned and hurried away.

Ben, who had been watching from the shop doorway, ran over. 'I'll call the police,' he said, thumbing his phone.

'Thanks, Ben. Then get off with those groceries – I'll stay with her till the doctor arrives.'

'What do you think's happened?' Ben asked as he tapped the number.

Kate narrowed her eyes.

'I don't know,' she murmured.

As she gently rested her hands on Shona Burgess's quivering shoulders, her gaze was drawn across the sunlit, jade-and-gold grass of the Green, drawn to the darkness which crouched like a malevolent spider at its heart.

She squinted at the gnarly, twisted bark of the Whispering Tree. It sat there as if it knew something. And it made Kate feel uneasy.

*

The problem, Richie Fanshawe thought resignedly, was that Jess was just too persuasive.

So now, thanks to her, he found himself wearing a pair of squeaky, uncomfortable shoes, sitting in a noisy bowling-alley and being giggled at by groups of girls on either side.

He'd failed to get even one of his three attempts so far to stay in the lane – every ball had veered into the side channel and rolled harmlessly past the skittles. Also, he had just paid a jaw-dropping sum for two small Cokes.

And to make matters worse, he was about to agree to spend half his summer holiday in the middle of nowhere. In a place which sounded as if its wi-fi was run by two cows and the local stream.

'Honestly, Rich,' said Jessica, hefting the orange 12-pound ball. 'You'll enjoy it!' She stepped up to the line and let the ball fly down the lane. It rolled dead-centre with a smooth, gentle rumble.

'A village miles from anywhere that I've never heard of?' Richie murmured. 'You've got to be kidding!' At the same time, he couldn't help feeling a small, proud skipping sensation inside – that she had asked him, of all people.

Then he saw Jess's ball – compact but effective – smash into the pins, sending nine of them flying. The tenth wobbled, but stayed upright.

'Yeeeesssss!' She punched the air with both hands, then swivelled with a squeak of shoe, licked her finger and chalked a mark in the air. 'I am so thrashing you, mate.' She plonked herself down on the couch. 'Look, admit it – you're not doing anything exciting this summer, are you?'

'What makes you so sure?' he retorted, unwilling to admit that she was right.

'Well – you're not, are you? I just know.'

'Thanks, Jess,' he said, scowling and folding his arms. 'You mean a saddo like me won't have anything lined up? I might be going… I dunno, I might be going to London with… with…' He picked out a name of one of the tall, willowy, short-skirted, popular girls – the ones who swore casually and went to parties and had gone out with boys since primary school. 'With Milly Croft.'

Jess made a *pfffff* noise. 'You are not going anywhere with Milly Croft. I don't think Milly Croft even knows you exist. You are *invisible* to Milly Croft.'

'You really know how to make a guy feel wanted.'

She leaned over as if to kiss him on the cheek, then, at the last second, ruffled his hair instead. 'It's a natural talent. Go on, your throw.'

Richie stepped nervously up, polishing his glasses. Jess had a large number of points on their lane's electronic scoreboard, he noticed, while he just had three sad-looking crosses. He reached for a new ball, deciding to go for one of the heavier ones. He gritted his teeth as the weight almost pulled his arm off, and tried not to keel over backwards as he stepped back for his run-up.

Jess was watching him in amusement. 'You, um, sure about this?'

'Quite sure,' said Richie, frowning in concentration. 'It's all a matter of physics, you know.' He gave the ball an experimental swing, ignoring the ache in his fingers and arm.

'Tell you what,' said Jess, 'if you get a strike this time, you can definitely come on holiday with me. Even though you pretend you don't want to. And if you mess up again, I'll ask someone else.'

'Who?' he asked, suddenly jealous.

She tucked her hair behind her ear and sat cross-legged. 'Not saying. But I'm pretty popular – know what I mean?'

Richie gritted his teeth, took a step back. Then he half-ran, half-slithered forward, hurling the ball in an ungainly but oddly effective manner.

Then, with a yelp of dismay, Richie suddenly lost his footing on the smooth floor and went head-over-heels. He landed with a painful thud, just as the ball itself left his hand, hit the wooden alley and thundered towards its target at an impressive speed.

He sat up, straightened his glasses. Jess, beside him, squinted at the ball's progress. It pounded forward, still staying on the central run of the alley. Neither of them dared breathe.

Two seconds later, Richie's bowling-ball hit the pins dead-centre, scattering them outwards, leaving not a single one standing.

Hands on hips, her mouth open in astonishment, Jess stared down at him, then back to the scattered pins, then back to Richie again. 'I don't believe it.'

'Like I said. Just, ah, a question of physics.'

She helped him up. 'Are you okay?' she asked, amused.

'Um...' He gave his arms and legs an experimental stretch. 'Yes, nothing broken...' He looked her in the eye. 'So,' he said, 'what was this village called again?'

'You're sure?' she said. She offered him her phone. 'Don't want to Snapchat the lovely Milly Croft, just to say you're free?'

Richie glowered at her.

Jess laughed. 'Stuck with me, then,' she said.

That night, she sat up in her bed. She felt groggy, and was uncertain for a moment where she was. Her eye was drawn to the television in the corner of the bedroom again. It was dark, but humming to itself.

She lifted the duvet off – for some reason, it was astonishingly heavy – and hauled herself over to the television. She pressed the off switch, but nothing happened. Again she pressed the switch, and again nothing happened. With an increasing sense of panic and frustration, Jess stabbed again and again at the button. For a moment, she wondered what had happened to the remote.

And the TV was wrong, too – it looked bigger, darker, chunkier than it should.

A pale shape appeared on the screen. The shape of a head. A girl with tomato-red hair, wearing blue-tinted glasses.

Jess took a step backwards in astonishment and rubbed her aching eyes.

'Emerald!' she exclaimed. Then, realising: 'Oh, so if you're here… it must be another dream, right?'

'Correct,' said the unstable image of Emerald on her TV screen, peering at her over her glasses. 'Now, please attempt to focus.'

Jess did. 'What's going on, Emerald?' she asked, hearing her own voice booming around her as if through a loudspeaker. 'Why do you keep appearing like this?'

'There is a problem. Interference with the chronostatic field. It is two-part interference… the worst kind. Jess, I have sensed… another force… more powerful.'

'Another force? What do you mean?'

'I do not know, as yet… Jess… You must…' The picture of Emerald was starting to break up, shot through with jagged lines.

'I must what? Tell me!'

The image collapsed in on itself, pixellating. 'Be careful when you sleep!' called the voice of Emerald Greene.

Then, just for a second, Jess was sure she saw a vast, black shadow unfurl itself from the television screen and move across the bedroom wall. Shaking, she steeled herself to focus on it; but this was a dream, and her eyes felt heavy and clogged. A sound echoed in her head – a soft, menacing, *snorting* noise, like –

Normal dream-reality reasserted itself. The television turned into a melon and exploded, showering the room with soft, pulpy fruit and seeds which dripped from the walls. Jess's headmistress, Miss Pinsley, was suddenly standing there, arms folded, wearing a pair of yellow washing-up gloves and tut-tutting to herself. 'Jessica Mathieson,' she said sternly, 'clean up this mess at once.'

And her father was there beside her, dressed as a jaunty janitor in a flat-cap and overall, carrying a bucket and mop. 'Don't worry,' he said, in a helium-squeaky voice more suited to a cartoon character, 'we'll get this tidied up in a jiffy.'

'Dad,' she said, 'you're dead. Go away.'

'Fair enough,' he said, and popped out of existence.

Jess, with a vague sense of anxiety, woke a second later in the darkness of her bedroom. She sat up, blinking.

A shadow. Real, this time.

She saw it out of the corner of her eye. For an instant, she was convinced that the dark shape was scrabbling at the window, and then she heard a skittering sound as something tried to get a grip on the slippery slates. That meant there was something on the roof.

Jess switched on the bedside lamp, hopped up on to her chair and pulled the long bar which opened the sloping window. Her heart pounding, she felt the chilly night air against her face. She heard the sound of distant traffic and the Cathedral bells chiming some early hour.

And – yes! There it was.

The houses on Chadwick Road were terraced in blocks of four, their slate roofs slightly staggered to account for the slope of the road. And something small, dark and agile was moving between the chimney-pots on their block, scuttling now along the roof of Number 42.

Jess squinted. She needed glasses, although she didn't yet want to admit as much to anyone.

The shape tensed, poised on the edge of Number 42's roof – and then leapt the gap to the next block of houses, passing briefly through the glow of a street-lamp as it did so. Jess caught her breath.

She couldn't be sure, but – it had looked like a black cat.

She closed the window and went back to bed.

Tomorrow, they were off to Little Brockwell – and something told Jess some answers might be forthcoming.

2
Rumours and Lies

Kate Trippett thought she knew all the children in Little Brockwell by sight. So she was surprised, that morning, to see that two new ones had arrived. They propped their bikes up outside the shop and came in. They were young teenagers, and she knew straight away that they were from the city.

Kate could also tell instinctively that they were neither brother and sister, nor boyfriend and girlfriend. Friends, then, but oddly-matched. The girl was slim and pretty, with brown hair and light freckles, a small, discreet piercing in her nostril and an assortment of ethnic bangles clanking on her arm. She wore a green hoodie with KEEP CALM AND GET KARMA on it, buttoned jeans with a frayed waistband and a pair of black Doc Marten boots. Kate noticed that she squinted, as if she was slightly short-sighted but didn't want to admit it. The boy, meanwhile, didn't look as if he should be with her at all. Nervous and jittery, he wore a bemused expression beneath his tousled fringe, and he kept re-adjusting his glasses on his nose. He sported an *X-Files* T-shirt and baggy jeans which stopped a few centimetres above his unfashionably sensible shoes.

Pretending to rearrange the greetings cards, Kate watched them. They were huddling around the copies of the local newspaper and talking urgently. Then they started looking at stuff on their phones, and pointing, comparing it with the articles in the papers.

Kate could tell the girl knew she was being observed.

There was something very watchful about her.

'Look at this,' the girl said, pointing to the poster on the wall. 'Little Brockwell Festival of Arts and Music.' She squinted at the names. 'Kick Violet, Spectronic, Frankie Thanks, The Delta Waves… Don't recognise any of them… Richie, are you listening to me?'

'I don't believe it!' The boy was gawping at a double spread in the magazine. Kate could see it showed a photo of a green-skinned man, a silver robot and a woman with a laser-rifle slung across her chest. 'They haven't renewed *Timeland* for a third season! I thought it was getting brilliant ratings!' He started frantically thumbing his phone, eyes flicking between it and the magazine to cross-check the information. Kate was amused.

'Richie,' said the girl, 'if you should ever see a life, grab it with both hands, will you?'

Kate decided this was the time to introduce herself. 'Can I help you?'

'Errrm,' said Jess, 'we're just looking. Thanks.'

'I can see that.' She folded her arms and nodded in a knowing but not unfriendly way. 'Most people come in to buy something, you know. It's not like the city here. You… are from the city, aren't you?'

'Does it show?' said the girl in embarrassment.

'Put it this way. Everyone knows everyone in Little Brockwell. So you can start with me. I run the Post Office and General Stores – which is where you are.' She extended a hand. 'I'm Kate Trippett.'

'Oh! Cool name. My sister's called that. Well, Katherine.' The girl waved a hand with a jangle of bracelets.

'A lot of us about. And you are…?'

'Jess Mathieson. My friend from another planet here is Richie Fanshawe. We're staying at Rose Cottage.'

'Oh, yes,' said Kate Trippett, as light dawned. 'You're

Rhiannon's friends? Looking after the house for the summer?'

'Y – yeah. Well, my Aunt Gabi is, anyway.'

'Who are they, child?' called a thin voice from the back room.

'That's my Gran,' said Kate. 'Her sight's almost gone, but she's got fabulous hearing. I expect she doesn't recognise your voices… do you want to come through and meet her?'

The newcomers exchanged a nervous look.

'It's okay,' said Kate, 'she doesn't bite.' She leaned forward and added in a whisper, 'At least – not without her teeth in.'

Behind the counter was a doorway with a bead curtain, and it led through to a darkened lounge which smelt of peppermints and musty furniture.

Jess gave a slight gulp of apprehension as they stepped into the room. Everything about it, Jess decided, felt *old* – the heavy curtains, big marble fireplace, the black and white photos in chunky gilded frames and the steady ticking of a long-case clock.

Like a queen at the heart of her domain, Kate's Grandma sat on a big armchair in the centre of the room. They approached cautiously.

She was thin, but not wizened – rather, she gave the impression of being lean and powerful, as if the arms and legs under her woollen cardigan and shawl contained hidden strength. Her hair was brilliant white, trimmed very short. She had a long, proud face scored with vertical lines, a thin mouth and a turned-up nose, and she wore round, tinted glasses over her eyes. Her hands gripped the arms of the chair firmly, without trembling; her fingernails were well-manicured, Jess noticed, and she seemed to have rings on every finger.

'Come closer,' she said, and her voice was clear and firm. 'I only get… impressions from over there.'

'These are the children staying at Rose Cottage, Gran,' said Kate. 'Jess and Richie.'

'Um – er – hello,' said Jess nervously. She was uncertain how to address the old lady, and really felt they should not be there at all.

'Just call me Grandma Trippett, child. Everyone does.' The old lady took both of Richie's hands in both of hers, much to his embarrassment. 'Ahh… ye've soft hands, for a boy! Need to get outside more, lad.'

Jess giggled at Richie's discomfort, and immediately put a hand to her mouth. 'Sorry.'

Grandma Trippett swung round towards her, like a predatory owl. 'Come 'ere, girl.'

Jess approached cautiously. The old woman reached out a hand and touched her forehead with the tips of her fingers. It was an unnerving sensation. The old lady only touched her skin very lightly, as if holding a porcelain vase. Then her knobbly hand traced the shape of Jess's face, from her forehead down across the bridge of her nose to her mouth and chin. Jess tried not to flinch at the cool, bony fingers.

'Gran can build up a picture of someone by touching their face,' Kate whispered to Richie, who was watching in fascination.

'Can she see at all?' he asked curiously.

'A bit. Not very well. But this is how she remembers people. She's got a photographic memory. Says it's her Romany blood.'

'Romany?' asked Richie.

'Her mother was a gypsy. Quite a scandal when my great-grandad married her, apparently.'

At last, Grandma Trippett drew back, nodding, leaving Jess slightly embarrassed. 'You're a comely young thing,' she said. 'You should beware that. Both a blessing and a curse, that is.'

Jess blushed.

'Though why you youngsters feel the need to stick bits of metal through your noses, I don't know,' Grandma Trippett went on. 'Yes, a blessing and a curse… I should know. I were young and pretty meself, once.'

Kate came forward to squeeze her hand. 'You had the boys queuing up to marry you, didn't you, Gran, after Grandad died in the war?'

'Was that the Second World War?' Richie asked.

Grandma Trippett chuckled. 'No, the Wars of the Roses, you young rascal. Of *course* it were the Second World War! How old d'you think I am?'

'Sorry,' said Richie. 'Actually,' he said, clasping his hands behind his back, 'we're currently in the longest period for centuries without a global conflict. Our generation's the first for ages not to be called up to fight.'

'Well, that's right,' said Grandma Trippett with a smile, 'and you remember it, lucky boy with your soft hands. What d'you want to be when you grow up, mm?'

'An astronomer,' said Richie proudly. 'Or a science-fiction writer. I've not decided which.'

'Hmmmm. Ambition. I like that, soft-handed boy. What about you, girl?'

'Me?' said Jess, taken aback. 'I don't know. I want to go to university, though, like my sister.'

'You're a fine young pair of people,' said Grandma Trippett, nodding her head approvingly. 'Tell me, Kate,' she said, turning to her granddaughter, 'any more news on the poor child?'

'Nothing,' said Kate. 'The police have even dragged the river. They've not found a thing.'

'What child?' asked Richie.

'Casey Burgess,' said Kate. 'Local twelve-year-old. Went missing yesterday.'

'And so soon after that Tyler Uttley business,' said Grandma Trippett.

'Gran!' Kate shot her a warning look. 'We don't want to be scaring these children. And Casey's mum Shona's already got enough problems, poor thing.'

Kate's Grandma clicked her teeth in disapproval.

'And nobody knows where she might've gone?' asked Jess, who, like Richie, was finding her curiosity piqued.

'She'll probably turn up,' Richie said. 'Kids do. Most people who go missing turn up again within 48 hours.'

'That's what the police said,' Kate agreed.

'And don't listen to gossip,' said Grandma Trippett, leaning forward and gripping the arms of her chair. 'Travelling folk ain't the kind to steal children.' She sat back again. 'Just you remember.'

Back outside, Jess and Richie wheeled their bikes along the main street of Little Brockwell.

'She was creepy, that old lady,' said Richie, shuddering. He was wondering exactly how old she was. Old enough to have been married *before* the war, so in her nineties, surely?

'Oh, I don't know,' said Jess. 'I quite liked her.'

'Just because she called you *comely*,' said Richie with a scowl. 'Weird old word. All she could say about me was that I've got soft hands. Of course I've got soft hands, I'm a scientist. I need to look after my hands.'

He became aware that Jess wasn't listening to him, but was staring across the Green. He followed her gaze towards the dark, brooding oak tree in the middle of the Green, little more than a trunk and a few twisted branches. It took Richie a moment or two to realise why the tree looked odd, and when he did, the reason was obvious – it was midsummer, and yet the tree had barely any leaves.

Jess, staring up at the black trunk, shuddered. 'I don't like it... It looks... *evil*, somehow.'

Sunlight seemed to come nowhere near the tree. An aura of shadow was cast around it, staining the Green like oil. Jess laid her bike down and hovered uncertainly on the edge of the shadow. She reached her right hand out, cautiously, and then withdrew it as if stung, staring in astonishment at her palm.

'What is it?' Richie asked. He stepped into the shadow. He felt a little chillier, he had to admit, but there was no sign of any strange sensation.

'My hand,' said Jess quietly. 'My hand reacted.'

'That tingling again? Like when you touched the witch?'

When she looked up, there was a cold, hard light in her eyes. 'I don't like this tree. Rich. Something's weird about it.'

Richie strolled over to the tree, looked it up and down. 'Seems quite harmless to me,' he said, and reached out for the bark of the trunk.

'Don't!' said Jess in alarm, but he was already touching it. The bark felt cold, smooth, almost like stone. It didn't seem to have the roughness of normal wood – rather it was unblemished and glassy in finish. Richie peered curiously at it.

'They call it the Whispering Tree, you know,' said a voice from behind them, and they whirled around to see a plump, middle-aged woman in an anorak and a clerical collar.

'Does it whisper?' Jess asked the woman in awe. 'You're the vicar here, right?'

'Rector, actually. Fenella Parsloe, Rector of St. Leonard's. You're new here, aren't you? Visiting for the summer?'

'That's right,' said Jess. She glanced over her shoulder at the tree again. 'The Whispering Tree. So...'

'Get right up close to it,' said the Rector softly.

'Isn't this a bit pagan for you?' Jess said cheekily.

The Rector raised her eyebrows. 'A harmless village tradition. Go on.'

Slightly in awe, Jess leaned against the tree.

Richie watched, scowling. He had never been that keen on going to church, ever since the Dean of Meresbury Cathedral had tried to stop their school from playing Dungeons and Dragons, claiming it was immoral and of the dark arts. He shuffled uncomfortably.

Jess pulled back, shaking her head. 'Mad. I could swear I heard voices.'

The Rector gestured to Richie. 'Go on. You have a listen.'

'Seriously?'

But he could tell he was expected to, so grudgingly, he put his ear to the cool, smooth bark.

At first there was nothing. Then, a soft, gentle susurration in the back of his head, overlaid with crackles and hisses as if it were trying to tune itself in on short-wave.

Richie pulled away, alarmed. 'That's… so weird.'

'What causes it?' Jess asked.

'Well, over the years, the more… sceptically-minded in our community have said it's to do with the sounds trees make as they grow… Or air currents inside the bark.'

'Like when you put a shell to your ear,' said Jess. 'And you hear the sea. Only you don't really.'

'Exactly!' The Rector beamed. 'Only, that's not the legend.'

'Go on,' said Richie, arms folded. 'Hit us with the legend.'

'Well… the story goes that when a villager dies, their spirit is absorbed into the Tree, so that they stay with the village.' She smiled at Jess. 'Like you say. A bit pagan.'

Richie shivered. 'What, so… Those are supposed to be their voices?'

'Yes. A chorus of voices, making up all the lost wisdom and knowledge of Little Brockwell… It's a strange place, this. Old English legends… You do have to wonder where they begin.'

'It's creepy,' said Jess, moving out of the Tree's shadow.

The Rector pulled a pair of glasses out of her pocket and perched them on her nose. 'Well, you shouldn't listen to everything people say.' Puffing a little, she walked over to the trunk of the Whispering Tree and patted it with the flat of her hand. 'There you are, look. Just an old tree stuck in the middle of our village green. Looks almost dead, but… well…'

Richie and Jess exchanged an awkward look.

'Never liked it much, myself, but, well… people come from all around to see the thing. It's mentioned in the guide-books, along with the chalk horse, and the church. And the pub.'

'I haven't seen many tourists,' said Richie suspiciously. 'Only us.'

The Rector thrust her hands into her anorak pocket. 'Yes, well, things have been tailing off in the last couple of years. And Little Brockwell isn't seen as a safe place to be at the moment.'

'We're going to be having a village meeting about it, I think. You'll see the notices up.'

'What about those travellers?' Richie asked. 'You don't think they're involved?'

'Oh, there are always people willing to point the finger,' the Rector said sadly, peering at him over her glasses. 'Fear, you see. Fear of difference, of change… That's what has always corrupted the human race. It was fear, all those years ago, which drove them to crucify Our Lord.'

Richie decided they'd better not get into that just now. 'So they definitely aren't around any more?' he persisted.

'No, the travellers moved on. North, I think. I believe they're camped somewhere near the Ridge, about ten miles from here, but I could be wrong… I expect you've been talking to Mrs Trippett? She's a fine old lady. Lived in the village all her life, you know…' The Rector glanced at her watch. 'Now, I really must go. A lady called Esme Hutton died the other day, and I have to prepare for the funeral… You two take care.'

'We will,' promised Jess.

The Rector went on her way, waving absently. Richie glanced over his shoulder as they wheeled their bikes along, and he wondered briefly how the Rector managed to move so fast, as she seemed to have disappeared from sight in just a few seconds.

'Whispering voices inside a tree?' Jess said aloud, gazing into the darkness of the tree-trunk. 'I know who'd be interested in *that*.'

'Yeah. So where is she?'

They wheeled their bikes back towards the road. Ahead of them, the street narrowed, rising where a humpbacked bridge spanned the local river, the Brock.

'Do you think everybody in Little Brockwell is planning to say hello to us at some point today?' Richie asked, raising his eyebrows.

'I know what you mean. I do feel a bit like an exhibit – *look out!*' She was suddenly pushing Richie out of the way as a small whirlwind came hurtling over the rise of the bridge, accompanied by the roar of an engine and a cloud of pungent exhaust fumes.

Jess fell on top of the bikes, and Richie sprawled on the verge some distance away, nearly banging his head on a bench. A black motorcycle zoomed past them, screeching to a halt in front of Kate's shop. The wheels carved a trench in the grass and a fountain of burnt earth shot into the air.

Jess got to her feet as the rider switched off his engine, and as he started to remove his crash-helmet, she strode towards him, her face showing righteous anger.

'You stupid, crazy *idiot!*' she snapped. 'Why don't you look where you're going with that thing?'

The helmet came off, and Richie saw Jess's jaw drop. The rider, dressed in black jeans and a leather biker jacket, was a teenage boy. He had a lean, tanned face, and chestnut-brown eyes behind a long, unruly black fringe. He ignored Richie and gave Jess a dazzling, white smile.

'Sorry,' he said. 'Didn't expect anyone to be around. Kids are all indoors these days. Scared.'

Jessica folded her arms, swivelled on one heel. She started toying with her hair. 'Well, I'm not a *kid*,' she said, 'and not much scares me.'

'Okay,' he said, and he sounded amused. 'Not much scares you, eh? Spiders, snakes? The Blue Screen of Death when you haven't saved your homework?'

Jess scowled and folded her arms. 'Who are you? And why are you making fun of me?'

'I'm not,' said the boy, as he locked his motorbike. 'Just having a laugh. Maybe I'll see you around?' He grinned, nodded and headed into the shop.

'Yeah,' said Jess. She shoved her hands awkwardly into her pockets. 'See you around, crazy idiot.'

'Well done,' muttered Richie sardonically from behind her, dusting himself down. He couldn't believe that she had let the boy go without more of a talking-to. 'You certainly gave him what for, didn't you?'

'Oh, shut up, Rich,' she said absently.

As they wheeled their bikes away, Richie noticed that she was still looking interestedly over her shoulder – not at the Whispering Tree, but rather in the direction of the General Stores…

The doorbell jangled as Ben Hemingway entered the shop. He placed his crash-helmet on the counter – very carefully – and pushed his tangled fringe out of his eyes. There appeared to be nobody around.

'Yo!' he shouted.

'I'm in the stockroom,' said Kate, poking her head out of

a side door. 'And please don't shout *yo* – it's so American.'

'Oh, right,' said Ben with a smile. 'Deliveries done... Hey, guess what?' he added.

'What?' Kate asked absently, coming through from the back room with a box of canned and bottled drinks. She started replenishing the cool cabinet.

'I just saw some kids I didn't recognise,' he said, coming over to help her. 'Almost got themselves run over.'

'Hmm. So I imagine you were riding with your usual care and attention?'

'I can't help it if they walk in the middle of the road. Anyway, who are they?'

'Jess and Richie. Nice young people... Jess's aunt is looking after Rose Cottage for the summer.'

'Uh-huh,' said Ben, and he hefted a small bottle of Coke, staring at it ruminatively. 'Um... how old is Jess, d'you think?'

Kate folded her arms and narrowed her eyes at him. 'I know your game, young man. Don't even go there.'

'Oh, come on! That's not an answer!' Ben told her, throwing the bottle from hand to hand. 'She seems kind of cool,' he said thoughtfully.

'Is, she now? Hmm.'

'So, come on. Younger than me?'

'I don't know, Ben.' She smiled indulgently. 'I'd guess maybe fourteen? Not one for you, if you don't mind my saying so, Mr Hemingway.'

'Really?' Suddenly, Ben fumbled the bottle of Coke and it slipped from his hands. He winced, shut his eyes, expecting to hear an explosion of glass on the tiles. It never came.

He opened his eyes, saw his cousin holding the bottle firmly in her right hand.

'Did you know I was square-leg for the girls' First Eleven?' Kate said. 'Hardly dropped a catch in four years.' She handed the bottle back to Ben. 'I'd suggest that you're just as careful,' she added, her expression impassive.

Ben took the bottle back. He frowned for a second, then shook his head and unscrewed the bottle. 'No worries,' he said, taking a sip of Coke. He rummaged in his pocket for change and opened the till to put the money in. 'What is it with this place?' he said to himself. 'Goes for months being duller than dull, then all of a sudden it gets interesting…'

The gorge was a cold, empty place.

It was infused with darkness, as if the very air had been filled with pitch. It was bordered on either side by looming, steel-grey mountains with jagged summits.

This was a place which – in the strict definition of the word – did not really exist.

There were places like this all over the world, hovering at the gateways of reality. They were especially strong in communities full of legend, full of tradition. Repositories of psychic energy.

The person who guarded this domain, who ruled over it, could not actually be said to 'exist', either, not in the sense that a highly sceptical, rational professor of Physics would allow. But in this world – this side-world, this netherworld, this meta-world – there was more to existence than tangibility, more than evidence, more than *proof*.

This place, these people, hovered in the jet-black shade on a summer's day. They lurked at the edge of vision, skulked in reflections and slinked through the shadows made by clouds across the moon. They were the sound of rustling in the hedgerows, the creaking of wood downstairs in ancient cottages, the gurgling of water in supposedly dry streams. They were more than Humanity could ever understand.

And yet they were trapped here.

Trapped in these liminal spaces, contained within shadow and darkness. Waiting to emerge.

In the fragment of dark sky which could be seen overhead, red-rimmed clouds clashed, throwing out daggers of crimson lightning into the land. The lightning-flashes illuminated the horseman.

He galloped like a desperate emissary, his cloak streaming out behind him and his eyes glowing like hot coals in the darkness.

He was returning.

With new information.

On the threshold of the Dark Horse, Aunt Gabi looked in awe at all the pub's crests and logos. The place had won quite a few awards. She entered, treading on a photocopied flyer advertising the Festival – she picked this up and pinned it back on to the notice-board.

They had settled in. Jessica had loved Rose Cottage straight away – it was dark, creaky, full of shadows and cobwebs and smelt of old wood and stone. She had bagged the front bedroom for her own, too, as it had a big bay window which let the sun in and offered a view across the rooftops of the village, out towards the hills and the chalk horse. There was something bewitchingly romantic about the giant horse, Gabi decided, something which made the place special.

Rhiannon had left them a note and a box of provisions to start them off. But it was just after midday, now, and Aunt Gabi could not resist the lure of the local pub for long. The Dark Horse was not that busy – a few regulars round the bar, one or two couples having lunch. There was an enticing aroma of steak-and-kidney pie, too.

The landlord greeted her like an old friend, shaking her effusively by the hand. 'Ah, Gabi LaForge, isn't it? Staying at Rhiannon's place?' He had a ruddy, honest face with bushy eyebrows and a gap-toothed smile. 'Have a seat. Harry Chambers – landlord, barman, general dogsbody and source of all that's worth knowing in Little Brockwell. Oh, and a lot that isn't, but we'll let that pass.' He winked.

'Thank you,' Gabi said, a little taken aback.

'What'll you have?' Harry asked her.

'Oh, just a sparkling mineral water, please. I'm working this afternoon.'

'How are your children?' Harry inquired as he levered the top from her bottle and poured the water into a glass with ice and lemon. 'A boy and a girl, isn't it?'

'Yes… Well, that is, they're not *mine* exactly. Jess is my niece – I'm her legal guardian – and Richie's her friend.' Gabi leaned forward, as she had sensed something more than a polite enquiry in Harry's tone. 'Why do you ask?'

He placed her drink on the bar. 'People around here have become very, very suspicious,' he said. 'Now, I'm not like that. A friend of Rhiannon O'Connor's is a friend of mine. But watch the children. There's trouble brewing in Little Brockwell, and I don't like it.'

'Heavens,' said Aunt Gabi. 'I came here for a bit of peace and quiet.'

And as if on cue, raised voices wafted through the open doorway from the beer-garden outside.

'What d'you mean, *simper*? I did *not* simper!'

Harry raised his eyebrows in amusement, and one or two of the other customers had started to look in the direction of the doorway. Gabi jumped up from her stool. 'Oh, dear,' she said. 'Excuse me. Minor domestic…'

Outside, Richie was trembling a little at Jess's hard stare, but he stood his ground. They were either side of a pub table, confronting each other almost nose-to-nose.

'Don't give me that,' he riposted. 'Just because leather-boy fancied himself! If he'd been an ugly git, you'd not have been so quick to forgive him for nearly running us over, would you?'

'Yeah, well.' Jess tutted, tossed her hair back. 'You're just jealous.'

'What, of that poser?' Richie sneered – but the barb had stung, he couldn't deny it. He was, he had to admit, quite relieved to see Aunt Gabi emerge from the pub.

'Well, this must be something of a record!' Gabi exclaimed, clapping a firm hand on each of their shoulders. 'Less than two hours up and about in the village, and you're already causing a commotion. Before I bang your heads together, any clues as to what this is about?'

'Ask *him*,' snapped Jessica.

'Ask *her*,' Richie retorted.

'Fine,' said Aunt Gabi. 'Sort it out yourselves. But just remember that I've come here to work on my uni stuff, so that I can eventually get a decent job and keep you and your armies of friends in biscuits. Therefore, I don't expect any bickering – right?'

Richie didn't dare look Jess in the eye. After a few seconds of trying to appear nonchalant, he risked a glance in her direction. Jess raised her eyebrows at him in a vaguely apologetic way.

Richie pulled a rueful face.

He hadn't really wanted to argue with Jess, but Motorcycle Boy had got on his nerves. He'd believed Jess would stand up to anyone, and he hadn't imagined she would be so easily swayed by a guy who so obviously loved himself. He supposed it wasn't really worth falling out over, and decided to let it go. They exchanged smiles, reluctant at first, then more open.

'Good,' said Gabi. 'Now, then, I'm going to order us some lunch. I've heard Harry's pies are world-famous. Come on in when you're ready.' She went back inside.

Jess turned to follow her, but Richie's attention was

elsewhere.

'What is it?' Jess asked, hovering on the steps down to the entrance.

Earlier, they had found that the sturdy, wooden post of the inn-sign was ideal for chaining the bikes to, but they hadn't properly looked at it. Richie, hands in pockets, gazed up at the swinging sign.

'Something I've been wondering about,' he said, absently holding up his phone to photograph the sign.

'What's that?' Jess asked.

Richie pointed upwards. 'A bit grim, isn't it?'

The sign depicted a black horse with red eyes, riding through what appeared to be misty marshland. The rider's face was not clear – he appeared to be wearing some kind of mask over his eyes, like a highwayman. A black cloak streamed out behind him in the wind. The name of the pub was written in gloomy Gothic script, red with a black border. The Dark Horse. Richie thought it looked threatening, as if the pub wanted to ward off customers rather than draw them in.

'Little Brockwell was a staging-post,' said Harry the landlord, who had come out to clear some glasses from a nearby table.

'That was something to do with old postal deliveries, wasn't it?' Jess asked.

'We were on the original mail-route between London and the North,' said Harry. 'The village was famous for stabling and horse-trading in the nineteenth century. And that's not all.' He pointed into the distance. They both turned to look at the hillside, where the white chalk horse watched over the village. 'That comes from much earlier times, of course.'

Richie squinted into the sunlight, shading his eyes to look at the horse. 'Definitely prehistoric,' he said, wanting to show off.

'Well, that's right,' said Harry. 'Thing is, you couldn't get a better landmark for a rider, now, could you?' Harry hoisted up the tray full of glasses. 'There weren't that many signposts in those days.'

Back inside, they sat down with Gabi, who was scanning the extensive menu. 'Wow. Full-scale gastro-pub stuff,' she said. She gazed into the distance for a moment. 'You know, I remember a time when kids weren't allowed in pubs – not even with an adult, and not even just to eat.'

'Well, that was then!' said Jess as she grabbed a bread roll from the basket on the table. 'They used to send us up chimneys, too. And down the pit. Thank goodness for the twenty-first century, eh, Richie?'

Richie was busy trying to decide if he wanted chicken pasta or a full roast dinner.

Harry, armed with a notepad, came hurrying over to take their order. 'Ah, yes,' he said proudly, 'the public house is a very different environment these days. We aim to provide a full and varied selection of quality cooking and to welcome the whole family.'

'Start us young,' said Jess from behind her menu. Richie kicked her under the table.

The young couple at the next table smiled, and Gabi looked nervously back. 'Kids, eh?' she said. 'Can't live with 'em…'

'Actually,' said the young woman, 'Mick and I were wondering… It's been such a long time since we saw anybody new in the village. We thought you might know something.'

'Ah. No. Sorry.' Gabi held her hands up in apology. 'We've… only just arrived. Total newcomers. Only really know what we've read in the papers, and even then…'

'You don't want to believe it all.' Harry gestured to the young couple. 'Mick and Zoe have got three lovely girls. They used to be in my girls' football team. But since all this… business, some of the other parents won't let their kids out of an evening, now. It's a real shame.'

'They ought to be questioning *them* lot,' said the young man, Mick.

'Mick,' said his wife, tapping him on the wrist. 'Don't start.'

Richie blinked. 'Do you mean the travellers?' he asked interestedly.

Mick, leaned back in his chair. 'Yeah, well… them lot. Got moved on a few weeks ago. Good riddance to bad rubbish, that's what I say.'

Harry sighed, as if sensing the beginnings of a familiar conversation. 'Any starters?' he ventured hopefully, pencil poised over his notepad. 'I recommend the avocado salad.' Nobody was listening.

'That doesn't sound very tolerant,' began Jess, but Richie kicked her again.

'If they were moved on,' Richie pointed out, reasonably, 'what makes you think they might know anything?'

'Well, they ain't all gone, have they?' Mick said.

'Mick!' Zoe admonished him. 'We don't *know* that…'

'It's true, though. There's still that one parked up at Corlett's Farm. It's an old farmyard, not used now,' he explained, leaning forward. 'Derelict buildings, up on the hill. Got hit bad by the foot-and-mouth all them years ago, then old Hector Corlett died last year and there were nobody to take the place over. Due to be pulled down before long. I dunno how they found out about it being empty, but…'

'What do you know?' Jess asked, curious.

Mick paused, looking around as if he didn't want to be overheard. 'Well, it's like this. My mate Del, he goes up that way fishing, like, and he saw this one the other evening. A girl, no more'n, well, your age… Parked there bold as brass in an old van, with a fire and cooking-pot and a washing-line and stuff.' He leaned back, shaking his head.

'So they haven't all gone?' Aunt Gabi said. 'Doesn't *prove* anything, does it? Come on, let's order.'

'I dunno where she come from,' Mick said with a shrug, returning to his pint. 'Del said he was pretty sure, like, that she weren't one of the last lot.' He clicked his teeth. 'Red-haired girl, he said. Weird, parked up there on her own in an old Volkswagen camper-van.'

Jess spluttered, almost choking on her drink.

Richie thumped her on the back as she coughed. 'It's okay,' he reassured everyone. 'I think she just had something go down the wrong way.' He too, had reacted with excitement to the news, but he was hiding it more successfully.

When Jess regained the power of speech, she fixed Mick with a hard stare. 'Your friend,' she said. 'He's *positive* she was red-haired? And in a camper-van?'

'Yeah. One of them old-fashioned, wossname… Dormobiles. Like people used to have when I were a kid.'

'What colour?' Jess persisted.

Mick thought. 'Erm… Green, I think he said. Yeah, green. Is it important, like?'

Everyone stared at Jess, and she took another sip of Coke to hide her embarrassment. 'No,' she said. 'Not really.'

And Richie understood the little smile she gave to herself.

'Kate! Kate, child!' Grandma Trippett's voice was commanding, urgent.

'All right, Gran!' Kate Trippett handed a customer her change. 'There you are, Mrs Pinkerton. I hope Trixie enjoys the new biscuits.'

Again, Grandma's voice called out, 'Kate! Are you there?'

'Sounds like Gran's not in a mood to wait!' said Ben. He was meant to be tidying the magazine racks, but he had been browsing his phone again.

As soon as Mrs Pinkerton, armed with a huge packet of

dog biscuits, had left the shop, Kate muttered a curse and told Ben to mind the till. She hurried through into the back room.

'What is it, Gran?' she said, looking towards where Grandma always sat. Only then did she realise that the armchair was empty.

Kate stopped in her tracks, then saw the shadowy figure of her Grandma over by the window – she had a shawl around her shoulders and was leaning firmly on her stick. With surprising speed, Grandma spun around to face Kate, using the stick as a pivot. Even though the tinted glasses covered the old lady's eyes, Kate could sense that she was somehow looking at her. Perhaps with something behind her eyes. Perhaps with her mind.

'Something ain't right,' Grandma Trippett said. 'It ain't natural.'

'I know. We're all upset, Gran,' said Kate. 'The police did their best. They're still looking into it.'

'I don't see as how the *police* will find anything,' said Grandma scornfully. 'That young inspector – came down in the last shower! No…' Grandma Trippett turned to look out of the window again, and the pale sunlight falling through the latticed panes cast eerie, mottled shadows on her face. 'No, the truth, if we ever find it... it'll be stranger than they could picture. I don't like to think about it.'

'Well,' said Kate, shivering a little, 'let's keep an open mind.'

'Tommy Taylor and Winifred Gilmore.'

'Who?'

'Tommy Taylor and Winifred Gilmore,' said Grandma again, and her knuckles were white on the handle of the stick. 'Disappeared from Little Brockwell, one summer's day between the wars. Vanished into thin air, they did, and never seen again.'

Kate frowned, not sure what to make of this. Her Gran

had an excellent memory, she knew, and didn't make things up. She decided to keep things as normal as she could. 'Did you want something, Gran?' she asked.

Grandma Trippett reached for a nearby bookshelf and took down a big, leather-bound photograph album. 'I want you to help me sort through these when you get a chance,' she said. 'There's some photographs in here I want to check over. Old pictures. I'll need that... machine you had for looking at 'em.'

'The magnifier? It's in the attic, I think.'

'Well, get it down again!' Grandma commanded, banging the floorboards with her stick and sending tremors through the house. 'Heavens, child, do I need to join the dots for you?'

'No, Gran. I'm sorry.' Kate ran a hand through her unruly hair. 'It's just that the shop's rather taking over at the moment. I've got to sort the accounts out properly...'

'Well, if you ain't the time, get that other young woman to help me. She had a bit of a spark about her. Bit of gumption.'

'Who do you mean?'

'The comely girl. The one who were here just afore!'

'Jess?' Kate frowned. 'She's just a kid. Only arrived in the village this week.'

Grandma Trippett made a little sound of contentment as she eased herself back into her armchair. 'She'll have an open mind, then.' Grandma leaned back, seemingly ready to go to sleep. 'An open mind,' she repeated softly.

Kate smiled indulgently and returned to the shop counter.

'How is she?' Ben murmured.

Kate wrinkled her nose. 'Bit odd, actually,' she whispered. 'Going on about some photos she wants sorting out. I mean, they must have been there seventy years or more... Goodness knows why they're suddenly so important now.'

'Ah, well. We don't know how Gran's mind works.' Ben

glanced at his watch. 'Do you mind if I go? I said I'd visit Dad this afternoon.'

'Oh, yes, you get off...' Kate tilted her head. 'How... is James? Any signs of improvement?'

'It's hard to say. The doctors say you get better days now and then, but not to get our hopes up, you know? Overall, we know Dad's just getting worse. It could be a year, could be less... before...' Ben looked down, his fringe obscuring his eyes.

Kate put a hand on his arm. 'Well, give him a hug from his favourite niece, okay?'

'Yeah, I will.'

'See you this afternoon,' Kate said. 'Hey, do you want a driving lesson when you get back? Harry said we could use their private road.'

Ben frowned. 'Nah, thanks, Kate. To be honest, I'm happy sticking with the bike.'

She watched him grab his jacket and head out of the shop, looking confidently up and down the street. Such a striking young man, she thought.

Ben's father – her Uncle James – had been in a private hospital near Westmeadow for the past two years, and the debilitating condition from which he suffered could only get worse. But Kate was thinking, now, about a conversation she'd had with her mother just a few short months ago, and she couldn't help wondering if they had told Ben yet. If they had let him in on the full, terrible truth.

She didn't really want to know.

3

Lost Souls

That evening in Little Brockwell, trade was brisk in the Dark Horse. A darts game was under way in one corner, and the contestants were becoming rowdy. In the television annexe, a sizeable crowd was watching a football match. The tables had filled up by eight o'clock and by now there was standing room only – Kate Trippett was squashed up against the bar with her regular glass of wine.

'It's like everyone wants the place to go on as normal,' Harry was saying, as he pulled pints at the bar. 'Good, in a way. That poor lad... they've found no answer to whatever it was that scared him.'

'In his imagination, wannit?' scoffed one of the lads at the bar. 'Kids, they make all sorts up.'

'Well, maybe,' Kate said, sadly. 'I'm glad this is a strong community. People seem very supportive.' A couple of the younger men – farming lads who'd taken a liking to Kate – murmured their agreement.

'I just told my girls what I always say,' said Zoe Parks, Kate's assistant from the shop. 'Come straight home and don't talk to no strangers.'

Kate Trippett was going to say 'any strangers', but she bit her tongue.

'Well, I don't know,' murmured Mr Alfred Bidmead, the antiques dealer, who was tall, elegant and white-haired, with a hawkishly intelligent face. He brooded over a pint of bitter, surveying the other drinkers over his half-moon glasses. 'I espied some young mothers today, collecting their charges from some event or other. Scooping them up in their arms and bundling them into their Range Rovers, as if they hardly dared brave the outside world for a second.'

Mr Bidmead spoke with a sharp, precise tone and always sounded vaguely superior. Kate had to admit that she found him a little intimidating.

'Well, we don't have no Range Rover,' Zoe snapped.

'Children could walk to and from school in the old days,' said Mr Bidmead, 'and knew they would come to no harm.' There was a mumble of agreement from one or two of the older men.

'And you could always leave your front door open?' Kate muttered under her breath, but the old man's hearing was remarkably good.

'You may joke, Miss Trippett,' said Mr Bidmead sternly, 'but your father, now, he'd have understood the import of my words.'

'Too soft, we are,' offered Bert, one of the older men. 'Too soft on the wrong-doers and the ne'er-do-wells. If we got them gypsies kicked out, for a start, it'd be safer to walk at night.'

'Travellers, Bert,' said Kate. 'And they're not all… Well, you sound very prejudiced.'

Nobody listened, though.

'That Miss Davisham, she were a good schoolteacher,' said another regular, and there was a murmur of approval. 'She were a good old-fashioned sort. Kept kids in their place but taught 'em well. Things have gone down'ill since she left Little Brockwell.'

'Yeah,' said someone else, 'where *did* she go all of a sudden?'

'Indeed,' said Mr Bidmead quietly, but nobody seemed to hear him, apart from Kate.

'Course, back when we were young,' said Bert

reflectively, 'there were always a bobby on the beat. He'd ride his bike up and down the High Street, and if he saw any mischief, he'd come riding along like the rushing wind, cape flying out behind him, and he'd clip you round the ear with his cape and you'd stop messing. Stung like mad, it did.'

'I bet it did,' said Kate with a shudder. 'How awful. That would never be allowed today.'

'Too right it wouldn't!' said Bert. 'There's your problem – too soft! No discipline!'

'Oh, please,' said Kate gently. 'We're a civilised society, or at least we pretend to be. I don't think *hitting* children is ever going to solve anything.'

Mr Bidmead, who had been watching the exchange with amusement, smiled grimly. 'This place is changing,' he said. 'And not for the better. Nothing is normal, you mark my words.' He pointed over to the football crowd. 'All that bravado's just for show. Those young chaps have kids, or little brothers and sisters, or little cousins.' Mr Bidmead took a sip from his pint and placed it on the bar with slow deliberation. 'For a long time I've feared that someone's trying to destroy this village. This community.'

Harry exchanged a glance with Kate. 'Come on, Mr B. That's a bit much. The kid's only been scared of his own shadow or something.'

'All the same,' said Kate thoughtfully, 'it's odd.' She pictured the crushed crisps again, and shivered.

The regulars fell silent, allowing Kate's comment to sink in. After a long pause – punctuated by thuds from the darts corner and a groan from the TV annexe at a missed goal – Mr Bidmead spoke first.

'This village will need to pull together,' he said. 'Rely on it.' He drank up and nodded to Harry, pushing his empty glass along the bar. 'Well, it's time for me to take to my armchair for another nocturnal chapter of Dickens…. I'll wish you all

71

goodnight.'

After Mr Bidmead left, there was a nervous silence among the regulars. It was broken by Zoe's husband, Mick.

'Anyone know what happened to them gippos?' he said. 'The ones what camped out on the Corley Meadow?'

'They were travellers, Mick,' said Kate, and this time the rebuke got through.

'Well – travellers, gippos, whatever you call 'em – where'd they go?'

Everyone turned to look at Harry. As landlord of the Dark Horse, he was privy to all the gossip and news – and as he knew the difference between the two, he was generally thought to be the best source of information in Little Brockwell.

Harry shrugged, though. 'I dunno, do I? They moved on. Council got an order to evict 'em. Far as I know that were the end of it.'

'Just a thought,' muttered Mick, taking a deep gulp of his Guinness. 'They got strange ways, them people. Children can be… taken in, y'know. Stories of a glamorous life on the road, all that.'

'Oh, come on,' retorted Kate crossly. 'You're suggesting Tyler Uttley was frightened by the travellers? And that Casey's gone off with them? I've never heard such nonsense. They're not criminals, they're just people who don't have a permanent home.'

'Scroungers, if you ask me,' Mick said. 'Living off the dole, ain't they? All of us lot here have to work for a living. Why can't they?'

'Some of them do, you know,' said Kate. 'They're not all on the dole. Imagine how it must feel to have the whole of England scared of you, just because you're different.'

As Kate spoke, she was remembering the flash of sunlight she had seen up by Corlett's Farm, but she kept that to herself for now.

Mick took a sip of his pint. 'All right. I'm just saying to cover every angle. That's all.'

'Well, I'm sure they are,' Harry said. 'Very capable types, our coppers. Now, then – who's for a refill before the half-time rush?'

'It must be her! It *has* to be!'

Jessica, striding up the sunlit meadow towards the ridge, wore an expression of determination. It seemed she wasn't going to stop for Richie, who was puffing and panting some way behind her. Finally, she took pity on him, stopping to lean on a fallen tree and to look out over the valley.

'Come *on*, you lumbering creature!' she shouted.

Jess admired the view. Her home town of Meresbury was an old and beautiful city, but there was nothing like this. All right, this place probably didn't offer much to do, but it was very restful if you didn't actually have to live here all the time. The green meadow, speckled with buttercups, climbed steeply away from the village. Dandelion-clocks floated in the warm air and a dragonfly whizzed past Jess's face. Little Brockwell nestled in the vale, a cluster of slate and tiled roofs. The proud stone tower of St Leonard's church jutted above everything, while the river was a thin thread of silver and gold, sparkling with sunlight.

Her home town was elegant, but this place had a timeless beauty.

Plus, she reminded herself, it had a fit boy on a motorbike. So it scored more than home just for that.

Richie caught up with her and collapsed gratefully across the branches of the fallen tree, wheezing and gasping.

'It… might… not… be her,' he eventually managed to say. 'Don't… get your hopes up.'

'Everything happens for a reason, Richie. It would be too big a coincidence if it wasn't her.'

'And a pretty big coincidence if it was,' Richie pointed out.

'No, no,' Jess answered, hurrying on up the path. 'Like I said, something odd is going on in Little Brockwell. And you know her and odd stuff. She'll be drawn to it, like a moth to a flame.'

At the top of the hill was a rusty five-bar gate, leading into a farmyard. Jess and Richie climbed over, their hands smearing with orangey rust, and dropped on to the ground. They could see now that the farmyard was in terrible condition – muddy, pitted and churned. Two vast metal barns cast cold shadows and blocked out the sun, while an old red tractor, looking as if it hadn't been used in years, stood sentinel nearby like a rusty sculpture. There was an all-pervading smell of manure, hay and mustiness. An eerie silence buzzed in their heads.

'Like a ghost town,' Richie whispered.

Around the corner behind the barn, they found a path leading up to a tumbledown stone farmhouse with a roof of cracked slates and a jungle of weeds for a garden – and here, they stopped dead.

There, parked at the garden gate, was an old, olive-green Volkswagen Dormobile camper-van, splattered with creamy mud. The concertina-like roof was up, but the windows were curtained and there was no sign of any life.

Open-mouthed, Jess and Richie turned to look at each other. 'It *is* hers,' said Jess. 'I'm sure of it.'

'You know what?' Richie murmured. 'I'm almost convinced.'

'Look!' Jess exclaimed. She darted forward. Just in front of the van was a neat campfire in a hollow. Above it, three sticks had been laid out in a wigwam-shape, supporting a hook from which a metal billy-can was hanging. The fire was not burning, but ashes still smouldered in the hollow. Jess reached out and touched the billy-can with the tip of one finger – it was still warm.

She peered inside the container, wrinkling her nose. 'Looks like some kind of stew,' she said. 'The fire's not lit – but I reckon it was, less than an hour ago.' She was pleased with her deduction.

'Okay, Shirley Holmes,' Richie said, folding his arms and looking around nervously. 'So where is she, then?'

Jess straightened up and hurried over to the Dormobile. She pressed her face up against the windows, trying to see if there was a chink in the curtains. 'Emerald?' she called, tapping on the glass. 'Emerald?'

There was no answer.

'Right, let's split up,' Jess said.

Richie groaned. 'No, no, no! In movies when someone says *let's split up*, you just know that something awful's about to happen to someone, and you're sitting there going, *why* are they being so dumb as to go off on their own? Let's stick together.'

Jess walked up to him, peered into his bespectacled, blinking eyes. 'You're not scared, are you, Rich? C'mon, be a man!'

'I don't want to be a man just yet. My brother says it's not much different from being a boy, except you have to pay income tax.'

Jess rolled her eyes. 'I'm just going to take a look around the house. Wait here.'

Despite Richie's protests, Jess scurried round the Dormobile and picked her way along the cracked crazy paving into the garden. Some of the grass was so tall that it looked like green ears of corn, waving in the breeze at head-height.

She tried the door of the farmhouse. It seemed to be locked, so she went round to the front window and peered in through the grubby, cobwebbed glass. Woodlice and ants scuttled for cover on the window-sill. The downstairs level of the house, Jess saw, was a big, open room with a flagstone floor, totally empty except for an old fireplace dividing the kitchen from the lounge area. There were cracks in the plaster, as well as a big tide-mark of damp across the far wall, and Jess felt the window-ledge crumbling as she leaned on it. She decided to step back before it gave way, and brushed the dust from her top, tutting.

She saw the movement out of the corner of her eye, and whirled round – not quickly enough.

A dark-clad, dark-masked figure.

Jess screamed as it cannoned into her, slamming her down face-first on to the earth. A hand clamped over her mouth.

She struggled, trying to squirm out of a powerful grip, but whoever was holding her down had immense strength. As the panic rose in her stomach, she told herself she had to keep moving, keep fighting the weight on top of her. She kicked, punched the air, tried to scream. *Where was Richie?* Jess found a corner of soft flesh and bit as hard as she could into the palm of her assailant – there was a squeal of pain from above her, and Jess pressed the advantage, levering her body up and lashing out with both booted feet.

Jess bit again, harder now. The assailant struggled to keep a hand over her mouth – for a second, Jess's mouth was free to scream, '*Richie!*' before her head was smacked into the ground again, sending a sharp, angry pain through her skull. Still Jess wriggled. She pulled a hand free, scratched at something which felt like heavy woollen cloth.

Now she had a lever, and rolled herself over.

The attacker, still trying to hold her down, was dark-clad and masked, slight but powerful. Jess bit, scratched and swore, fighting like a demon now that she had the advantage. She jerked her legs back as hard as she could and flipped them upwards, then kicked hard, giving her opponent the full force of two Doc Martens in the shins. With a grunt, the figure shot backwards into a flower-bed.

Richie was running up the path, now, and hovered on the edge of the fight, uncertain what to do.

Jess hurled herself forward like a wildcat, gripped the attacker's wrists and pinned them down. Her opponent struggled, growling angrily. In the struggle, something came free – the black scarf which had been wrapped around the figure's face.

A shadow fell over them both. In a split second, Jess realised that Richie was holding a cracked flowerpot and lifting it high above his head.

'*Richie, no!*' she screamed, and leaped up, pushing him aside just in time.

Richie staggered back, dropping the flowerpot, as Jess rolled over.

As one, Jess and Richie scrambled to their feet and turned towards the assailant, who was now slowly standing up.

The figure pulled its dark hood down, releasing a tangle of bright, glossy, tomato-red hair. Jess and Richie saw a hard, strong pair of green eyes, looking intently at them from a pale and high-cheekboned face.

'Well,' said a familiar voice, 'you certainly did not waste any time.'

It was their old friend, Emerald Greene.

Livvy Parks – ten years old, bright-eyed and light-fingered – lifted the window of the schoolroom and dropped on to the parquet floor. She stayed on all fours for a second, making sure she had not been heard, then she tiptoed over to the door.

Her nose twitching, Livvy looked up and down the corridor. Opposite, the school office was dark and quiet. Down the far end, the door to the kitchen was open. She could hear the sound of rhythmic snoring as the caretaker, in between doing some odd jobs in the holidays, took his afternoon nap.

Livvy sniggered. 'Just too easy,' she said to herself, and slipped back inside the classroom.

She hurried over to the teacher's desk and slid her penknife into the top of the drawer. It gave easily, with a sharp cracking sound – Livvy held her breath, but there was no change in the rhythm of the snoring.

Livvy pulled the drawer open, rummaged through the pens, paper clips and drawing pins. She reached right to the back and her hand came into contact with something flat, oblong and hard. With a cry of triumph, she caught hold of the wire of a headphone, and tugged hard – the iPod came free of the clutter at the back of the drawer.

'It's not stealing,' Livvy reminded herself. It was her property, and Mrs Chaney had confiscated them in the last week of term. She'd said she would give them back at the end of the day – but Mrs Chaney had ended up talking to a parent and Livvy, before she'd had a chance to ask, had been whisked away in the car by her mum, Zoe. 'I need to see her!' Livvy had protested, but to no avail.

So, Livvy had taken matters into her own hands. This was the first day she'd had the chance. She knew it was wrong to break into someone's desk, but she reminded herself she was only reclaiming what was hers.

Livvy pocketed the iPod. She tried to put the drawer back in, although it was wonky and wouldn't fit properly. As she struggled with it, her fingers brushed against a battered metal tin which made a clinking noise. Livvy bit her lip. She really knew she shouldn't, but she picked the tin up and shook it gently. It rattled with coins. She opened the lid and looked inside. The tin was packed with money – coins and notes.

Without even thinking what she was doing, Livvy slipped the tin into the top pocket of her shirt. Then she scampered across the dusty floor to the window again. The caretaker's snores still reverberated up and down the corridor.

She had to climb on to the radiator. The window, which had an old, worn sash, had started to close again on its own and the gap wasn't big enough to squeeze out of any more. Gasping with the effort, Livvy steadied herself with one hand and eased the window up with the other. She climbed on to the ledge, swung her legs round and dropped on to the playground as the window slammed shut above her. She winced, realising she had grazed her knee.

'Almost there,' she murmured. Now, she only had to make it across the playground and back the way she had come – through the hole in the fence, the hole which led to the Meadows and freedom.

Livvy scurried across the playground, glancing once over her shoulder at the school building. There was no sign that the caretaker had woken up. Smiling to herself, Livvy patted the tin in her pocket and felt a surge of confidence.

A cloud passed over the sun, casting a shadow across the playground. Livvy frowned, suddenly feeling chilly.

And then, with a sound like rushing wind, something huge and dark emerged from behind the bike-sheds.

Livvy yelped and stopped in her tracks, almost falling over. She swallowed hard, tried to ignore her thumping heart and looked up in terror at what she saw.

It was, simply, a man on a horse.

But there was something terrible about him, something unearthly. The horse had a jet-black, shining pelt which rippled like water. It had piercing, scarlet eyes and proud nostrils which gushed steam. The rider, meanwhile, was taller than any man she'd ever seen. He was dressed in black – boots, a soft velvet cloak, gloves. A cowled hood shadowed his face, so that all she could see was a pale chin and a thin-lipped mouth. He held the reins firmly with one hand, while the other hand grasped some kind of lance or pole, adorned with red and black flags.

And there was something horribly familiar about this horseman, about this moment.

It stirred something in her subconscious – a memory – no, surely a *dream* –

'Can I… help you, mate?' said Livvy nervously. 'You lost?'

The rider gave no answer. All Livvy could hear, above the distant murmur of traffic, was the sound of the horse's breath. It sounded icy cold, like a mountain stream.

'The gymkhana's next month, you know,' Livvy said, backing away. 'You're a bit early.'

The horse reared up, whinnying, its dark mane streaming against the sunlit sky. Livvy, startled, fell over backwards and scrambled to her feet again, backing away slowly but still somehow held there, entranced by the dark knight.

The rider's mouth fell open with an unearthly hissing sound, and he bared sharp, yellowing teeth at Livvy. He lowered the lance, pointed it at her accusingly. The shadow of the lance fell across the playground, dark and accusing, touching Livvy with a chill.

And then the horse charged.

Hoofbeats echoed on the playground tarmac as the dark whirlwind came for Livvy. Shaking with terror, the girl ran. She slammed up against the playground fence, the smell of creosote in her nostrils, scrabbling for a hold on the knotted wood. The hoofbeats thundered louder and louder.

Livvy waited until the last possible moment and then hurled herself aside. The tin fell from her pocket, scattering coins and notes across the playground, but Livvy didn't care any more. She did a somersault roll into the side of the school building as the horseman tore past her, the lance slicing deep into the fence where she had been a moment ago.

What happened then was impossible, but Livvy saw it

with her own eyes.

The horseman twisted out of shape, a blur of black and red.

A terrible sound echoed across the playground, like the neighing of the horse mixed in with human screaming and the noise of shearing metal. Like water running into a plughole, the horse and its rider seemed to become an angry whirlpool, vanishing into the fence without leaving the slightest mark on the wood.

Livvy stared open-mouthed for several seconds, her mouth sandpaper-dry and her heart pounding so hard she could feel it in her ribcage and her throat. She looked one way, then the other. Nothing. The scattered notes blew in the breeze, skittering across the tarmac like rubbish, but otherwise all was quiet.

And then she started shaking.

Livvy Parks fell to her knees and began to sob uncontrollably, her tears staining the sun-bleached surface of the playground.

After a few seconds, raindrops began to spatter down, mingling with Livvy's tears, blackening the grey tarmac. The rain became a shower, and then a torrent, lashing the village, filling every sun-baked crevice with brackish, life-giving water.

And Livvy Parks knelt in the playground – the rain flattening her hair and making her skin glisten – and stared straight ahead, unmoving, seemingly unaffected by the downpour.

Kate looked up from the till as the bell jangled, and felt a slight chill as she saw that the new arrival was Mr Alfred Bidmead. He wiped his feet on the mat and smiled.

'Good day,' he said, and nodded at the streaming window-panes and the water rattling down off the awning.

'Suddenly, not the best of days.'

'Indeed,' she said, without much affection. 'What can I do for you?'

Mr Bidmead removed his hat – a touch of old-fashioned propriety. 'Sorry to bother you, Miss Trippett. Is your grandmother awake?'

'I think she's watching telly. Can I do anything for you?'

'No, no...' Mr Bidmead allowed his hand to trail along a nearby shelf. 'I think not.' He looked up suddenly, directly at Kate. 'You were very outspoken in the pub. I liked that.'

She folded her arms. 'Thanks. I think.'

'You're welcome.'

There was an awkward silence.

'Mr Bidmead,' she said, 'are you worried about what's going on in this village?'

'Very much so. Which is why I need a word with your grandmother. If I could.'

Kate looked him up and down for a minute, wondering what secrets the old antiques-dealer was keeping to himself for now. Then she nodded towards the back room.

'Thank you,' said Mr Bidmead, and smiled.

Her old, tired eyes were closed, but she heard the door creaking. Then she made out his unmistakable, slow, sad footsteps. One, two, three, four.

They stopped.

He took two more paces, and now she knew he was this side of the counter, by the door to the back room. She could smell the clean, strong wool of that long coat he wore, and she could hear his breathing now.

She clenched the arms of her chair.

'Come in, then, Alfred, if you're coming,' said Grandma Trippett.

Alfred Bidmead, of Mr Bidmead's Antiques Emporium,

cleared his throat. She could see him, now, a pinkish-black blur, and was aware that he had found a seat on the green leather armchair at right angles to her. The chair creaked as he settled, and she heard a clatter as he laid down his walking-cane.

There was silence.

'Are you well?' he asked.

Grandma Trippett felt herself rocking with laughter. 'Concerned for my welfare, are you, now, Alfie Bidmead? You always were a sly little boy.'

He gave a laugh of his own, uncertain and croaky. 'I'm sixty-nine, Auntie Emily.'

She made a dismissive noise. 'Don't call me *that*. You haven't called me that since you were little. Silly, it is, kids calling random adults Auntie this and Uncle that.'

'Sorry. But yes, you're right. At times, I do still feel like I'm still that child.'

'We're all children,' she said darkly. 'When there are forces gathering that are older than any of us... Older, maybe, than the human race.'

She saw his head turn towards her. 'Have you told anyone of your concerns?' he asked sharply.

'*Phhwwww*. Who'd listen to me? They all think I'm half daft. Just because I don't get around the way I used to.'

'You know there are new children here,' he said. It was information, no more and no less – he sounded neither concerned nor pleased.

'I know. I made sure to call 'em in for a chat.'

'And?'

'City kids,' said Grandma Trippett. 'From over Meresbury way. They shouldn't be in danger.'

'But all the same... We need to be aware.'

'An' what about that one in the camper-van?' she asked. 'Something about her makes me... Well, she makes me fret.'

'She doesn't come down to the village much, Emily. I can sense a way about her, though… I think she's more than just a teenage girl.'

Grandma Trippett tutted. 'I don't like this, Alfie. There's not been this kind of tension in the village for years.'

'Perhaps decades,' he ventured.

She knew he was right, but did not say so this time. 'Just make sure you let me know what's going on.'

'You should get yourself a smartphone, Emily.'

'And you should get yourself a better sense of humour, young man.'

He held his hands up in defeat, and stood. 'I have things to attend to,' he said. 'Research. I'm sure we'll catch up again soon.'

She heard him turn to go, counted the footsteps again until he was by the door into the shop. Then she called his name again. Sharply, crossly, as a mother might call a disobedient child.

'*Alfred.*'

She sensed him stop, turn around.

'Yes?' he said.

'If you try to… use this, somehow… To try and find her… You know it will not end well.'

There was an uncomfortable silence.

'I know,' he said, eventually.

'Promise me. Promise you won't go looking for her. She's gone, Alfred, she's lost… She's lost for ever.'

The silence was longer this time. It crackled with almost electrical tension. Then she heard him move, swiftly, his long coat swishing in the air.

'I have matters to attend to,' he said, his voice betraying no emotion.

'I am sure you do,' she said softly, and closed her eyes.

*

'I must apologise for my over-enthusiasm,' said Emerald Greene, as she rummaged in a cupboard for her mugs. 'I did think for a moment that I had intruders. I could not see your faces clearly.'

They were inside the camper-van, sitting around the small table. Raindrops were landing with loud plopping noises on the roof of the van and streaming down the windows. It was turning into quite a heavy shower. Jess was relieved they'd made it inside the van.

'That's… quite all right,' said Jess, rubbing a bruised shoulder. 'I've had worse knocks on the hockey pitch, Em. Don't let it worry you.' She winced. 'So, how are you keeping?'

Emerald frowned. 'How am I keeping what?'

Richie jumped in before they got too confused. 'Look, what I don't understand,' he said, 'is why you've hidden yourself away up here?'

Emerald Greene placed three mugs on the table. 'It is complicated, Richard. When I returned to this zone six weeks ago, the chronostatic barrier around Rubicon House began… fluctuating. It was not safe for me to remain within its environs… So, I gathered the equipment I needed and decided to… travel for a few days.'

Jess took a sip from her mug and gave a wince at the strong kick of Emerald's coffee. She didn't ask where – or when – Emerald had travelled to. She knew these questions could end up leading to all sorts of complications, and that the answers would come out in due course, if they were relevant.

'So you ended up here, in Little Brockwell,' said Jess.

Emerald Greene smiled back. 'So I did.'

'Is it something to do with that tree?' Jess asked. 'Or the weird things happening here?'

Jess couldn't stop staring at her. She was scarcely able to believe that this was Emerald again, here and now. They had said goodbye in the woodland clearing months ago, seemingly for ever. And now, something had drawn her back. Inside, she was fizzing with excitement to see Emerald Greene again. Emerald was mysterious, weird, interesting – and she always brought danger and adventure with her.

'Possibly all of the above,' said Emerald Greene.

Emerald did not look quite the same, Jess noted. She was taller, but then she supposed she and Richie were, too. Her tomato-red hair was shorter, a tousled, ragged bob now. She still wore her blue-tinted glasses, but with more fashionable frames. And instead of her old cagoule and shabby clothes, Emerald had acquired a more bohemian look – a blue-velvet coat with wide lapels, a green silk shirt, a pair of black suede jeans. She had also gathered an assortment of items around her neck: sun and moon pendants, a digital stopwatch, a string of glass beads. She smiled more often, too, and more mischievously.

'Em,' said Jess carefully, 'you do know that… you've changed?'

'Pardon?' said Emerald, blinking.

'You look… different,' Jess explained cautiously.

'Surely not.' Emerald scrambled to the front of the van and flipped down the mirror on the sun-visor. Craning one way and the other, she pulled faces. 'No, no, you are quite wrong. The chronomutic fields have caused no imbalance, thank goodness.'

Jess and Richie shook their heads.

'I think she means… your clothes?' said Richie, with a hopeful glance at Jess.

'And your hair,' added Jess.

'Oh, I see. My apologies.'

Jess's heart leapt at the old, familiar phrase. 'You've had a makeover,' she said. 'You know, like on YouTube.'

'Yes, I did a little… image reprogramming.' Emerald sat down again. 'To be less conspicuous. You approve?'

'It's great,' Jess said, deciding it probably wasn't a good idea to get into just how conspicuous Emerald Greene actually looked. 'Now, can you *please* tell us why you're here? I mean, it's not just a huge coincidence, is it?'

'Ah,' said Emerald Greene, and she sat back, pressing her fingertips together. For a moment there was silence, punctuated only by the pattering of the raindrops on the roof and the windows. 'Coincidence. Well, it is not that rare.' Emerald raised her eyebrows. 'Do you know anyone who shares your birthday?'

'No. Don't think so.'

'I do,' said Richie. 'Jake Haines, in my Maths set.'

'There you are,' said Emerald. 'In a class of thirty, the odds are actually in favour of two of you having the same birthday.'

Jess frowned. 'What does that prove?'

'Coincidences happen because they are statistically *likely*. You are interested in mysteries, and so am I. We were fated to investigate this one together.' Emerald's face broke into a broad, delighted grin. 'It is exhilarating – is it not?'

'Well, I'll say this for you, Em,' said Jess, hefting her mug with a smile. 'You still make a fine cup of coffee.'

'I'll drink to that,' agreed Richie, raising his mug.

'Just a minute!' Jess exclaimed, and started looking around the van in concern. 'Emerald, where's Anoushka?'

'Oh, yeah!' said Richie, thumping his mug down on the table. 'That cat!'

Emerald Greene spread her hands. 'Well,' she said, 'there was a small problem. He… lost his life last week.'

Jess felt her face draining of blood. A hard, painful coldness filled her stomach. 'Oh, no… Em, I'm so sorry!' She touched her friend's hand, felt cold skin.

Emerald Greene looked faintly puzzled. 'There is no cause for concern. He is quite well. Anoushka!' she called.

'Anoushka, you may come out. We are among friends – old friends!'

There was a scurrying sound from outside. A flap, which neither Jess nor Richie had spotted before, opened in the main door of the van, and a familiar black figure darted in and leapt up on to the table. Anoushka crouched there, fixing first Jess, then Richie with a beady, green-eyed stare. The emerald in his collar seemed to pulse with a dim light for a second, and then a drawling voice said:

'Well, if it isn't the Terrible Twins!'

'Anoushka, you sly old thing!' said Jess, and scratched him behind his ears. Anoushka lay down and purred with contentment. '*She* told us you were dead!' Jess added, narrowing her eyes at Emerald Greene.

'*She* certainly did *not*,' retorted Emerald. 'I said he had lost a life, as indeed he did. Luckily, it was only his sixth. Anoushka has three left.'

Richie blinked, opened his mouth to speak and then shut it as if realising how ridiculous he might sound. He looked from Anoushka to Emerald and back again.

'Rrrrright....' said Jess, stroking Anoushka uncertainly.

Richie managed to speak. 'I thought that was just a... well, a myth or a metaphor or something. You trying to tell us it's actually *true*?'

Anoushka tutted and lifted his head for a second to bare his sharp teeth at Richie. 'Honestly, young man,' he said, twitching his ears, 'do they teach you *nothing* in your human schools?'

The rain eased quickly. The sun was low in the sky, painting the clouds orange, when Ben Hemingway parked his motorbike on the wet cobblestones outside the church.

He was just locking the bike when he saw two familiar figures hurrying down the hill into the village. He gave them a wave. They slowed to greet him – the boy quite reluctantly, he thought.

'Hi, Jess,' he said. 'Had a good walk?'

She glanced nervously over at her friend. 'You go back to the cottage, Richie. Tell Gabi I'm on my way. I'll catch you up.'

Richie muttered something and hurried off, stony-faced.

Ben raised his eyebrows. 'Guess I'm I not his favourite person?' he enquired innocently.

'Oh, don't worry about him. He's still bitter that you almost ran us over. I've forgiven you, though.' She looked at him with unnaturally bright, wide-awake eyes. 'So... You know my name now. Good research skills.'

'Yeah, I thought so. Go anywhere nice?'

She glanced away for a second – guiltily, Ben thought. 'Just... to look up an old friend,' she said. When she looked back at him, her wide mouth turned up at the edges in a slightly knowing, not-saying-any-more kind of way which he found interesting.

'Right!' He folded his arms and leaned against the bike. 'You seem in a good mood.'

'Oh, just buzzing from three cups of hyper-strong coffee.'

'Ooh, strong stuff, that. Lay off it. Keeps you awake at night.'

He tried to keep his tone light, bantering, teasing – maybe flirting? It occurred to Ben that it had been a while since he'd done this. After the disaster that had been him and a self-obsessed emo-girl called Amber Bancroft – still very fresh and raw in his mind – he'd told himself he was going to keep away from all that for a bit, at least until his new school.

And then along comes this one.

'Thanks for the public health warning,' she said. 'So, tell me – is this little place always pretty boring, then?'

'Depends,' he said. 'People make their own entertainment in a small village.' He offered her a stick of chewing-gum, which she accepted gratefully.

'Thanks. Well, we've only been here a day, so I... expect I'll find things out as I go along.'

As she folded the gum and popped it in her mouth, she tucked a stray strand of hair behind one ear and began swivelling on her heel, hands folded behind her back as she chewed. Ben decided this was rather cute.

'I expect you will,' said Ben.

He was already liking her a lot more than the brash, over-confident, sweary girls from the village. And definitely a lot more than Amber Bancroft.

'So... You've got a motorbike. Not that I'm saying that automatically makes you cool, or anything.' She was reddening now. 'Hey, you need to be seventeen to ride a proper motorbike! Are you seventeen?'

Did he detect a slightly accusatory note? 'Had my birthday in March,' he said, sounding slightly hurt. 'What about you?'

'Oh, I'm four – um, sixteen,' said Jess quickly.

She almost lies convincingly, he thought in admiration. Very cool. He could have taken it further, got her tangled up in knots of deception, but he didn't. 'Well, I hope you're staying around.'

'Yeah! Is there, like, anything happening around here? Does anyone go into town? To gigs or clubs or anything?'

Ben gave a little laugh, which made his dark fringe dance. 'Well, there's table-tennis on a Monday night. And chess on a Thursday...'

'I... actually didn't... mean that kind of club?' Jess ventured.

Oh, dear, he thought, she thinks I'm being serious. 'Well, the Festival's happening. There's DJ night at the Horse, and Battle of the Bands.' He glanced hopefully at her.

'Really?' she said. 'Isn't that a bit lame?'

'C'mon, it's the Little Brockwell Music and Arts Festival. World-famous. Not.'

'It's not exactly Glasto.'

'Too true. Don't knock it, though! Round here it passes for excitement. Always assuming it's not cancelled, of course, with all the stuff that's been going on. Anyway… I might be there.'

'Oh, well, yeah! I might be going, actually,' Jess gabbled.

'If nothing better comes up,' Ben added, amused.

'Y – yeah, sure. I mean, well, I don't know. I may not be there. But if I am, I might see you there, yeah?' She gave him a hopeful look.

And there I was, Ben thought, worried I was losing my touch. 'Might do,' he said, and smiled. He waved his phone. 'Stay in touch?'

'Sure, yeah!'

Jess took her own phone out. Numbers and social media details were swapped with brisk efficiency. As they said goodbye for now, and Jess hurried on her way, Ben turned back to his motorbike. He was about to put the crash-helmet on when he caught sight of a movement in the churchyard.

He stared over the gravestones and saw the lean, white-haired figure of Mr Bidmead, standing there on the church path and watching him intently. The antiques dealer, in a long dark woollen coat and a broad-brimmed hat, had his hands folded on the ebony handle of his walking-cane.

As Ben frowned at him, wondering what he wanted, Mr Bidmead lowered his half-moon spectacles and gave Ben a look of disdain. Then he twirled his cane and continued on his way through the churchyard.

Well, that could be about any number of things, he thought ruefully. He was used to being disapproved of. He pulled his crash-helmet into place, kick-started the bike and revved the engine.

*

There was a girl lying by the Whispering Tree.

If anyone had been watching, they might have thought, perhaps, that there was nobody there at first. Just a shadow among the shadows, made to look humped and three-dimensional by a trick of the light. But then the shadow moved, stirred. It sat up. It shook its head, and it had a tangle of hair, which seemed to turn from black to brown in the blink of an eye.

Jess, still looking over the new details that had just been added on her phone, didn't notice the shape at first.

He stared at the shadows by the Tree as she passed. She narrowed her eyes. Focused on the shape. The girl.

She tried to tell herself that the girl who had just sat up, as if waking from a long sleep, looked perfectly normal. But she wasn't, and Jess knew it.

Jess watched the girl for a second or two. She looked tired, disorientated, as if she wasn't quite sure where she had woken. Jess jumped over the fence, hurried over to the girl.

'Are you okay?' she asked.

The girl, who was younger than Jess and skinny and freckled, struggled to focus. 'Yeah. I think so. Where am I?'

'Little Brockwell. On the Green. Is that… where you think you should be?'

'I… dunno. It was dark… And there was this horse and rider…'

Jess felt a shiver pass through her, as she realised something. She lowered her voice and spoke urgently to the girl. 'You're Casey,' she said. 'Casey Burgess.'

It was only an educated guess, but it turned out to be right. The girl looked at her properly for the first time.

'Yeah. Who are you, anyway? You don't live round here.'

'It's a long story.' Jess looked around. There was nobody else in sight for the moment, apart from three old ladies gossiping outside the Village Stores. She hoped to see Kate

Trippett, or the Vicar, or some other responsible adult, but couldn't. 'Stay there,' she said to Casey. 'Don't move. People have been looking for you.'

On her phone, she found the number of the Village Stores and called it. Seconds later, Kate answered. 'Yes?'

'You'd better come outside,' Jess said. 'And call Mrs Burgess. Tell her Casey's here. And she's fine.'

They met in the vast and cavernous nothingness, lit only by flickers of red lightning.

The Queen of Shadow, her face bone-white beneath her fantastically twisted, burnished crown, sat on her black throne, flanked by two silent horsemen. Ravens sat on the back of the throne, surveying the Palace with beady-eyed superiority.

She looked her visitor up and down with her crimson eyes. The emissary from the other side, she thought. A person who was betraying not only family and friends, but the whole of Humanity.

She had insisted that the emissary be cowled and cloaked, as was only respectful in her presence. Beneath the hood, the kneeling figure was blurred, shimmery, not properly focused here in this realm in the place that did not really exist. The place halfway between reality and dream. At least, that was how the humans explained it.

The Queen knew that this interference was only to be expected. The temporal fields, after all, were strong, and very few could pass between the worlds without some measure of disturbance.

'Speak,' she said.

The emissary spoke, in a voice like a scratched recording. 'The one you said would come. She's here, in the village. She's been here for several days, now – watching.'

The Queen drew back, hissing from between sharp yellow teeth. '*I knew it*!' The Queen's mouth did not seem to

93

move as she spoke, but her eyes were constantly moving back and forth like restless animals. 'If she knows of the search for the Perfect Soul, she could jeopardise all our plans.' Clouds of reddish light spilled from the eye-sockets as she breathed, hitting the black pillars of the Palace and condensing there in jewelled clusters.

'She's bound to start asking questions,' said the emissary. 'She knows the other two, as well. It's as if they're all friends. From a long way back.'

'She can be dangerous to approach. We must be circumspect for now. Watch, learn, gather intelligence.'

'I don't like it. Things could go wrong.'

'*Nothing will go wrong!* We know that the Perfect Soul is in the village. It only remains to be found.'

The emissary's cowled head lifted for a second – but at a warning hiss from the Queen, it was rapidly lowered again. 'And if I find it for you... Then what you have promised me will be mine? You can still deliver?'

'We do not break promises!' The Queen hissed her words, practically spitting them.

And the emissary's head bowed in acknowledgement.

'Now, go.' The Queen raised a long, bony hand and waved it dismissively, settling back in her throne. 'I have matters to take care of.'

As the emissary withdrew, bowing low, something large and round floated down from the high vaults towards the Queen's outstretched hands.

It was like a globe of heavy, polished stone, black like jet, and yet it floated as lightly as a bubble on the breeze. Its surface was pitted, ancient, and yet there was something almost alive about the way it moved, slowly floating down into the hands of the Queen.

The Queen took the globe in both hands and began to study it intently.

After a second, an image started to form on the surface of the globe. It was like a reflection at first, like the fragile image of a window-pane on a bubble. Then it gained colour, depth, movement. The globe fizzed and crackled as the image sharpened, came alive.

The globe showed a village green. Timbered cottages, a red telephone box, a shop. And there in the centre, the twisted, black form of the Whispering Tree.

'*At last*,' said the Queen, and the breath of her voice sounded like a ghostly wind in the trees. 'At last, after all these centuries… the time is almost upon us.'

4
Close Encounters

The wi-fi in Little Brockwell was pretty rubbish, Jess had found. But right now, waiting for Richie and Emerald to join her, she discovered that if she leaned at a certain angle against the end one of the Meadow Cottages and pointed her phone towards the Church, she could get enough to check out Ben Hemingway online. Again.

He was a bit of a joker on Twitter, she noted, the sort of guy who would retweet funny memes and post pithy one-liners which may or may not have been his own. Not always the obvious stuff. Jess gave a wry grin and she flicked through his Instagram, his Facebook. He didn't usually like to post photos of himself, she noticed – more stuff from the world around him, like a muddy pair of football boots in the hall, a Starbuck's cup with his name spelt KEN (caption: 'How hard can it be?!') and so on.

She felt a little frisson of something, though, when she saw how many girls were in his friends-list. Oh, no. Ben was Mr Popular, it seemed. She scrolled through them. Georgie Popplewick, Caitlin Derbyshire, Mia Henderson, Amber Bancroft, Izzy Kane, Maddy Atkinson… Cute-girl names, popular-girl names. They all had big hair and duck-face pouts, and some of them definitely weren't wearing enough in their profile pics.

Jess scowled, closed Facebook down and shoved her phone back in her pocket. She reminded herself that these girls didn't necessarily all live in Little Brockwell – and even if they did, maybe they were just people from Ben's school. Maybe girls he barely knew. People accepted all sorts as friends online, after all. She clung on to that thought.

She looked up as Richie approached. Emerald was following behind – in her usual restless, agitated way, her gaze darting up and down, back and forth all the time as if she could see things coming out of the hedgerows. Richie was carrying his big birdwatching binoculars with him.

'Upwards!' said Emerald as she sailed past, not stopping.

'Okay?' Richie asked, hands in pockets, looking Jess up and down.

She blushed. 'Why shouldn't I be?'

'Just asking.' Richie nodded at Emerald's retreating form. 'Come on. We'd better keep moving. You know what she's like.'

'I do,' said Jess, with a heavy sigh.

'Did you tell her about Casey?'

Jess nodded.

'What did she say?' Richie asked.

'Oh, you know. She just did that Emerald thing where she puts her head on one side, to acknowledge the information. Like she's filing it away for the future.' Up in front of them, Emerald Greene was striding ahead, long legs making short work of the hill leading out of the village. 'Come on. We'd better keep up.'

A fleet of shiny cars had assembled at the Village Hall. The young children came scurrying out of the Hall one by one, some with painted faces, some armed with pictures, collages or cardboard swords. They were scooped up by their hunted-looking parents and bundled into the waiting cars, and then doors slammed and tyres squealed as the families headed back home as fast as possible.

The parents were forming a protective shield, now, run with military precision.

In a meadow high above the village, Richie and Jess leaned on a fence and watched the operation. Jess held the binoculars, although Richie was hovering, trying to grab them for a turn. 'Wait!' she was saying. 'Just wait a minute!'

Behind them, Emerald Greene strode up and down in the long grass, her velvet coat billowing behind her like a cloak. She was holding something up to the sky – an instrument like a pen with a small mirror on the end – and occasionally she would stop, squint, readjust and then pace up and down some more.

'These kids – ' Richie began, then he turned to look at Emerald Greene. 'Emerald, what are you *doing*?' he asked.

Emerald squinted into the mirror again before snapping the device shut and pocketing it. 'Calibrating, Richard – altering some data. You were saying?'

'Tyler, Casey… just vanishing, then coming back like that,' he said. 'It's impossible, isn't it?'

'Richard, have you learnt *nothing* from your experiences? It has happened, therefore it is not impossible. Uncanny, yes. Wildly improbable, I grant you. But nothing is impossible.'

'Sure, Em,' Jess murmured, scanning the horizon. 'You've obviously never tried to get your toothpaste back in the tube.'

'I do not like the word,' Emerald said. 'I prefer *unencountered*.' She suddenly held out her palm, and the binoculars flipped out of Jess's hands and into Emerald's. Jess was pulled off balance and had to clutch at the fence. Emerald, oblivious to Jess's frantic hand-signals, continued to look through the binoculars, nodding to herself and humming a little tune. 'Yes, yes… look at them. Scurrying like mother hens…'

'You can understand it, though,' offered Richie, pulling the strap free. Jess straightened up, rubbing her neck gratefully and looking daggers at Emerald.

Emerald swung the binoculars round slowly. 'In this

time, parents live in fear of someone harming their children. Perhaps rightly so. There are evil people whose desire is to abduct and hurt children. A tiny minority, of course, but it still means that no child can take the small risk of talking to any stranger... The price paid for your safety is a loss of freedom.'

'Is it like that in your time, Em?' asked Richie boldly, folding his arms.

Emerald ignored the question. 'Monitored day and night, by nannies, childminders, webcams. Shuttled to and from school in armour-plated cars...' Emerald drew a sharp breath, continued surveying the landscape.

'Why are they still doing it?' said Jess, idly tearing the leaves off a dandelion and scattering them. 'That's what I don't get.'

Emerald did not remove her eyes from the binocular lenses. 'Doing it?'

'I mean, aren't they scared? Don't the parents want to keep them at home?'

'In unusual situations, it is often best to carry on as normal,' said Emerald Greene. 'And if their children are at the Little Brockwell Arts Festival events, they know where they are. Not playing in gardens or yards or streets, unsupervised.'

'I suppose so.'

'But these parents are too literal, too single-minded. They do not think to consider the deadliest threat of all.'

Jess and Richie both felt a creeping chill, despite the warmth of the summer morning. They looked at one another, raised their eyebrows, then looked back at Emerald again.

She swung round to face them, removed her glasses so that they could see her green eyes, cold and hard and resolute. 'The darkness, you see... the darkness we are fighting can go where parents cannot watch their children. The one place they always leave unguarded. The one place where they are simply, terrifyingly, *alone*.'

There was a moment's silence. Then, Emerald Greene threw the binoculars to Richie, who surprised himself by catching them. Emerald, hopping with some agility over the stile, landed on the road and headed off down towards the village.

Richie nudged Jess, indicating that they should follow, and they hurried after Emerald along the twisting lane.

'Where, Em?' Jess asked, as they hurried to keep up with her long, confident strides. 'Where do you mean?'

Emerald Greene stopped suddenly in the middle of the road, whirled round to face them. Jess and Richie, caught unawares, stumbled to a halt and backed up a pace or two.

'You mean you do not *see*?' asked Emerald incredulously, spreading her arms wide in exasperation. 'Forgive me. I thought I had made myself clear.'

'Well, you hadn't,' Richie told her. 'As usual.' He folded his arms. 'So, go on, then. What is it? What's the place you're talking about?'

Emerald lifted her hand and pointed a finger at Richie, moving it closer and closer to his head until it was right between his eyes.

'Their dreams,' she said, her voice soft and fearful. 'The darkness comes for them in dreams.'

Jess and Richie looked at each other uncomprehendingly.

'Come on,' said Emerald. 'There's someone we all need to go and see. Someone very, very important...'

In her mind's eye, Emily Trippett was nine years old, and running. Running away from something vast and dark and terrible.

It was galloping, galloping down the street, the dark cloak spreading out behind it as Emily ran, her feet like lead, breath burning in her lungs. At the Brock Ford, the horse's hooves sent up sprays of white as the beast pounded full-tilt through the water, not slowing for a second.

Emily ran, ran, ran, with the horse getting closer and closer. The creature's hoofbeats were thundering in her head, and the hot steam of its breath was heating the air right behind her neck.

She slammed up against the gates of the farm. Nowhere to run. Her dress splashed with mud, her hair awry, Emily Trippett turned to face the darkness.

There were two horses, side by side, jet-black pelts gleaming with water and sunlight. And between them, the dark figure of a woman. Pale face, jet-black hair, red eyes.

The woman held out a long, pale arm.

She extended her bony, pale fingers and smiled, a broad, chilling stripe of red across her white face.

'Emily,' she said. 'I know you, Emily.'

Emily Trippett backed away, shaking her head.

'Take my hand, Emily. We can have an agreement.'

'No.' Emily heard herself say the word without her lips moving.

'Think about it, Emily. Death shall have no dominion. Death hovers over you, Emily. How would you like to banish it for ever?'

Emily shook her head, backing away.

'Time has no meaning here, Emily. You could be nine, nineteen or ninety, but you are always a breath away from death. That could change. It could change now, Emily!'

The horses' hooves kicked the water, sending up glittering sprays in the sunlight.

She backed away further.

The woman's hand seemed to grow, to extend, reaching for her. The taloned fingernails turned it into a grasping, pale claw.

Emily gasped.

And then she woke.

As usual, it took Grandma Trippett a second or two to readjust to her surroundings, to hear the tick-tock of the clock, to smell the wood and peppermint and cinnamon tea of her room behind the shop.

Sunlight filtered in through a chink in the heavy curtains, and motes of dust danced in the beams. She breathed in the heavy air of the village summer, heard Kate bustling around in the shop and chatting to customers.

Her old heart slowed again. She was back – back in the new century, and safe.

The bell of the shop rang, and there was a murmured conversation outside. She felt a slight, almost electrical tingle in her fingertips. Grandma Trippett hoisted herself up with her stick, hobbled over to the mirror as fast as she could to check that she was presentable, and leaned on her stick to greet her visitors.

'Gran,' said Kate, smiling as she peered round the door. 'Jess and Richie to see you. And they've brought a friend!' She ushered them in. 'Got to get back to the shop,' Kate added. 'I'm short-handed today – Zoe didn't come in.'

Grandma Trippett narrowed her eyes as three young people entered.

'Hello,' said Richie. 'You said you wanted to see us?'

Grandma Trippett's weak gaze was fixed on the blur of red who had entered behind Richie and Jess. Even with her limited vision, Grandma could tell immediately that there was something extraordinary – unearthly, even – about this girl.

'This is Emerald Greene,' said Jessica. 'She's… well, she's an old friend of ours. She's interested in helping us solve the mysteries of Little Brockwell.'

The red-haired girl stepped forward, holding out a milky-white hand, and Grandma Trippett shook it uneasily.

'Delighted to make your acquaintance,' said Emerald, her eyes sharp and searching.

'Likewise, I'm sure,' muttered the old lady, and shuffled past her, heading for the wooden dresser against the far wall. 'Now, then… Mysteries, eh?' She lifted something from it – a leather-bound photograph album bulging with unsorted pictures. Richie, perhaps seeing that she was unsteady, took the heavy album from her. 'Thank you, boy,' she said. 'Now, where's that enlarger thingy?'

'I believe this is what you require?' said Emerald Greene. She was examining a device on a nearby desk, rather like a portable television with a metal tray beneath it.

Grandma Trippett was watching Emerald Greene with a mixture of mistrust and interest. 'Yes. That's it. There's a good few hundred snapshots in here, and there's one special one I'm looking for. I need one of you keen young people to help me sort 'em out.'

'I will gladly help,' said Emerald, seating herself in front of the magnifier with her hands neatly folded in her lap. She tried to catch Grandma's eye, but the old lady was having none of it.

'You, boy,' said Grandma Trippett, ignoring Emerald and pointing her stick at Richie. 'This should keep you out of mischief for an afternoon.'

'Me?' said Richie, looking over his shoulder as if he hoped Grandma Trippett was talking to someone else.

'Yes, you! Got sharp eyes, have you?'

'Well – yes, I s'pose so. With my glasses on.'

'Good!' Grandma, who had always found that being decisive rather took the wind out of people's sails and made them less likely to protest, pulled out a chair and sat Richie in front of the viewer with a stack of photographs. 'I'll tell you what we're looking for in a moment.'

Emerald Greene, who had been examining the pendulum of the long-case clock with close interest, suddenly looked up. 'This a very handsome clock,' she said. 'Has it always been yours?'

'No,' said Grandma Trippett, scowling at the girl. 'I bought it last year from Mr Bidmead, if you must know. In prime condition, it were.' Cheeky girl, Grandma thought, asking all these questions. She wasn't like the others, that was for certain.

'Ah, yes,' said Emerald thoughtfully. 'The antiques dealer… Well, it is an extremely fine timepiece.' She looked up sharply, breaking off from her reverie. 'Come on, Jessica,' she said quietly. 'We have other investigations to pursue.' And she headed back out into the shop – not meeting her gaze, Grandma Trippett noticed.

Jess, smiling in slight embarrassment, was about to follow, but Grandma Trippett called her over and sat her down. She slipped an arm around the girl's slim shoulders and peered closely at her, using the remnants of her sight to focus on the girl's face.

'Listen to me, girl,' she said, in a low and conspiratorial voice. 'Listen closely… your friend there.' And she nodded towards the door.

'Emerald?' said Jess. 'What about her?'

'I'll tell you what about her… You should watch her.' Grandma leaned forward, lowering her voice to a whisper. 'There is something… fey about that 'un. She and the darkness may be enemies, but they've more in common than you could imagine. There's death in her eyes – wears it like a shroud, she does. The look of one who's seen terrible things.'

Jess drew back, blinking uncertainly. 'You're trying to scare me.'

'I think that'd be difficult, child,' said Grandma. Pushing back the bangles on Jess's wrist, she seized the girl's right hand in both of hers. Grandma felt her cold skin, and shivered inwardly. 'As I thought. An unearthly chill! Where have you been with your friend, mmm? What have you seen that you don't dare tell?'

Jess drew her hand away. 'It's nothing. It doesn't bother me.'

'Did something touch your hand, girl, mm? Something

not of this world? You can tell me, you know. I'm aware of such things.' The old woman leaned forward. 'And I have certain... healing capabilities. There are herbs, tinctures which can help.'

'I've... got to go,' said Jess awkwardly, jumping up. 'Emerald will be waiting.'

Grandma Trippett stood up, leaning on her stick, and her dark-shaded eyes gazed once more into nothingness. 'Go, then. But I'm still here – if you need me.'

Jess, still unsettled from her conversation with old Mrs Trippett, found Emerald Greene standing by the churchyard gates. A short way up the church path, by the door, a group of mourners in black lined up to shake hands with the Reverend Parsloe.

'The family and friends of Mrs Esme Hutton,' said Emerald Greene quietly, as she stood with her hands behind her back and her head on one side, as if listening to some ultrasonic signal. 'An elderly lady of ninety-three. Sadly passed away last week.'

Jess remembered how the Rector had mentioned it to her and Richie yesterday.

'You know,' said Emerald Greene, 'it is amazing that one does not see more funeral processions. When you consider how many people must die each day...' She slipped her blue-tinted glasses on, hiding her eyes. 'In a way, Jess, I find myself appreciating these ceremonies. They serve as a timely reminder of the fragility of life, of how the dead are just a heartbeat away from the living.'

Jess raised her eyebrows. 'I love hanging out with you, Em. You're so cheerful.'

'Thank you.'

Sarcasm, Jess remembered, usually bounced right off Emerald. 'So, um... were you hoping to crash the wake and nick a few ham sandwiches, or are we heading somewhere?'

'Dynamic as ever, Jess,' said Emerald Greene delightedly, and spun round. She lifted the compass from her neck, peered at the dial and adjusted her direction slightly, pointing at a row of cottages leading off behind the churchyard. 'Number Five, Acorn Row,' she said, her arm stuck out like a scarecrow's. 'While Richard is being distracted by an old lady with an obsession, I believe we will find some answers there.'

Jessica was puzzled. 'You don't think Grandma Trippett knows what she's talking about?'

'Not necessarily,' said Emerald Greene, and her face gave nothing away. 'Come with me.'

Jess folded her arms and stood her ground. 'Look, to be honest, Em, I'm a bit confused... And why were you so interested in Grandma Trippett's clock?'

'Trust me, Jessica!' called Emerald over her shoulder, striding across the street now.

'Emerald,' Jess groaned, scurrying across the sunlit street to keep up with her friend, '*why* do you always assume I'm not going to understand anything?'

'I find it saves time,' said Emerald. She pointed over the hedge into the well-tended garden they had found themselves standing next to. 'Go on. Look.'

Nervously, Jess lifted herself up on tiptoe and peered over the hedge. The first thing she saw was a garden sprinkler, spraying silvery water across a green lawn. A blaze of red roses covered the far fence, and a wooden swing stood beside them.

Sitting in the swing, hardly moving, was a pale, blonde girl of about ten in a blue dress. She looked almost as if she was meditating. Jess suddenly felt a creeping chill – there was something unnerving about the way the girl was sitting there on the swing, almost motionless, staring into space with her hands neatly folded in her lap.

'Come on,' said Emerald Greene, opening the garden gate. 'Let us go in.'

'Em, we can't just – ' Jessica tried to grab her friend's sleeve, but Emerald was already striding across the lawn towards the girl. 'Why do I let her get me into trouble?' she asked the world in general.

Emerald was squatting down in front of the girl. 'Her name is Livvy Parks,' she said, not seeming to care if Jess was listening or not. 'Her mother, Zoe, works in the shop and did not turn up for work today. You remember Kate Trippett mentioning that? Well, I think we have found the reason why.' Emerald waved a hand in front of Livvy's blank face. The girl did not respond – she did not even blink.

'Hey!' There was a shout from the house, and the sound of a door opening.

'Uh-oh,' said Jess, biting her lip. 'We're in for it now.'

They straightened up as Livvy's mum, Zoe, marched towards them across the garden. Her face was white and she had obviously been crying a great deal. Zoe Parks slowed, though, when she caught sight of Jessica, and her expression softened.

'Oh, it's you,' she said. 'You could have come to the door. If you girls have come to see Liv, you'll not get much out of her, I'm afraid.' She sniffed and wiped her nose on the tea-towel she carried.

'Do you know… what…?' Jess asked tentatively.

Zoe Parks rubbed her tired, sunken eyes and sat down on a nearby deckchair. 'Dr Baker says it's just shock. She needs rest.' The tea-towel slipped from her fingers and fell to the grass. Jess leaned down and picked it up for her. 'Rest,' Zoe said, and laughed bitterly. 'Look at her! It's something… *unnatural*, innit? Look at my little girl! What's up with her?'

Emerald Greene was staring into Livvy's expressionless eyes. 'Dr Baker will have made the best possible diagnosis,' she said, 'allowing for the limitations of his craft, Mrs Parks. He would be… a practitioner of medicine, yes?'

'He's the local doctor,' said Zoe Parks, puzzled. 'And who the *hell* are you?'

'Sorry,' said Jess. 'This is Emerald, a friend of mine. She's from...' Jess decided they'd better not go into that just now, especially as she wasn't all that sure herself. 'From London,' she said, crossing her fingers and hoping that would explain a lot of strange behaviour. 'Emerald, can you snap her out of it?'

'Snap her out of it?' repeated Emerald Greene sternly, peering over her glasses. 'That could be lethal. Livvy is in a state of catatonic induction.'

Jess skimmed a hand above her head. '*Voooom*. Catty-what?'

'Well, put crudely... a trance brought on by shock.'

Zoe was looking curiously from her daughter to Emerald Greene and back again. 'Like hypnosis? Why should I believe you? Some London girl who thinks she knows more than the doctor!'

Emerald waved a hand at Zoe. 'Mrs Parks, do you want to find out what has caused this state in your daughter?'

'Of course I do, but – '

'Then kindly allow me,' said Emerald.

And she knelt down and touched Livvy's temples with the tips of her fingers.

The Queen of Shadow sat upright in her polished throne and listened.

It was an odd kind of listening that she did, and in fact listening was not really the word for it. It was more a kind of combination of all of her senses, reaching out through the darkness and across the dimensions.

In all the millennia of her banishment to this realm, she had never sensed a presence in any way complex enough to be interesting. But this one... It swirled with a complexity, a profundity which she had never encountered before.

She sat forward, bared her teeth.

This was something new.

'You know,' said Richie, 'it would really help if I knew what I was looking for.'

'You young people,' Grandma Trippett muttered. 'So impetuous. Patience, boy, hmm! We'll know it when we find it.'

He slipped another black-and-white picture under the viewer – about the fortieth, he thought, in twenty minutes. He wasn't in the mood for local history today, and at the back of his mind there was a nagging uncertainty about where Jess had gone with Emerald Greene.

Richie had always found something slightly untrustworthy about Emerald, something slippery. He sensed that Grandma had come to the same conclusion in a very short space of time, but he didn't say anything.

This picture showed a beautiful young woman with dark, wavy hair. She wore a black dress and a white beret, and she was laughing – showing white teeth – as she brandished a cocktail glass. Richie looked at the picture for a minute, then looked at Grandma. 'That's you, right?'

'Aged eighteen,' she said. 'When I was just Emily. Carefree Emily… Day before war broke out, that were taken.' She drew a sharp breath. 'Still, nothing there… Next one, boy, come on.'

'My name's Richie,' he muttered. 'If you call me *boy*, I can call you *old lady*, all right?'

Grandma Trippett chuckled, her whole body shaking and her ears glowing red with mirth. 'All right, all right! You cheeky monkey.'

Richie slipped the next photo under the viewer. It was larger than the one before, and he had to adjust several controls on the side of the machine to get the picture to fit in the viewscreen. 'There,' he said eventually. 'Got it... That's the village green!'

The picture was obviously posed, but for Richie it immediately conveyed something of the atmosphere of the day. Six men in shirt-sleeves and six young women in plain dresses stood round a maypole on the Green, each holding a ribbon as if about to begin their dance. A crowd had gathered, among them several children – including one little girl with bobbed hair and a white dress, who had flowers gathered in her arms. She was staring off to one side – as if shyness did not allow her to look at the camera. Just to the left of the crowd, Richie could make out the menacing shape of the Whispering Tree creeping in at the edge of the picture, looking as spiky and fearsome as it did today.

'When was this?' Richie asked.

'Earlier than the last. Ten years afore.'

'How do you know?'

'That's me, there, you daft 'un!' And Grandma pointed to the small, shy girl with the flowers. 'I remember that day clear as anything. A beautiful May Day. The heat were... electric. Hottest May I can recall... And there's three of my sisters too.' She pointed to the girls who were ready to dance round the Maypole. 'There were seven of us altogether, boy. Margaret, Lucy, Agnes, Ruth, Esther, Mary, Emily. Seventh daughter of the house, that were me. Some said that made me special, in some way, but I don't know about that.'

'So this is definitely the one you want?' Richie asked.

'It is. All right, boy – Richie, I mean – take a look at that photo and tell me if you see anything... untoward.'

Richie, sensing his heartbeat quickening, leaned forward and peered at the enlarged picture...

*

111

In the garden, Jess watched with growing unease.

As Emerald Greene reached out to Livvy, Jess felt a tingling in her own right hand – that odd, cold pins-and-needles sensation which she had come to know and fear. The hand, touched a few months ago by the cold fingers of a wraith, now acted as a kind of indicator of supernatural activity. Fearful, Jess took a step back and began to chew her fingernails.

'Careful, Em,' she breathed.

The sun was high in the sky, like a white-hot lance cutting through a sheet of blue metal, bathing the garden in golden light.

Zoe Parks and Jess held their breath, hardly daring to look at one another. There was no sound but the gentle swishing of the sprinkler as it soaked the patchy garden behind them.

Emerald Greene's face wore an expression of intense concentration. Still touching Livvy's temples, she lowered her own head as if in pain, then jerked it suddenly upwards.

Zoe gasped and moved forward, but Jess held her back. 'It's all right. I think she knows what she's doing.'

'*We were lost*,' said Emerald softly. It came from her mouth and yet it was not quite her normal voice – it had a deep, resonant quality which sent a chill up Jess's spine. Livvy, meanwhile, appeared not to have moved or spoken, and indeed not to have altered her trancelike state.

'What?' Jess crouched down, aware that the cold numbness in her hand was making her tremble, even despite the heat of the summer sun. 'What did you say, Em?'

'*We were lost, but now we are found once more. In the place of shadows they will come to us, and when darkness falls across the land, we will come to them. One by one, they will fall. And be taken from this land to a place of safety.*'

'The children,' said Jess, her eyes wide in horror.

'*One by one. The Tenebrae will come until we have that which is ours by right. That which was sworn to us generations ago. The*

Tenebrae will come. Tenebrae. Tenebrae.'

'What's she sayin'?' asked Zoe in alarm, backing away.

'Tenebrae!' shouted Emerald Greene, and suddenly, without warning, she let go of Livvy's temples, leaping back as if she had been stung.

Jessica was the only one to notice that, behind them, the sprinkler jerked slightly and spluttered for a second – as if its power flow had been momentarily interrupted – before it resumed its graceful spinning.

Livvy Parks gasped out loud.

She gripped the ropes of the swing so hard that her hands turned white and bloodless. Then she let go, splayed her palms out in front of her and stared at them as if seeing them for the first time.

'How did I get here?' she asked in a small voice.

And then, Livvy was crying and her mother was hugging her tightly, and Emerald was on her feet beside Jess, shaking slightly, running a hand through her bright red hair.

Jess looked back and forth in alarm. 'Is everything…'

'Yes, yes. Fine,' said Emerald. She pulled a green silk handkerchief from her pocket, dabbed her perspiring forehead and let out a deep breath. 'Mrs Parks, your daughter will be all right now. Make sure she has plenty to drink, and a long rest.'

Zoe Parks hugged the sobbing Libby close to her, and her eyes briefly flickered to Emerald in thanks.

Jess was frightened. For the first time since Jess had known her, Emerald Greene looked as if something had truly rattled her.

'One more question, if I may?' Emerald addressed the request to Zoe Parks, who nodded reluctantly. Emerald leaned in to Livvy. 'What did you see?' Emerald asked Livvy gently, leaning forward again.

Livvy lifted her tear-stained face and pushed her hair out of her eyes. 'It was… like a man on a horse,' she said, frowning.

'Only… it wasn't. Not like a normal man, if you know what I mean. Sort of… dark. And not really there.' She bit her lip. 'You gonna think I'm crazy.'

'Not at all,' said Emerald Greene, straightening up with a new look of determination in her eyes. 'Livvy, this horse. I have to ask you something about it. Was it the first time you'd ever seen anything like that?'

'Well…' Livvy wrinkled her nose. 'Yes and no.'

'Where had you seen it before?' asked Emerald urgently.

Zoe Parks folded her arms. 'Come on, what's with all the questions? Is this some kind of school project?'

Jess held her breath. She knew the answer was important, even if Livvy's mum did not.

Livvy looked from Emerald to Jess, to her mother and back to Emerald again.

They were all waiting, there in the hot garden in Little Brockwell, for her to give an answer – an answer which, Jess could sense, was of supreme value to Emerald Greene. To the only person who might have worked out what had happened to the other children.

'Two days ago,' said Livvy.

'And where?' persisted Emerald, her voice low and urgent, fingers making an odd beckoning gesture as if trying to coax the answer from Livvy. 'Where did you see it?'

Livvy rubbed her eyes. She looked from Emerald to Jess, to her mum, and then back to Emerald again.

'In a dream,' she said. 'In a bad dream.'

'Well?' said Grandma Trippett impatiently. 'Can't you see it?'

Richie had been staring at the photograph for several minutes and his eyes were beginning to ache. Was this all some kind of practical joke by the girls – to trap him in this musty room on a summer's day, with only a mad old woman and her photos for company, while they went out and had some fun?

He just couldn't see what she was getting at.

And then, with the force of someone slapping him right between the eyes, he realised.

'The church,' he said. 'You can't see the church!'

The camera had been angled towards the cottages in front of the church, and the village store could be seen in the background. Behind the maypole and the Whispering Tree, the church should have been clearly visible, silhouetted against the sky.

But there was nothing. The sky was blank.

Grandma Trippett clapped him on the shoulder. 'You're not such a daft 'un, then!'

'Yes, well, and you're not such an old…'

'Fruit-cake?'

'Oh, I wouldn't say that – ' Richie glanced down. The old lady was presenting him with a plate, on which there was a rich, brown slice of home-made cake full to bursting with marzipan, sultanas, cherries and nuts. 'Oh, I see,' he said. 'Thanks. Brilliant!'

He took a bite. It was the juiciest, tangiest, most delicious fruit-cake he had eaten in a very long time. As he found himself incapable of speaking while eating it – something he sensed Grandma Trippett would disapprove of anyway – he gave her a big thumbs-up.

'So,' said Richie at last, holding his plate in one hand and manipulating the viewer with the other, 'what have we got here, then? Can this thing do any more magnification? No, seems we've got it on full...' He took another bite of the splendid cake, then suddenly let the slice drop on the plate. 'Of course!' He spun round to face the old lady. 'Mrs Trippett, I don't suppose you've got a computer? With a scanner?'

She snorted in contempt. 'Computers! Overgrown calculators, ain't they? No, of course I've not got one. No need.'

'Oh.' Richie looked crestfallen. 'Does Kate have one?'

'Maybe. I don't know. Busy in the shop, though, ain't she?'

'Anyone else you can think of?' asked Richie hopefully.

'Rector's got one,' said Grandma Trippett. 'Uses it for the Parish Magazine. Dare say she'd let you borrow it for a bit, if you ask nicely – and say I sent you?'

'I will. Thanks!' He grabbed his jacket, and hurried out.

'So what was behind that little demonstration?' panted Jess, struggling as usual to keep up with her friend.

They reached the stile at the entrance to the Green, where Emerald swung around with a flourish of her coat. Then she turned slowly back, looking thoughtfully at the dark, imposing form of the Whispering Tree.

'You do not understand the importance?' Emerald said, raising an eyebrow. 'Livvy Parks has seen the Darkness and did not disappear! Even though her dreams had already been invaded.'

Emerald suddenly vaulted the stile, and was striding towards the Tree with a determined expression. Jess groaned, leapt the stile and hurried after her.

'Yeah. Right. I'm kind of having trouble with this, Em. Is this… this Darkness thing something real? Or something imagined in people's nightmares?'

Emerald was in the shadow of the Tree, circling it. She was bobbing up and down, making a humming sound to herself.

'So this is where she was found… What kind of tree is this?' she said suddenly.

'An… oak, I think. Does it matter?'

Emerald Greene lowered her glasses and peered disapprovingly at Jessica, like someone much older. 'Of course it matters. Everything matters.' She turned back to the Tree, reached out and touched it, then pulled back as if stung. 'How

116

remarkable.'

'What?' Jess said excitedly. 'What have you found, Em?' This, she thought, her heart pounding, was just like old times. A mystery, and Emerald Greene here to investigate it.

'Could be nothing… You said you heard voices?'

'Yeah, but not really. It's just the bark drying in the sun, or air inside it or something.'

'How very *rational* of you,' said Emerald, managing to make it sound like an insult. She leaned into the Tree. She drew closer and closer, until her ear rested against the bark.

Jess held her breath. In the warm, glutinous sunlight, and the stillness of the summer day, everything seemed to stop.

'Well?' Jess said after a few seconds.

Emerald rummaged in her pockets, frowning, and took out what looked to Jess like a doctor's stethoscope. She put the earpieces in the ears, placed the diaphragm against the bark and listened intently for a few seconds. Then she stepped back, pulled the stethoscope out of her ears and shoved it back in her huge pockets again.

'So is it a healthy tree?' Jess asked.

Emerald tapped one finger against her lips for a few seconds, thinking. 'Yes,' she said eventually. 'You know, I think it is *probably* just the bark drying in the sun. Or air being displaced as the tree takes on water.' Emerald Greene spun round, and fixed her with her most cold, hard, serious stare. 'Oh, and to answer your previous question – both.'

'Sorry, what was my previous question?'

Emerald tutted. 'Do keep up. The Darkness! It is both real, and inside people's heads. And it has allies in the village, I would expect.'

'Allies? You mean people working for it?'

'Yes. Person or persons unknown,' said Emerald enigmatically.

Jess decided to let that go for now, but stored the

information for future use. 'Right... Okay, and what was that word you were saying with Livvy?' she asked.

'Word?'

'Back there in the garden, when you did your crazy witch-doctor thing on little Livvy. Casting out the evil spirit, or whatever you were doing.'

'I was breaking the catatonic induction.'

'Yeah, well. You said all that weird stuff, about being lost and found... And you said *ten*-something?'

'*Tenebrae*,' said Emerald Greene, and the word hung in the air, vast and dark and heavy like a cloud across the sun.

'What's that, then?'

'Well, it has several meanings. *Tenebrae*, in the Church of your time, is a religious ceremony, I believe – a service during the period you call Holy Week, in which candles are extinguished one by one.'

'Sorry, Em. Never really bothered much with church. I think I'm an agnostic, actually.'

'*Tenebrae* is also, in a more general sense, the Latin word for "darkness". You study French, do you not? *Les ténèbres*? Comes from the same root. I saw something, very briefly, through Livvy's eyes, and that was the name... *it* gave itself as it spoke to me. A collective name, I think.'

'The horseman?'

'Yes, that... was one manifestation. We must be aware, alert for others.'

'So... what is it? What *are* they?' asked Jess, puzzled.

'A darkness, a living darkness given form and shape and sentience by...' Emerald Greene pinched the bridge of her nose with her forefingers as if concentrating hard. 'By something with the power over life and death.'

'Em?'

'Yes, Jessica?'

'This is all sounding rather familiar.'

'Jessica, I know this much. We are dealing with a force more malevolent, more terrible than the people of this village can imagine.'

'Great,' said Jess. 'And I thought I was on holiday.'

There was a sudden commotion over by the farm buildings, and they turned as one. Anoushka emerged from behind the old tractor – looking a little bedraggled – and hopped on to Emerald's shoulder. The emerald in the cat's collar seemed to pulse with light, and Jess thought she saw Emerald's own eyes shine briefly in response.

'I have been making discreet enquiries, Miss Greene, as you requested,' the cat said, in his usual fruity tones.

'Yes, Anoushka. And?'

'The travellers moved on two days ago. The convoy headed north across the gritstone ridge… My intelligences believe they were making for the village of Bardleton, some eight miles from here. There is a patch of common land just outside the village.'

'The travellers?' asked Jess, confused. 'I thought we'd ruled them out? Grandma Trippett said – '

'I *know* what the old lady said,' snapped Emerald Greene, and Jess was shocked at the unusual harshness in her voice. 'This is my investigation. I leave no stone unturned.' With that, Emerald hopped over the iron gate and landed on all fours, like a cat, on the muddy farmyard.

'Is there… anything else I can do?' Jess asked.

'You have your evening planned, I believe,' said Emerald Greene, straightening up.

Jess thought of Ben, and felt herself turning red. 'Well… Kind of.'

'Enjoy yourself, and forget about this for a while. Anoushka and I have other avenues to pursue. And tomorrow – we should know more.'

Emerald tapped the side of her nose, and she and

Anoushka headed off, back towards the camper-van.

Jess waved, uncertainly.

The Rector bustled around, clearing papers and cups out of Richie's way as she sat him down and logged him into her battered computer. As soon as he had mentioned that he was on an errand for Grandma Trippett, the Rector had been falling over herself to help.

'In fact,' she said, shoving some tatty papers into an already bulging filing-cabinet, 'if you're a bit of a whizz with computers, can you stop it flashing up these messages saying my printer's out of paper when it quite clearly isn't?'

'Sorry,' said Richie. 'I think miracles are more your department.'

The Rector chuckled, appreciating the joke. 'Can I get you anything, ah, Richie?… All right, then. I'll leave you to it. Give me a shout when you've finished. I'll be over the road in the church.'

Richie placed Grandma Trippett's photo in the scanner and scanned a digital copy of the image, which took a few seconds. As soon as it was done, he clicked the mouse impatiently, pasting the image into an online app where he could manipulate it.

The photograph filled the screen. Richie adjusted the frames, expanding the right-hand side of the picture where the missing church should have been.

He changed a few specifications here and there to alter the image's tone, its light and shade and its resolution. Then he tapped the mouse and sat back to watch the results of his handiwork.

A diagonal line swept across the screen from bottom left to top right, enhancing the lighter and darker shades of the image a little more each time it passed. A series of bleeps provided a soundtrack to the process. The computer was at least a decade old, and so Richie knew it would take a minute or two over this simple task.

Richie yawned, stretched. The hot summer afternoon was making him feel drowsy, and he wondered if he should have taken up that offer of a cold drink after all.

Suddenly, he sat bolt upright in the Rector's chair, looking at the screen. He clicked frantically on the Zoom command, got the picture to home in on the one small corner where something very, very interesting was happening.

The image-enhancing program came to an end. Richie looked at what he could see on the screen –and his jaw dropped.

'No way,' he said to himself, and then again, because he could think of nothing else to say, 'Absolutely no *way*!'

He quickly opened his Instagram account and posted the image – and just to be sure, he saved a backup to his Dropbox as well.

Then, he sat there unmoving, staring open-mouthed at the computer screen, suddenly feeling more unsettled and alone than he had felt in a long time.

'Hello, Mrs Burgess.'

Shona Burgess jumped visibly as her name was mentioned. She had just got off the Westmeadow bus, carrier bags in hand, and had been about to cross the street when she spotted the strange girl in the long velvet coat.

She knew who she was. People had seen her, up at Corlett's Farm and hanging around the village. Weird-looking kid with red hair and blue glasses. Emerald, she remembered she was called. Something to do with those other new people.

But some people said she was clever, that she knew stuff. That she could help. Shona eyed her warily.

'Is Casey well now?' asked the Emerald girl, falling into step beside Shona.

'What's it to you?' Shona asked suspiciously. 'Are you friends with her?'

Emerald smiled. 'Not especially. But I do take an interest. I am... concerned, you might say. I am collecting... reactions.'

'Reactions?'

They had come to the gate of Shona's terraced cottage. She dumped the bags down so that she could stare the girl out, narrowing her eyes, folding her arms. Emerald just responded with an implacable, unblinking gaze, her green eyes like polished jade. The girl's calmness unnerved Shona, made her shiver.

'Yes,' said Emerald softly. 'To the horses.'

Something echoed in the back of Shona's mind. 'I dunno what you mean,' she said, and leaned down to pick up her shopping.

'Here, let me help you.' Emerald had hold of two of her carrier bags and was marching up Shona's garden path to her front door. Infuriated, Shona followed her.

'I don't need your help,' she said. 'Any of you.'

'I am just concerned about Casey.'

'No, you're not. You're just another of them, aren't you? I reckon they sent you to find stuff out, about whether I'm a fit mother and all that.' She shoved the key aggressively into the lock. 'You can tell them all to bog off and mind their own business.'

'Tell who? Sorry?' The girl seemed genuinely confused.

'Social workers! Do-gooders!' She snatched her shopping from Emerald.

'I am sorry. I have no interest in those people. I only want to find out about the horses, and Casey.'

Shona stood on the threshold for a long few seconds, and then put her shopping bags down carefully in the hallway. She turned towards Emerald, arms folded.

'You really want to know?' she said. 'Casey's fine. Bit

shaken up, but quiet… Not quite her usual perky self, but she'll be good.'

'Just like Tyler Uttley. And Livvy Parks.'

Shona glowered. 'Maybe. I don't get on with them other families much.' Emerald held her hands up, sighed. Shona guessed village politics were not something she was interested in. 'All right. What do you want?'

Emerald gave Shona a hopeful smile. 'The horses, Mrs Burgess… tell me.'

Shona closed her eyes, and was silent for several seconds. 'They only came once,' she said eventually.

The telling sentence hung in the warm summer air. For a few seconds, there was silence. No traffic, and even the birdsong seemed to stop.

'Yes,' said Emerald. 'That's usually enough.'

'It wasn't… like a dream,' Shona said. 'Not really.'

'You were how old then?'

'I was twelve.'

'And living here, in Little Brockwell?'

Shona nodded. 'Lived here all my life.' She nodded into the hallway. 'This was me mum's house. And me gran's.'

'Interesting.' Emerald pressed her fingertips together and looked over them. 'So tell me what you saw.'

For some reason, Shona found herself trusting this strange red-haired teenage girl, wanting to tell her everything. It was unusual. Shona was not, by nature, a trusting person. Her ex-husband, teachers, social workers, even her daughter Casey – she tended to assume by default that they were all lying to her. But this one seemed to have no reason to lie. She was genuinely asking questions because she was interested, and because she wanted to help. It was an unusual feeling, trusting someone.

'It was… I didn't really see. More of a… feeling.' Shona shook her head. 'This is stupid. It were a nightmare. Just a nightmare from over twenty years ago. Why do you want to know?'

'Please,' said Emerald. 'Tell me.'

'But it was just a bad dream.'

'Bad dreams are rarely just bad dreams. They can be echoes of the past, portents of the future, or both. Especially in a place like this. A powerful place, steeped in history. A place where ancient forces converge.'

Shona looked her up and down curiously. 'You really talk funny, you know that?'

'It has been noted. I'm working on it.' Emerald gestured. 'Please. Tell me.'

A cloud passed across the sun, drenching the house and garden in a cold greyness.

Shona Burgess shivered. Now, rhythmic accordion music began to echo across from beyond the church, and the sound of tinkling bells. She tried to ignore it. She didn't much care for the Morris dancers. Found them sinister.

'Like I said. I was twelve. I… thought I heard horses on the street, or maybe imagined them, I dunno. I either went to the window or… imagined I did… maybe dreamed I did.'

'Do you remember what time of day this was?'

Shona frowned. 'Well, it were night. Middle of the night. Everyone were asleep. Maybe two, three o'clock. Is that important?'

'Maybe. And maybe not.' Emerald gave her a reassuring smile. 'They exist in a rather fluid relationship with Time, you see. All of this may just as well have happened yesterday.'

'Right.' She gave Emerald a curious look. 'Are you, like… Do you *write* stuff, or something? Is that what this is all for?'

Emerald ignored the question. 'Tell me what you saw in the street.'

Shona sighed, leaning against her door. 'Like I say, I'm not sure I even saw it. But it was like I knew it was there. A horse, big black one. Evil dark, like it soaked up the moonlight. I heard it, too. Snorting and clopping.'

'It went past this house?'

Shona nodded. 'It stopped just over there in the street.'

'And was there a rider?'

She frowned. 'I dunno. Not really sure.'

'And what happened then?'

'It just went away.'

'Galloped off? Trotted?'

'No.' Shona shook her head, finding it strange to talk about this after all these years. 'Just disappeared. Like… faded into the darkness. Like when you turn the telly off, you know?' She mimed thumbing a remote-control. 'Like someone made it… go.'

Emerald smiled broadly. 'Thank you, Mrs Burgess,' she said. 'You've been very helpful.' She nodded, and turned to head off back down the path to the road.

'You'll let me know? If you find out anything?' Shona called.

Emerald looked over her shoulder briefly. 'Everyone will know, soon enough,' she said enigmatically.

And then she walked away, heading out of the village, without looking back.

Now, the village was alive with activity.

Jess strolled down the main street, thinking hard about what had happened with Livvy – as well as the Tenebrae and the travellers and everything else. People were putting bunting up in their gardens, she saw, while others were decorating their doors with leaves and flowers.

She could hear the sound of accordion music and the tinkle of bells drifting through the air. Shadows lengthened as a warm afternoon gave way to a mild evening. Jess even found herself whistling along to the music as she headed towards the main square.

As she rounded the corner into the square, she saw a group of villagers gathered around, watching a group of men in white costumes and ribboned hats perform an ornate dance. A top-hatted man with an accordion was providing the musical accompaniment, and the audience clapped along.

She watched them open-mouthed for a while. The dance seemed to involve a lot of waving of sticks, which had pieces of metal attached to them so that the sticks made a jangling noise.

Occasionally, the men would meet up in the middle and clash their sticks together with a loud percussive crack, or wave handkerchiefs in the air, or make wild, feral 'Hai!' noises as if doing karate.

'Sad, isn't it?' said a voice behind her, and she felt a gentle hand in the small of her back.

She whirled round, and saw the dark, twinkling eyes of Ben Hemingway.

'Oh… hi!' She felt herself blushing. 'You again,' she added.

'Yeah, me again. God, it's like I actually live round here or something.'

'Oh… sorry… I just meant…' She saw his smile, and her apology tailed off into a giggle.

'They do this every year,' he said, deadpan. 'Morris dancing, it's called. I think they enjoy it.'

'They must do!' She was aware that she was grinning stupidly, now. She thrust her hands into her pockets, swivelling back and forth, trying to make it look as if she just casually happened to be standing beside Ben. 'So, um…' she said. 'You know a lot of people.'

He turned, his face giving nothing away, but he half-raised his eyebrows. 'Oh, yeah?'

'Mr Popular on Facebook and Instagram, aren't you?'

'Oh, that.' He waved a hand. 'People get too hung up on that. I don't think it's real life…'

'Oh, no,' said Jess hurriedly. 'Nor do I, really.'

'Look at this bunch! I dunno which one's Morris. Think he's the big bloke with the sideburns?'

Jess laughed. 'I expect so. What's it all for?'

'Old pagan ceremonies. Bringing out the forces of nature and all that. Or some sort of male bonding ritual for middle-aged blokes.'

'Yeah, mid-life crisis,' Jess said. 'If they weren't doing this, they'd be buying sports cars.'

'And running off with their secretaries.' Their eyes met in complicity. 'So, how'd you find this place?'

'Oh, pretty easily. We've got Google Maps.'

She was quite proud of her little joke, and felt warm inside when Ben did a comedy eye-roll and acknowledged it. 'Yeah, yeah. I mean what d'you think of our poxy little village?'

'It's… different. Not like Meresbury. I expect it would drive me mad if I had to live here all the time.'

'Oof, you hurt me, City Girl. But yeah, it does. The drugs help, though.'

Jess did a double take and her eyes widened. 'Really?'

'I'm joking.' He gave her arm a playful tap. 'It's more cider, if I'm honest.'

'Cider. Right.'

The Morris dancers were taking a bow, now, and Jess and Ben politely joined in the applause.

'So, that little guy you hang out with,' Ben said, leaning into her. She could feel the warmth of his mouth against her ear. 'He your boyfriend?'

She did an over-exaggerated, comedy laugh. 'No way! Nah, Richie's just my mate. He's kind of like a brother. You know. Great and annoying in equal measure. I expect he'd say the same about me.'

'Cool,' said Ben. 'Well, you can't avoid people round here, so… we still on for later? Down at the Horse?'

'Sure! Yeah!' She hated the way she sounded in her head – too eager, too loud. She tried not to show that she was cringing. 'Um, what should I wear?'

'Whatever you like. They're not too fussed about that round here.'

'Oh. Great.'

'Actually, there might be a few posers there. Some of the idiots I had to go to school with. I'll introduce you, if you're unlucky.'

'I'll… look forward to that,' she said uncertainly, twirling a lock of her hair around one finger.

'Yeah, not too much.'

'All right. Not too much.'

'Don't want them cramping our style, do we?' he added, and he winked. 'See you later, babe.' And he strolled off, disappearing down one of the small, winding streets between the houses.

Jess realised she was still playing with her hair, and pulled her hand down with a tut of annoyance.

'Babe,' she said to herself. 'Seriously – *babe*? Who does he think he is?'

But she was grinning uncontrollably, and as she wandered back towards Rose Cottage, she felt buoyed up, light, full of a warm, late-summer joy.

The shadows were longer and deeper, now, as she rounded the corner into the lane where Rose Cottage was. Terraced stone houses lined both sides of the street. She passed an old telephone box, now refurbished as a wi-fi information point, and glimpsed the fields and hills between the cottages.

She heard the whinnying of a horse – a normal countryside sound, one she'd got used to – and looked over her shoulder, only half-interested. She could not see it at first, despite looking up and down the road.

'Hello?'

The lane was abandoned, deserted. Even the distant jangle of the Morris-men had stopped. And so, for a second, had the chirrup of birdsong.

Jess felt a chill, now, a shiver quite wrong for the time of year. She turned in a full circle.

There was the whinnying again, and now the clip-clop sound of hoofbeats on the tarmac. But which way was it coming from? It was echoing off all the stone and slate, bouncing around the village.

There! Just a flash of darkness, passing between houses at the far end of the lane... Big, black, bulky. She was sure she had seen it. But it had moved incredibly fast. She'd had a brief glimpse of a velvety pelt, and a rider in some dark clothing or other.

She ran to the T-junction, looked up and down. There was nothing to be seen. The birds had started to sing again, as if some brief suspension of normality had now been lifted, and a world briefly knocked out of kilter was now back on its usual bearing.

Jess rubbed her eyes and made her way back towards the house. Occasionally, she glanced over her shoulder, but she saw nothing more.

The sun thickened to a yellowy-orange, looking like a giant egg-yolk as it sank in the cloudless sky.

Shadows gathered in the children's playground. It would normally have been busy with the pre-bedtime bustle – this evening, though, a little boy of seven or eight had the slide all to himself while his stern-looking parents hovered close by, arms folded. Otherwise, the playground was deserted.

Or maybe not. A keen observer might have made out a tall, red-haired girl in the shadow of the nearby trees, wearing a velvet coat and blue sunglasses. A lithe Burmese cat was curled up on her shoulder, watching the children closely.

'Anything, Anoushka?' asked Emerald Greene.

'My senses are... clouded,' said the cat softly, in a voice that only his mistress could hear. 'The enemy is watching and waiting, and yet does not act. I cannot fathom why.'

'Timing is all, Anoushka,' said Emerald grimly.

As she stepped out of the shadows, the boy's parents glared in her direction. Emerald tilted her head, interestedly, as if observing a scientific experiment. She walked forward, approaching the playground, and Anoushka hopped off her shoulder and trotted beside her.

The parents were zipping up the boy's coat now, ready to hurry off.

'Please,' Emerald said, holding pale hands up in the evening light as she approached them. 'I mean no harm. I merely wish to warn you to be on your guard. This area is a potential energy nexus.'

'A what?' The father, who had ugly thick eyebrows and a tattoo on his forearm, narrowed his eyes at Emerald. 'You off your trolley, girl? Who are you, anyway?'

'C'mon, Keith.' The woman tugged at his arm as the little boy clung to her skirt, looking up at Emerald Greene with fearful interest. 'Come on, let's go 'ome!'

Emerald squatted down and stared at the boy with wide, green eyes. 'Does your son suffer from any unusual sleep patterns? Nightmares, sleepwalking, enuresis?'

'Enya-what?' The father sounded angry, now, and had his fists clenched.

'I know what she means,' the mother said, stern-faced. 'Yeah, he used to wet the bed. Didn' everyone? But 'e don't no more. He's a good lad... What are you – student or somethin'?'

'Yes,' said Emerald softly, with a mischievous glint in her eye. 'I am a student of unusual phenomena, and this village is full of them.' She straightened up. 'Dark forces are at work in this place. Ancient powers are gathering, biding their time... It could be perilous to venture out alone after nightfall.'

The mother picked the boy up and backed away from Emerald Greene. 'Who d'you think you are, frightenin' my son?'

'You teenagers,' said the father, waving a finger in Emerald's face, 'you're all as bad as each other. Get back to your drugs an' computer games an' all that stuff and keep it to yourself! Unnerstand?'

Emerald spread her hands. 'I am merely warning, not threatening. Please do not take my friendly advice the wrong way.'

'Yeah, well, don' you take it the wrong way if I tell the coppers about you, missy.' The man took out his phone and there was a quiet beep as he thumbed it. 'I think she's one o' them from up on the hill. Look at all them necklaces. Gippo rubbish, innit?'

Emerald Greene took off her glasses and looked the angry father in the eye. 'Please do not alarm yourself. I am on your side. There is no need to inform the authorities of my presence.'

'On our side?' said the man uncertainly, and the hand holding the phone wavered slightly.

'Keith!' The boy and his mother were halfway up the path, now, heading back to the road. 'Keith, leave 'er and let's get 'ome.'

Anoushka slunk around Emerald's legs as the girl's green eyes shone like two polished orbs. They could have been reflecting the dwindling rays of the sun, or they could have been shining with their own strange, interior light.

'You do not need to inform the authorities of my presence,' said Emerald again – casually, as if she were chatting to a friend.

For a moment, the boy's father looked on the point of

becoming even angrier. The hand holding the phone up to his ear started to shake, and he turned bright red.

'They are not interested in me,' suggested Emerald, in the same low, casual tone.

The man visibly relaxed. He lowered the phone, thumbed it to lock. 'No. Well.' The man blinked and wiped the beads of sweat from his forehead. 'Just… just you…' He gestured at Emerald with his phone, then blinked again, shaking his head as if he had forgotten what he was going to say.

'Have a pleasant evening,' suggested Emerald.

'Yeah… Um, yeah. You too, miss.'

He hurried off after his wife and child. As he reached them, he paused for a second, looked back at Emerald Greene and scratched his ear. Then he took his little boy's hand – and the family headed off, seemingly oblivious to Emerald's presence.

Emerald Greene replaced her glasses, clasped her hands behind her back and, impassive, watched them go.

Richie opened the door to the church uncertainly. The Rector was there, sitting with her head bent in prayer in the front pew.

He found the old building imposing, slightly frightening, and he felt a slight chill as the door creaked and slammed shut behind him.

'Oops,' he said. 'Sorry.'

The Rector turned to face him, her glasses low on her nose, and gave him a stern look for a second before breaking into a broad smile.

'Come in,' she said, straightening up. 'God's house is open to all, you know.'

Yeah, thought Richie as he walked nervously up the aisle – but I don't think I believe in God. At least, not the kind of God some people really seem to get into.

He was thinking of a friend his brother Tom sometimes

brought home – a theology student called Demelza. Her eyes were bright whenever she spoke of Jesus, and she always looked kind of serene and wore a small, fish-shaped badge on her lapel. Richie recalled Tom saying in admiration that she was in Bangladesh or somewhere this summer, helping flood victims. Richie didn't think he could do stuff like that.

He stopped beside the Rector. A square pool of late-evening sunlight lay on the stone floor between them.

'Want to know, then?' he said. 'What I found on your computer?' he held out his phone.

The Rector looked kind, Richie thought, like someone's mum or auntie. She probably made a good priest because of that.

'Not sure it's my business,' she said in her no-nonsense voice. 'You can tell me if you want to.'

Richie let his gaze wander, up to the altar and beyond, to the big stained-glass window with its bold renditions of saints and angels. He shivered momentarily. He was thinking of all the odd things he had once seen – not in Little Brockwell, but back in Meresbury, a few months ago, just after he and Jess had first met Emerald.

'Reverend Parsloe,' said Richie, 'do you believe in *evil*?'

'It's a cornerstone of my faith,' she replied softly. 'The power of the Holy Trinity guards against evil and fights it.'

Richie took a deep breath. 'There's evil in Little Brockwell,' he murmured. 'Not... like the Devil and stuff, or whatever the Bible says. It's... different.' He looked her in the eye. 'I think it feels like part of the village.'

She did not seem perturbed. 'You're talking about the Tree?' she asked, peering over her glasses.

'That's got something to do with it. Yes.'

'*Something* to do with it?' she said quizzically.

Richie avoided that line of questioning. 'Reverend Parsloe – about those kids. What do you think they saw?'

'I hope,' she said, 'that God will watch over us.'

'That's not what I asked,' he said.

'Richie, if you've come to convince me that children can be spirited away by dark horses, or eaten by the Whispering Tree, then...'

He scowled. 'I don't know what to think any more.'

'You really mustn't let your imagination get the better of you... The Council have been wanting to cut the Whispering Tree down for years, you know, but there's some sort of unbreachable preservation order on it.'

Richie adjusted his glasses, licked his lips. He touched the phone in his pocket and wondered whether he should tell her now, come right out with what he knew.

'Yeah,' he said. 'I expect you're right. Anyway, I've got to be home for my supper now. Thanks again for letting me use your computer.'

'That's all right. Any time.'

Richie turned to go.

'Richie?' the Rector called over her shoulder.

'Yes?'

'You're right about one thing,' she said, and she peered over her glasses, her face serious. 'Evil is not something abstract, something invented – it comes from us, from deep within us. And yes – I believe there is evil here.'

'Right,' said Richie, and it felt cold to him then, in the church.

'Tell your friend,' said the Rector. 'The one in the long coat.'

'Emerald?' Richie was surprised. 'You... you've spoken to her?'

'I've seen her round and about. She's not as stealthy as she likes to think, a lot of the time. So tell her... Tell her to do her job, and I'll do mine.'

'Okay,' he said, unsure what this meant. 'I will.'

The Rector returned to her prayers – and Richie, feeling more uncomfortable than ever, hurried to the door and out into the welcoming summer evening.

5
Innocence and Experience

'You having a good time?' Ben shouted in Jess's ear, passing her a drink.

She grasped the over-warm plastic tumbler of Coke, smiling bravely. In all honesty she wasn't sure if she was, yet.

The pub had a canopy and a small stage set up in the pub beer-garden, with a rather tatty, faded banner draped across it saying LITTLE BROCKWELL SUMMER FESTIVAL. Jess wondered if they just dug out the same banner every year.

Pounding beats drifted across the air as the evening settled in – Eighties and Nineties rock, Aunt Gabi's kind of stuff. Gabi, though, was being strong-willed and staying in to work.

Dave Dazzle, the sparkly-shirted Westmeadow College DJ, was bouncing on his podium, occasionally mumbling into the microphone. Nobody was dancing, but a few people swayed grudgingly. A rather tacky mirror-ball spun behind him, scattering green and gold dots on the black backdrop.

'This guy's a laugh!' Ben said, and punched the air as Dave Dazzle merged the beats with precision.

'I s'pose so!'

Jess wasn't sure, but if she was spending the evening here with Ben, she didn't really care how cheesy the music was going to be. She had heard a lot worse. But already, more people had gathered in the pub garden than she had expected – mostly a few years older than her, gossiping and laughing in cliquey groups. She realised a lot of them probably went to school locally, at Westmeadow Academy or the College, and so they would all probably know each other.

She felt shy and awkward, but tried to be confident. *I'm sixteen, remember*, she lied to herself again. And hey, I'm with *Ben Hemingway*.

Some of them were smoking, which made her eyes sting. The boys and young men wore crisp shirts and sported gallons of sticky hair-gel and pungent aftershave. But Ben looked great, she thought, in his biker jacket, T-shirt with the name of a band she'd actually heard of, and black jeans. His floppy hair was looking a bit tidier tonight, so that it only occasionally fell over one eye rather than being all over the place. He looked a bit unshaven, too, since yesterday. More than stubble, but less than a beard. That did something for her, something she couldn't quite name. She liked it.

The girls in their skimpy summer dresses, though, made Jess feel overdressed – and she was sure that the glossy creatures were glancing over at her, sneering and gossiping. She deliberately turned away from the girls. She was here with Ben, she reminded herself, and they were not.

'So, um… you like them?' She looked down at his T-shirt, and immediately she kicked herself. If he didn't, he wouldn't have the T-shirt, would he?

Luckily, he just grinned. If he thought it was a stupid question, he didn't show it. 'Yeah, they're cool. Have you heard their new album?'

'Um, not yet.'

'I'll play it to you later, maybe?'

'I'd like that. Thanks!'

'I like the, ah…' Ben thumbed the side of his nose and pointed to hers.

She felt herself blush. 'Oh, that. Yeah. It's new. Well, new-ish.'

'Did it hurt?'

'Um… a bit. When the needle went in. But not for long. And it felt a bit weird for a day or two, but I'm used to it now.'

'How do your mum and dad feel about it?'

She debated for a second whether to hedge her answer, but decided to be completely straight with him. 'Um, I live with my auntie. She's totally cool with it. She's… just a cool person. Generally.'

'Ah.' Ben sipped his drink. He glanced at the stage, then back at Jess again. 'So your parents… where…?'

'Dead,' she said casually. He looked shocked, and she found that she almost enjoyed that.

'Right. Um, so… how long…?'

'When I was little.' She felt comfortable with him, was happy to reveal things this early on without any pressure. 'Gabi's not got kids of her own, so she's always looked after me and my sister. And Kat's away at uni. Well, travelling now. Don't see much of her.'

Ben clinked his glass against hers. 'Well, here's to Gabi. She sounds great.'

'She is.'

He'd got them both drinks from the bar inside – a Coke for her, and she wasn't quite sure what his was. Behind them, a sullen, dreadlocked girl of about twenty was serving the outdoor customers out of a hatch. Unlike Harry inside, she didn't seem that bothered about checking anyone's age.

Jess was sure those girls over there were still talking about her. She didn't know their names, but she knew their type. Some of them looked like Ben's Instagram friends, those duck-face-pouty girls. They might as well have been her school's self-centred, vacuous little band of Populars with their Popular Names: Molly, Zara, Abi. The ones who strode through the corridors with hair-tossing confidence, and lived for boys, wild parties and illicit thrills. Every school had them.

'It's busy!' Jess said, looking around as the pub garden

started to fill up. 'Do you know... that lot?' She looked over at the girls.

Ben grinned. 'They come out of the woodwork in the evening. Not cool to be seen round the village during the day... Look out, here comes trouble.'

One of the girls, an ash-blonde vamp in heels and a blue Oriental satin dress, had sashayed over for a refill. She jogged Jess's elbow with deliberate force, splashing Coke across her top.

'Oi!' Jess snapped. 'Careful!'

The girl ignored her. 'Hiya, *Ben*,' she said, stroking the sleeve of his jacket with a taloned hand. She was drenched in a summery, flowery perfume. 'Fancy *you* being here. Didn't think it was your scene.' She giggled and tucked her hair behind one ear.

Oh, *please*, thought Jess. You are so obvious.

'Yeah. Hi, Georgie.' Ben looked uneasily from the girl to Jess and back again. Jess raised her eyebrows at him. 'Um, Jess, this is Georgie Popplewick... We were at school together.'

'Hello!' said Jess. She tried to sound friendly, but was still pointedly rubbing at the stain on her top.

'Whatever,' said Georgie, barely looking at her. She carried on talking to Ben. 'You wanna come round Holly's later? Her mum and dad are out.'

Ben looked awkward and scratched his ear. 'Not really,' he said. 'Thanks anyway.'

'Aw, come on. She's, like, totally having a party.'

'Can you be *partially* having a party?' Jess asked. 'Just wondered.'

Georgie Popplewick shot her a look of disgust, then turned back to Ben. 'Come on, Ben. Say you will.'

'No, really,' he said. 'We were going to hang out here and, well, just chill, y'know. We're good.'

Jess felt a warm glow, and a rush of pride that he was

including her in his plans. *We.* She imagined Georgie Popplewick didn't get many knockbacks.

'What,' Georgie said, still not properly looking at Jess, 'you're with *her*?'

'Yes,' said Ben. 'That okay with you?'

Georgie Popplewick didn't quite know how to respond. Her mouth opened and closed again.

'Weird about those kids,' Jess ventured, filling an awkward silence. 'Some odd things going on.'

Georgie Popplewick turned towards her properly for the first time. She looked her up and down with undisguised disdain, taking in everything: Jess's unruly hair, black vest-top, green-and-white checked shirt knotted around her waist, white jeans and green Converse Shorelines.

'That look is *so* last year,' Georgie sneered.

Jess almost took a step backwards. 'Well, *sorry*,' she riposted. 'I didn't realise I was in the fashion centre of the Universe.'

Georgie wrinkled her nose and turned away, with a contemptuous shake of her blonde mane. 'Hanging out with kids, now, Ben? Better watch yourself.' And she gave a knowing smile as she sidled past them to the bar.

'*You* watch yourself, you cow,' muttered Jess, but it was swallowed up by a deafening drum-break from Dave Dazzle.

'Sorry about the Poppy,' Ben said, embarrassed. 'She fancies herself.'

'Oh, really? Can't say I noticed.' Jess drained what was left of her Coke and thrust the glass at Ben. 'You can get me another drink.'

He grinned. 'You want to dance in a minute?'

'Yeah, sure – *if* this guy puts something decent on!'

Richie had kept the photo to himself at supper, not knowing whether to tell Jess about his discovery.

If Aunt Gabi had sensed any tension, she hadn't shown it. Richie suspected that her writing had reached a crucial point, because she brought reams of paper to the table and scribbled frantic notes in between forkfuls of shepherd's pie (microwaved – even Gabi, whose lack of cooking skill was legendary, couldn't really get that wrong).

After that, Richie reflected, there had been a frantic flurry of activity. Jess had spent what seemed like an hour in the bathroom getting ready for her date with Motorcycle Boy, while Gabi scoured the internet for something, oblivious to the world. Richie endured some television for as long as possible before grabbing his jacket, pocketing a torch and slipping out of the back door.

Richie was used to making his own entertainment – especially these days, when he found his parents too busy arguing with one another to bother with him. Thankfully, astronomy and sci-fi provided an escape, and recently, he'd even managed to persuade Rachel Casera from school to watch the new *Timeland* DVD with him. She had been polite about it. He seemed to remember her words were something like, 'It's not exactly a chick-flick, Richie, but I'll give you points for effort.' Rach remained a decent prospect for something more than friendship, and he knew he was going to keep trying.

Jessica, he knew, saw him as a brother – a geeky little brother who was good for a laugh. Richie accepted that, and filled the role happily.

He hurried along the road, picking out a path with the torch-beam. He was still rattled by his discovery, and the village at night was not the most welcoming of places. The streets of Little Brockwell were quiet, although he could hear the thump of the disco and the babble and clink from the pub.

Richie reached the Green and hurried across the damp grass, his breath ragged and loud in his head. He stopped, about two metres away from the spiky bulk of the Whispering

Tree, and shone the torch at it.

The twisted, charcoal-black bark did not seem to reflect the light properly. Only the feeblest glow showed him that the trunk was even there.

Richie took a step back. He tried to picture the old photo in his head, and turned so that he could see the floodlit church.

Although he hadn't told anyone yet, he had solved the mystery of the vanishing church tower – it had been obvious, in retrospect. But there was still the matter of the thing which had, for decades, obscured it on the photograph. Back then, the technology hadn't existed to reveal it. But now it did. And he knew who had it.

The torch flickered.

Richie frowned. He moved back from the Whispering Tree and the torch beam returned to its full brightness, but when he stepped forward again, closer to the Tree, it dimmed once more.

And then he heard the sound.

There was something approaching from the street.

It was disturbing the air behind him on the Green, whizzing across the ground at high speed. Richie turned, gasped, shone his torch full-face into whatever it was. He caught a glimpse of a broad, white disc of light, then heard a yelp and saw something dark crashing to the ground next to him.

With his heart thumping and his whole body shaking, Richie held the torch out in front of him like a weapon. 'Don't move!' he shouted.

The beam picked out an upturned, old-fashioned bicycle with a wicker basket, its wheels spinning crazily in the torchlight. He swung the beam round to the side of the bike, and a familiar figure covered her eyes with her hands.

'All right, whatever you say! Honestly, Richard, you *really* should not be out and about causing havoc at this hour.'

'Emerald!' he gasped in relief. 'Am I glad to see you!'

'Are you?' she asked, puzzled, straightening her coat and righting her bicycle. She gave the headlamp a thump to get the beam back on.

'Yes, yes!' he said impatiently. 'It's just an expression.'

Emerald Greene stepped round Richie, brushing the grass from her coat. She hoisted her bag on to her shoulder. It was an old leather rucksack which had seen better days – better decades, even. 'All right,' she said wearily. 'Tell me what you need explaining this time.'

'Um… Well, what are you *doing* here, Emerald?'

'Just getting some context,' she murmured, surveying the Whispering Tree first from one angle and then from another. Tapping her index finger thoughtfully against her top lip, she went on, 'This tree has been here for approximately three thousand years, you realise?' She began to furrow in her battered rucksack. 'It is, in fact, one of the oldest living things on the planet.'

'Yes,' said Richie, swinging his torch back round again. 'And Casey reappeared here… And the Rector doesn't like it.'

'And the Rector does not like it,' repeated Emerald Greene thoughtfully as she rummaged in the bag. 'Well, the Rector would not. She has faith – the irrational belief in the unprovable.'

Richie wasn't quite sure he got that, but it sounded typically Emerald-like. 'What are you up to now?' he asked.

Emerald handed him something from her rucksack. 'Hold this for one moment.'

Richie blinked in puzzlement. It was a pink stick of rock, wrapped in plastic and stamped with the message *Welcome To Bognor Regis*.

'And this, too.'

An Ordnance Survey map. Oh, well, at least that's useful, he thought – until he realised it was a map of the Isle of Arran.

'And this.'

The next object was a black cylinder, about the size of a stick of rock.

'Ah – here we are!' Delightedly, she waved the flat oblong of a small, flip-top computer. 'Lucky I never throw anything away,' she added.

'What's this?' Richie asked, holding the black tube up and sniffing it.

'Oh, just cadmium explosive. Be careful with it.'

Shuddering, Richie handed it back to Emerald along with the rock and the map.

'Now, then…' Emerald flipped open her palm-top and began punching keys in rapid succession. Richie tried to read the illuminated screen over her shoulder, but all he could see was a series of complex numbers which made little sense to him.

Emerald saw him peeking and moved away, snapping the computer shut in irritation. 'Did you realise,' she said, 'that the gravity and temporal balance fields within a radius of three metres of this tree are totally at odds with what one would expect?'

'Did I realise?' Richie repeated faintly. 'Um… would it surprise you if I said no?'

'Excellent,' said Emerald, eyes wide and bright with mischief. 'It is likely that nobody else has noticed, either. That means we can leave that worry aside for now. Important lesson for the day, Richard – never test the depth of the water with both feet.'

'I'll bear that in mind,' said Richie. 'So, did you come all the way down from your little camp just to do a moonlit study of Little Brockwell's oldest resident?'

'I am investigating,' said Emerald Greene primly, flicking the bike-stand back up and wheeling her bicycle back towards the road.

Richie followed her, waggling his torch insistently. 'Any line in particular?'

'Allow me to recap,' said Emerald, and she rode along the village street, with Richie scurrying beside her. 'Several children in this village have had a very odd experience, and there does not, at present, appear to be any obvious link between them. And Anoushka's intelligence, gleaned on his travels, tells me of another. A child from the traveller community, called William. He went missing just three days ago – shortly before your arrival in the village. And returned, just like the others.'

'But… we didn't know about that!'

'They are private people,' said Emerald Greene, frowning intently. 'Their community has its own rules. If it were not for one of their cats being talkative after sharing a fish with Anoushka, we would be none the wiser.'

Anoushka had joined them, Richie realised – he wasn't quite sure when, but one minute Emerald's bike-basket had been empty, and the next the cat was sitting there, bright and alert, eyes to the front.

'And you're going to find them?' Richie asked. 'The travellers?'

'Absolutely,' said Emerald, and she gave him her glittering, not-quite-there smile. 'Jess is… otherwise occupied, so would you like to come?'

'Now?' said Richie in horror. 'But they're in Bardleton, Jess said, about eight miles away! And it's after dark!'

'Very observant, Richard. I see you will become an astronomer yet.'

'That's sarcasm,' he said accusingly. 'You don't do sarcasm!'

'She's learning,' Anoushka said from the basket.

'I am learning,' repeated Emerald, folding her arms. 'So, do you have a bike?'

'Hang on,' Richie said. He had come to an important decision. 'Look, I need to show you something. I'm not sure about it at all, but it might affect things.'

Anoushka and Emerald both seemed to turn identical stares on to him, penetrating and unearthly. 'What?' said Emerald, with a dangerous, knife-sharp edge to her voice.

Richie swallowed hard, and looked down at Emerald's mini-computer. 'Can you get Instagram up on that?' he asked.

Jess and Ben were propped against the back wall, now, hemmed in by gaggles of teenage boys and girls. She wondered where they had all come from. Not Little Brockwell, surely?

More people were dancing. Dave Dazzle had ramped things up now, coming into the 21st century with a bit of deep house, trance and dubstep. The beer-garden was steadily becoming darker, hotter, louder. Jess could feel the music reverberating through the stone paving, the beats juddering through her body. It was quite exciting, and every time she looked up at Ben, who was leaning next to her in a protective, interested way, she felt her heart beat a little faster.

She was feeling more relaxed now and could feel her face flushing with excitement – she hoped she didn't look too red.

Ben was talking about his work in the shop. 'It's all right, really,' he was saying, 'and it'll do for a summer job. Get some cash, before I start at sixth-form college. If my results are any good, of course.'

'In Meresbury?' Jess asked, hopefully.

'No, Westmeadow,' he said, and they exchanged a rueful grin.

She drained the last of her Coke, plonked the glass down and impulsively grabbed Ben's arm. She pulled him right down so that her lips were up against his ear. 'I wanna get some fresh air,' she shouted, knowing her words would vibrate in his eardrum. 'Away from all these people.'

Ben grinned, gave her the thumbs-up. 'Take a drink with us?' he mouthed.

As he turned towards the bar, she grabbed his jacket again, let her hand run all the way up his sleeve as she leaned in to tell him, recklessly, 'Get me a *proper* drink.'

Ben grinned. 'You sure?'

'Yeah, why the hell not?'

She caught sight of Georgie Popplewick over in the corner, sipping something long and orange and flanked by two attendant harpies. She was glowering at Jess.

And Jess folded her arms, put her head on one side and shot a brief look of triumph in the older girl's direction.

The look Georgie Popplewick gave her in return could have withered fresh fruit.

Something about Emerald Greene's expression made Richie shiver. 'So,' she said, 'what will I be looking at?'

'One of Grandma Trippett's old photos, cleaned up with some useful software. Take a look.'

Richie peered over Emerald's shoulder, and Anoushka hopped up, silently, on to her other shoulder. All three of them looked at the enhanced picture on Richie's Instagram, which had appeared with pin-sharp clarity on the screen. It was almost identical to the original which Richie had viewed in Grandma Trippett's living room, but with one significant difference. The foreground was still the same – the maypole dancers in their Sunday best, each holding a ribbon, and to the left, the dark edge of the Whispering Tree – but in the background, something had changed.

On the right-hand edge of the photo, behind the crowd of onlookers, there was a figure, one which had simply not been there in the original photo. Huge, dark and menacing, it blotted out the sky where the church would have jutted above the trees and houses. Although it was no more than a shadow, with hardly any detail to speak of, the shape of the intrusive figure was unmistakable.

It was a horse.

Richie and Emerald peered at the photo. They looked at each other, then back at the screen.

On the picture, the jet-black horse supported an armoured, cowled rider with a long lance. The man – figure, creature, Richie wasn't sure what to call it – appeared to be watching the Green and the people on it, but was unobserved by any of them.

'Look at the size,' said Richie. 'Use the people as a scale… that thing is *enormous*. It's much bigger than a stallion.'

Emerald Greene drew breath. '*Tenebrae*,' she hissed through clenched teeth.

'What?' asked Richie.

'They were here, back then,' Anoushka said, restless now on his mistress's shoulder, his fur rippling. '*They were here!*'

Emerald Greene closed the program, folded the computer shut. Her eyes were distant, Richie thought, almost alien. She had the look of someone who had seen something beautiful, but also terrible.

'They have always been here,' said Emerald Greene softly.

'So… what are you thinking?' Richie asked.

'The camera can see things hidden from the eye,' murmured Emerald, 'but it can be equally unreliable. All the same, I did not know they had ventured so far abroad in their search. I need to know what has galvanised them after all this time…' Emerald jumped on to her bike. 'Obtain transport, Richard. Meet me by the bridge in ten minutes – or I go without you!'

And suddenly she was gone, riding off into the darkness.

*

'Good night for seeing the stars,' Ben said.

Jess and Ben had left the DJ, the Dark Horse and the crowd behind them and were lying on their backs, up on the hillside – right in the eye of the chalk horse. The lights of the village lay below them. Very occasionally, the distant sound of the music drifted up on the breeze.

'It's beautiful up here,' murmured Jess. 'So peaceful.'

Ben, holding the Mere Valley cider they had smuggled out, took out his penknife and folded out its bottle-opening attachment. His hands shook a little – Jess realised he had to be more nervous than he was letting on – but he deftly flipped the metal cap from the bottle. 'Cheers,' he said, and took the first gulp before handing the bottle to Jess.

She propped herself up on one elbow to take it – but hesitated, wary of the fizzy, golden liquid and the pungent fumes which rose from it. Like fallen apples, she thought, the ones which got trodden underfoot and were crawling with wasps. Beautiful, heady, but dangerous.

'Don't tell me you've never had it before?' he asked, with a smirk.

'Yeah. Loads of times.' Didn't even sound convincing to herself, she thought grimly. She raised the bottle once, said 'Cheers!' in an overly melodramatic voice and took the smallest gulp she could get away with.

It was all right at first – fizzy, sweet. Then the kick took her by surprise, sharp and pungent in her mouth, spreading up into her nostrils. She pulled the bottle from her lips, trying hard not to cough, and wiped her mouth with her hand.

'Good stuff,' she said hoarsely.

Ben took the bottle back. 'I could have got you something else, if you'd have preferred.'

'Nah.' She leaned playfully into him, brushed her arm against the warm leather of his motorbike jacket.

'Look,' Ben said, and he took something out of his pocket

– a small, metallic cylinder. He clicked a button on the side and it unfolded into a portable telescope, about half a metre long.

Jess, even despite her exposure to Emerald Greene's collection of weird and wonderful objects, was impressed by the device. 'Wow,' she said. 'So you and Richie have something in common!'

'What?' Ben asked, confused.

'He's an astronomy-nerd, too,' she teased, and she put the glass to her eye. 'Hang on, I can't see a flipping thing!'

'Ah,' Ben said gently, and his hand was warm against hers as he took the telescope from her and turned it the right way round. 'I think you'll find it's better like that.'

Jess laughed in embarrassment, feeling nervous as he guided her hand, angling the telescope slightly up. 'Oh, right. Yeah.' She shivered with excitement as he touched her, and hoped desperately that she didn't seem like a silly little girl.

'Can you see the Plough?' Ben asked, his hands on her shoulders. 'Look, over there. Logical name, really, as it's shaped like a saucepan.'

'Hmm, makes sense. Not.'

'What sign are you?' he asked gently, rolling over so that he could slip an arm around her shoulders.

'Oh, *pleeeeeease*. Not corny old star-signs!' She passed the telescope back to him.

'Just thought you might like to see it.'

'Oh, okay. Virgo, if you must know.'

'Ah, well. Just a moment.' He scanned the sky for a few seconds, then handed her the telescope again, pointing and guiding her hand. 'That really bright star, there, see it? The one with a blue tinge? That's Spica, or *Alpha Virginis*, the brightest star in Virgo. A binary… And one of the fifteen brightest in the whole Northern sky, in fact, so you can pick her out on a clear night.'

'How far away is it?' Jess murmured.

'Ooh, she's about 270 light years away.' Ben paused. 'Virgo... so you've got a birthday coming up, then?'

'Um – yeah.' She lowered the telescope, feeling herself go hot and cold as she suddenly remembered the lie about her age, which had seemed so trivial at the time. Needing to do something with her hands, she took the cider-bottle. 'Um, Ben...' she began, 'when I said I was sixteen, I – well, I may have rounded up a bit.'

'It's okay,' he murmured. 'You don't have to tell me.'

'No, but – '

'Don't spoil it,' he said, his brown eyes soft, amused. 'Really.'

Jess took a longer, deeper drink from the bottle. This time, when she pulled it from her mouth, she couldn't help coughing and spluttering, and found that she was giggling without intending to. Her face was very hot, she realised, and she didn't quite feel as steady on the sloping hillside as she had done.

Whooah. So this was what it was like.

'The horse,' she murmured, handing Ben the bottle as she gazed across the vast, chalky back of the creature, standing out pale against the dark grass. 'It's beautiful, isn't it? Beautiful.'

But she realised it was time to stop talking.

He had moved closer to her. He'd slipped a hand round the back of her head, and his fingers were tangled in her hair. Well, she thought, with a sudden adrenaline rush, heart thudding – here we go.

She tilted her head, the way she had seen people do in films.

It was only at the last possible millisecond that she realised this was to stop their noses from colliding.

After thirty minutes of riding along the ridge, Emerald and Richie made out the hamlet of Bardleton below them – a small cluster of lights nestling in a hollow.

Anoushka started to purr in satisfaction. Emerald Greene looked down at him and gently scratched his ears. 'You have something?'

'The meadow,' said Anoushka. 'Down there, beyond the pond… you can see camp-fires burning.'

Richie was sceptical. He wasn't sure how anyone could make that out at this distance – but then again, the cat's eyesight was much better than his could ever be. He glanced over towards Emerald Greene and saw her looking through a pair of slim, silver binoculars.

'Are they infra-red?' asked Richie, impressed.

'Of course,' Emerald replied casually. She lowered the binoculars. 'All right. Let us go.' She glanced at Richie, saw him looking uncertain. 'No need to be afraid,' she said, and it seemed to him that she had, for a moment, softened her no-nonsense tone. 'They are only people.'

'Of course,' said Richie, and polished his glasses nervously.

'Now, Richard – I realise that you and I have not worked together closely before. There are a number of rules to be followed.'

'Rules?' he asked, sounding suspicious.

'Indeed.' Emerald ticked the points off on her long, white fingers. 'First of all, do not disappear or go off on your own. Secondly, do not contradict me, or question any decision I make. And thirdly – you let me do all the talking.' Emerald raised her eyebrows. 'Clear?'

'Clear.'

'Oh, and something else,' said Emerald, and here she lowered her voice. 'I mentioned to Jess that I thought the Enemy had allies in the village. Now, I know that to be true. Someone has been working on behalf of the Tenebrae, manipulating us all like chess-pieces.'

'Why?' asked Richie, aghast. 'What could they stand to

gain from it?'

Emerald held her hands out, carefully examining her fingernails in the moonlight. 'The Tenebrae are eternal,' she said. 'They have shown that they can transcend normal barriers of Time, maybe even hold back death.'

'Hold back death?' Richie shivered. 'How?'

'I do not know yet. But perhaps… perhaps it is someone who, for some reason, feels the onset of Time. Someone who fears the approach of death, and thinks they stand to gain victory over death by siding with the Darkness.'

Someone who fears the approach of death. Richie felt a shiver at those words, and was about to say something. But Emerald was still being brisk.

'All right? Ready?' Emerald turned her hands around, palms up, so that they were spread out in a kind of shrug, or maybe a gesture of openness. 'Just be aware of that. Trust no-one!'

'Not even you?' asked Richie.

'You may mistrust me if you wish, Richard,' she said, smiling back. 'That is your privilege. Now, let us proceed! Anoushka!'

The cat jumped back into the bike-basket and Emerald pedalled off down the hill towards Bardleton at a rapid pace.

Richie gave a curt, mock salute in Emerald's direction, then rode after her.

Twenty minutes later, Richie was wondering if this had been a good idea.

The camp near Bardleton was a ramshackle collection of caravans, Transit vans and the kind of old wooden gypsy-wagons which Richie had only ever seen on TV. They were grouped in a rough circle around the centre of the field. Several roaring camp-fires burned there, casting an orange glow over the scene.

Richie couldn't quite believe that he, Emerald and Anoushka were now sitting on a woollen rug near one of the fires, watched with amusement and suspicion by the travellers. Their arrival had drawn a large, diverse crowd at first, Richie noticed. He saw dreadlocks and dungarees, braiding and patchwork, and a few people who looked pretty much like his neighbours back in Meresbury. However, when a tall, weather-beaten man had stepped out of the shadows – introducing himself as Kim – he had taken charge and the onlookers had melted back into the shadows.

'You're a long way from home,' said Kim, as he offered them some mugs of fruit tea. He had sharp blue eyes, a lined face and shoulder-length, greying hair, and the others seemed to defer to him to some extent. 'People might be worried,' he added sternly.

Richie waved his phone. 'Hey, no problem. Twenty-first-century technology, you know? We're just a beep away.' He wasn't sure how Kim had intended his comment, but he wanted to make it clear that they hadn't walked in unprepared.

To Richie's surprise, Kim laughed out loud, as did some of the others. 'Wonderful! The boy thinks we're savages.'

'No!' said Richie hotly.

On the other side of the camp-fire, girls and boys were nudging each other and muttering.

'Richie,' said Emerald Greene under her breath, 'please, leave this to me.'

Richie took a sip of his tea. It tasted of apple and cinnamon, zinged in the roof of his mouth and warmed him from within.

Anoushka, who was under strict instructions to keep silent, hopped from Emerald's lap and curled up near the fire, not far from Kim's feet. Kim leaned over, stroked Anoushka's fur and scratched behind his ears. To Richie's astonishment, Anoushka did not respond by hissing, clawing or even moving. He just opened his heavy-lidded eyes for a second and seemed to settle back to enjoy the feeling.

'What a beautiful cat,' murmured Kim. 'Yours?' He looked from Richie to Emerald in turn.

'Mine,' said Emerald Greene. 'And he has used six lives, so he has great experience.'

Kim laughed again. 'I like that.' He ruffled Anoushka's head. 'Burmese?... He's the darkest one I've ever seen. Very striking.'

'Anoushka is a special breed,' said Emerald Greene softly. 'There is more to him than meets the eye, I assure you.'

For a fleeting moment, Richie wondered if a look of understanding passed between Kim and Emerald. When Kim spoke again, it was in a slightly softer tone – as if, perhaps, he had noticed something in Emerald Greene which he could understand and respect. Something which linked them. A vagabond heart and a distrust of authority.

'So,' Kim murmured, 'what brings you young people out here at this time of night?'

Emerald Greene leaned forward. For a moment, Richie was alarmed - she looked so stern, strong and grown-up, her face in shadow and the firelight playing on her rich red hair.

'Two children vanished from Little Brockwell,' said Emerald, 'and both returned a day later.' There was an ugly-sounding murmur from the other side of the fire, but Emerald held up a hand to forestall it. 'No, no. Please do not misunderstand... I am accusing no-one. I am here to ask about Will Carver, the boy who disappeared from your camp for twenty-four hours last Wednesday and Thursday.'

Kim's expression hardened, and he prodded the fire, not looking up at them. A flurry of sparks flew up. 'Now, why d'you want to know about him, mmm? Will's fine. He's back with his family. That's the end of it.'

'I expect the police have asked questions. But you do not

trust the authorities, do you, Kim? No reason why you should. You are not exactly easy for them to deal with.'

Kim's eyes narrowed, and now he looked up at Emerald through the flickering flames, his face deeply shadowed. 'You got something to say, Miss, then get to the point. Why are you bothered about Will?'

'I am bothered about *all* humanity,' said Emerald Greene, in a deadly serious voice. 'Their safety is my concern.'

There was a brief silence, punctuated only by the crackling of the fire. Scented woodsmoke drifted across, and Richie tried not to cough. He looked hard at Emerald, really hoping she was not going to push things this time.

'You're not from some daft religion, are you?' asked Kim eventually. But he answered his own question. 'No. All wrong for that. And you're certainly not the press.'

Richie decided to step in. 'One of... the other children it happened to is... well, a friend of a friend,' he said awkwardly. As he was an honest person, force of habit made him cross his fingers behind his back. 'We're just worried. We want to find out all we can.'

'Strange, isn't it?' said Kim darkly, and now he looked up. 'When it's two kids from the village, kids who live in nice houses, the authorities go crazy. One of ours does a bunk and it's hard to get anyone to care. What does that tell you?'

'That society is unjust,' said Emerald Greene perkily, 'and that our assumptions about others are based on deep prejudices. So, now that we have that agreed, can we talk about this properly?'

Don't antagonise them, Emerald! thought Richie, shooting her a desperate glance. Up to now, he'd been doing quite a good job of hiding how frightened he was, but Kim's stern expression had made his stomach plummet to his boots.

Kim stood up, and indicated that they should move away from the fire. Emerald, Richie and Anoushka walked beside him, Richie still hanging on to his mug of herbal tea.

'Will may be back with his family,' said Emerald softly. 'But all is not well, is it? He is… changed, somehow?'

Kim walked, not answering at first. But then he spoke, very softly, addressing his voice to the sky rather than to Emerald and Richie.

'He's twelve. Been with the community for a couple of years, now. Tammy Carver, his mum, was a bit of a waster. She went out west, somewhere, and we've no idea if she's even still alive. We've put out feelers, tried to get hold of her, of course.'

'Of course,' said Emerald Greene gently. 'It would have been the first idea, I imagine.'

'No joy, though.' Kim took a deep breath. 'That night, he was seen on the edge of Little Brockwell. Sunset, it was. He was playing on the ford, skimming paper boats. One of the girls saw him, called him in, and he said he'd be there in a moment.'

'That was the last anyone saw of him for a day?' asked Emerald Greene carefully.

Richie saw an odd look – strained, hollow – pass across Kim's face before he turned to Emerald Greene with a rueful smile. 'Yes,' Kim said. 'Like he vanished off the face of the Earth.'

At the very edge of the camp, where their bikes were chained to a pole, the firelight faded into shadow. They came to a stop, and Emerald, hands clasped behind her back, turned to face Kim.

'And when he came back…?'

'He just wandered back into the camp like nothing had happened,' said Kim, arms folded, his expression giving nothing away.

'Did Will suffer from any kind of… sleep disorder?' Emerald asked.

Kim's eyes narrowed and he took a step towards her. Richie saw Anoushka tense, down on the ground, and he felt his own pulse-rate quickening. Where had that question come from? What was Emerald *playing* at?

'How...' Kim murmured. He ran a hand through his greying hair. 'How could you possibly know that?'

Emerald closed her eyes for a second, smiled indulgently. 'Many people ask me that question. I put it down to a natural talent for investigation.' She raised her eyebrows. 'So the answer would be yes?'

Kim looked hard at her for a few seconds before answering. 'Will sleepwalked,' he said.

'Often?' Emerald asked.

'Well... it depended,' said Kim carefully.

'And would he generally... get far?'

'Usually no further than the edge of the camp, but... There was one time one of the girls found him on a bridge above a motorway. Standing there, gripping on the barrier with all that noise underneath him, and all those bright lights. As if he just couldn't see them.' Kim shook his head. 'She walked him back. Next day, he was fine, didn't remember a thing... After that experience, though, we set up a rota to watch him. Me, two of the mums, some of the older lads. Managed to make sure he didn't get himself into any dangerous situations... But then it stopped.'

Emerald Greene looked up. 'Stopped?' she repeated sharply.

'Yeah. For months. We thought he was cured. Then it started again, just a few weeks ago.'

Emerald folded her arms. 'Several weeks before, Will had been showing recurrent signs of his sleepwalking condition – and nobody wondered if the two events might be in any way related?'

'Course they did,' said Kim scornfully. 'But come on, sleepwalkers wake up. It's not a big thing.'

But Richie knew Emerald Greene had that light in her

eyes, the fire of discovery, illuminating the whole of her face. And he sensed that what they had heard tonight was of the utmost importance.

'All right?' said Ben, his forehead against Jessica's.

'Mmm, yeah,' she said, giggling. 'Awesome sauce.'

Ben's mouth was warm, firm but gentle. At first their lips just pressed against each other, playfully, for no more than a second or two at a time. Jess kept laughing every time her mouth was freed, and she was sure that she was blushing more deeply than she ever had before. Her body shook as if she was being pummelled by invisible forces. She wriggled on the chalk to move closer to him, aware that she was probably covered in the stuff, and not caring.

After about a minute or so of this teasing, his mouth opened wider and she responded, sliding her arms firmly around the soft leather of his jacket and pulling him close. She knew what to do, thanks to Abby Thomsett's extensive descriptions at school lunchtime about what she and Kian Mills got up to. The tips of their tongues met, tickled each other in a gentle, flirty conversation. Well, it felt right, she told herself. Thanks, Abby.

But then something made Jess break abruptly away, so quickly that she almost overbalanced on to the chalk and had to steady herself.

'What's the matter?' Ben asked, concerned.

'Nothing,' she mumbled, pushing her hair back and looking from side to side. 'Nothing, really.'

'Isn't it… what you wanted?'

'Yeah, yeah… it's good.' She met his gaze, carefully. 'Too good. Kind of… all at once, you know?' She sat down, drew her knees up to her chin. 'Sorry,' she said, smiling shyly at him. 'Not really… done this, before.'

She fumbled for the cider bottle, took another long drink.

It was really going to her head now, making everything blurry, but at the same time it was getting easier.

'Hey, nobody's an expert,' said Ben, and his fringe fell over his eyes again. He moved to slide an arm around her shoulders. 'You're shaking. Are you cold?'

'Yeah, a bit.'

He took his jacket off, wrapped it round her and put her arms through the sleeves. 'There. Nothing like a bit of dead cow to keep you warm. Hope you're not a vegan.'

Jess laughed. 'No,' she said, smiling shyly at him again. 'Although I've nearly gone veggie a few times. Dunno what's in meat these days, do you?'

'And what stopped you?'

'Well, I like bacon too much. Frying bacon in the morning, that's just gorgeous.'

'Too right,' said Ben, and they exchanged a complicit grin. 'My dad liked a fry-up,' he added, 'before he got ill.'

'Oh… I'm sorry. Is it serious?' Jess asked, concerned. She drank again, passing him the bottle.

'He's in a private hospital. Not far from here. I visit him whenever I can, but… there's nothing they can do.' He took a drink. 'You heard of Klemmer's Syndrome?' he asked.

'Can't say I have.'

'It's a blood condition,' said Ben. 'It affects people differently, though. I mean, Dad was fine for years. You wouldn't have known there was anything wrong. But then it started, and… he's just been getting weaker.'

'That's awful,' she murmured. 'I'm so sorry… What did… I mean, how… when it started…'

'Well, the first thing was when he got clumsy – knocking things over, dropping stuff – then his co-ordination totally went. It's awful to see… He used to play football, rugby. Now he can hardly walk.'

'I'm sorry,' said Jess.

This was uncertain territory. Grown-up stuff. She wasn't sure whether to feel sorry for him, or to admire the matter-of-fact way he told her, or just to feel sad.

'I suppose we're just used to it now,' he said.

Jess hesitated, as if coming to a decision. Then, emboldened by the cider, she got her phone out of her pocket, swiped the screen a couple of times. With her hands trembling, she showed it to Ben. It was a photograph, a small copy of the one which was permanently on her bedroom wall. It showed an attractive young couple in outdated denim jackets – a dark-haired man and a frizzy-haired young blonde woman, smiling together in a bar somewhere.

He took it, looking at it, then looking up searchingly at her, but she didn't meet his eye.

'My mum and dad,' she said. 'That was taken the day they met.'

'They look… nice,' he said. He handed the phone back.

'I don't show that to just anyone,' she told him. She pulled the jacket close around her. It was warm, soft, enveloping and smelled faintly of engine oil and some kind of musky aftershave – just a hint, not gallons like the sweaty boys in school. Less is more, she thought. He knows it.

She glanced at him, shyly. His eyes invited her. This time she did not need further encouragement.

They kissed again, gently. And then more urgently. It felt strange to Jess, like she was suddenly someone else, someone older and more daring and adventurous, moving her mouth against his, forgetting the ridiculousness of it now and enjoying it. Remembering to breathe through her nose.

Excitedly, she slipped her hand into his hair, pushing so that his mouth almost crushed hers. But then she felt resistance. He pulled gently away from her. He was looking over her shoulder, startled.

'What was that?' he said. He seemed to tense up.

'What?' Jess looked round in alarm, but she had not seen or heard any movement. However, something was happening, something which meant that Ben had to be right – for she could feel her hand tingling again. 'I… didn't hear anything,' Jess said, as they both stood up together, and she pulled her cold, prickling hand inside the sleeve of the leather jacket.

'Over there,' Ben said, pointing down towards the treeline, where a broad path cut across the ridge. He put the telescope to his eye.

They were both stained with powdery chalk, like a pair of ghosts in the starlight. Jess wanted to laugh, but hiccupped instead. She clung close to Ben, needing to do so but hating herself for it at the same time. The cider-bottle was still there on the chalk eye of the horse – she scooped it up and took a long, stinging gulp from it. Getting the hang of this, she thought, then pulled a face as she felt the sharp after-kick.

'Can you see anything?' Jess asked.

'I think it was just a dog,' he murmured.

'Long as it wasn't a wolf,' she joked.

And then, for a second, something made her turn towards the west – away from where Ben was directing the telescope, to where the dark ridge met the slightly paler, blue-black sky.

Her heart missed a beat.

'*There!*' she yelled, and suddenly pulled Ben around.

Too late – as she watched, the silent shadow flitted away, sinking down out of sight behind the ridge.

'Where?' Ben was asking. 'What are you looking at?'

Jess was staring, staring across the chalk horse at the darkness beyond, knowing full well what she had seen.

'It was something – a *shape*! Like a – a man on horseback! It was there!'

She was certain. It had been vast and black, silhouetted for an instant against the night sky. And if it was indeed a horse, it had been *huge*…

163

Like the one she had briefly glimpsed in the village.

Jess ran from the eye and scrambled across the curve of the chalk horse's head, trying to find something – a rock, a tussock – for a better vantage point. After a few metres, she gave up, flapping her arms in frustration in the too-big jacket.

She turned back towards Ben. 'It *was* there! Just for a second, as if someone was watching us!'

'Peeping Toms on horseback?' Ben said with a grin, scrambling up the slope after her. But his eyes were genuinely worried, and he was scanning the ridgeway panorama as intently as Jessica. He put the telescope up to his eye and swung it in a wide arc across the ridge from east to west.

'Anything?' Jess asked. The tingling in her hand was starting to abate, now, as quickly as it had come on.

'Nope.' Ben lowered the telescope. The night breeze ruffled his fringe and he pushed it back out of the way. 'I'm not saying you imagined it… I'm sure you saw something. But whatever it was, it didn't hang around very long.'

'I'd better tell Emerald…' Jess murmured. 'Wish she'd been here.'

'Emerald?' he asked.

'Oh, a friend of mine. A very clever friend. She has this kind of… intuition, about things that we'd call strange or unusual.'

'Is she in Little Brockwell?'

'Yeah. Kind of.' Jess shivered. 'Ben, can we go back down to the village? I'm getting a bit creeped out up here.'

'Okay. No problem.'

But he did not move. He kept standing there, looking at the darkness beyond the chalk horse's edge. As if he could still see something.

'Ben?' she murmured, and put a hand on his arm. 'Ben, are you…?'

He shook his head. 'For a minute…' he said softly. 'I

thought…'

Then he offered her a hand and led her back the way they had come, and the two of them made their way back to the path, leaving the chalk horse silent and still in the starlight.

And in the nearby trees, two pairs of burning, red eyes – one above the other – watched them go.

The eyes had done more than watch tonight. They had started a process in motion. A process which, very soon, would lead to a result.

Richie kept his eyes to the front and concentrated on the cone of light which his bicycle lamp was casting. There was a decent moon tonight, at least, almost full, so they could see where they were going pretty well.

He gritted his teeth as the chilly night air rushed past, trying to ignore his growing worries about having been missed, and also the sensation – stupid, he knew – that there was always something just a few metres behind them.

He pedalled hard, and caught up with Emerald Greene, who appeared to be making her rattly old bike whizz along without very much effort at all.

'He seemed scared,' Richie called out.

Emerald glanced at him. 'No, it wasn't quite that. I sensed he had suspected there was something more to Will's story. Something he did not dare discuss, which he would have thought seemed foolish. The sleepwalking connection, you see. He hardly dared make it – did you notice?'

'But where does that get us?'

'Pay attention! I happen to know that Tyler Uttley, the first boy to see the Shadows, was being referred to a sleep clinic. He suffered from terrible nightmares. Livvy Parks – she had bad dreams, too, but not on a regular basis. And the other day I accessed the medical records for Casey Burgess. She, too, suffered from a sleep condition – she was exhibiting all the signs of hypersomnia.'

'Of what?'

'Hypersomnia,' repeated Emerald. 'Inability to sleep, alternating with bursts of sleep so deep, so enveloping that it is almost impossible to rouse the subject.'

'And you looked up the girl's private *medical records*?'

'Richard, we are dealing with a matter of life and death. The normal processes have to be bypassed.'

'I'm not sure,' said Richie. 'I think we ought to call the police.'

'The *police*!' exclaimed Emerald Greene in contempt, and she braked, slamming her foot down hard on the tarmac. Richie managed just in time to pull up beside her. 'The police would just hamper this investigation, Richard,' she said scornfully.

'But… don't you think they ought to know?'

'Damage is done when bumbling idiots get involved, Richard… No, this is too serious to involve the normal authorities. Too serious by far.'

'If you say so,' said Richie doubtfully.

'I do. Now,' she went on, rubbing her hands together, 'let us ride home, Richie! I feel we are all in need of sleep!'

Their bikes sped on into the night.

Georgie Popplewick hadn't had a good night.

First of all, that DJ at the Horse really hadn't been all that. He had been embarrassing. And yet people seemed to enjoy it and were dancing and waving their arms. The bands had been a bit rubbish, too. And for some reason, tonight, people just weren't *listening* to her properly.

Then her dad had texted her and told her she had to be back by 11pm – like, how *old* did he think she was? And on top of that, there was Ben Hemingway – *Ben Hemingway*, who was, like, without doubt, *the* fittest guy from school – hanging round with some little dork who looked like she was barely old enough to be allowed out.

Georgie Popplewick didn't do not being the centre of attention, and she didn't do not getting her own way. So this weekend had been pretty bad.

And now, as if to rub her face in it, *all* her friends had gone off in a taxi to the Max Club in Westmeadow while she was in the loo, leaving her to walk two miles up a country lane home to her mum and dad's house.

It was almost as if they didn't like her.

It was embarrassing. Walking. Georgie Popplewick did not *do* walking. And now, halfway up the hill, her new high-heels had become so uncomfortable she'd had to take them off and carry them, and walk home in her bare feet. At least it was dry, she thought ruefully. And there was a moon, so she could see where she was going.

She shivered, though, as she hurried along. It was a bit of a spooky lane, especially in the moonlight with the weird shadows. And she had a good view of that chalk horse on the hill, which she'd always found a bit creepy. It was like it was watching her.

Not for the first time, she hated her mum and dad for moving to a middle-of-nowhere place like Little Brockwell four years ago when she started secondary school. The place stank of cows, there was no decent wi-fi, and the most exciting thing to happen was this lame little festival every summer. Before, they'd been in Westmeadow and she could just walk or get a bus into town, hang out with friends in Nando's, just *do* stuff. Now, she was like some country bumpkin.

Georgie was counting the days until she could go to university and get out of this grim place. Not that she wanted a degree – she just wanted to find a rich man so she never had to work. And universities, she was reliably informed, were full of rich young men. Even titled ones, sometimes.

A *ding-ding!* made Georgie jump out of the way just in time, almost staggering into the ditch. Two bikes whizzed past, and in the moonlight she saw two more annoying kids riding them – a geeky boy with glasses, and a girl dressed like a weird hippy with dyed red hair. The cyclists disappeared up the lane at speed, leaving Georgie sighing and trudging on.

'A mile,' she moaned out loud to herself. 'I've got to walk another *mile.*'

She got her phone out, looking for taxi numbers and cursing the fact that she hadn't thought to book one at the pub. All she got was the little symbol in the corner of the screen which told her the network coverage was as rubbish as ever in Little Brockwell.

'Honestly, this place,' she muttered. 'It's like a Third World village.'

She spun round on one heel, holding the phone up in hope. Against the moonlight, against the dark hills, and the stark figure of the white horse up there on the hillside.

It was then that Georgie Popplewick thought she actually *heard* a horse.

She heard the whinnying, and the gentle clip-clop of hooves. From behind her, she thought, in the lane.

She whirled around, her heart thumping. There was nothing.

Frowning, and slightly unsettled, Georgie activated the flashlight app on her phone and held it up. 'Hello?' she called. 'Anyone there?'

The lane behind her was empty.

'Must be hearing things,' she thought, and hiccupped a little in fear. She turned round again to continue walking.

And stopped dead.

The horse was in the lane ahead of her.

Dark. Huge. Silent, still and waiting.

Georgie felt a dark, primal fear, the kind of terror which she had not felt since, almost a decade ago as a seven-year-old in her bedroom in Westmeadow, she had woken up, gasping and sobbing, from a dream where she was being chased.

The dream came back to her now. Her heart thudded as she recalled it. The dream in which she was chased through a moonlit field by dark, red-eyed horses.

Steam gushed from the horse's nostrils. Its rider, she saw, was dark-cloaked, dark-hooded.

'I don't know who you are,' said Georgie softly, 'but I just want to get home. Please, get out of the way so I can get home.'

And then a figure emerged from behind the horseman.

It was a woman with long, dark hair and a deathly pale face. She wore a dark, trim-fitting suit, a stylish black hat, black gloves and black riding boots.

It wasn't that she had walked up the lane, or had been standing next to the horse. It was as if she had suddenly appeared, out of the night. As if she was part of the night.

Georgie was shaking in fear, her mouth dry, coldness spreading within her. There was something wrong with this woman. Something evil, unearthly. Not criminal, not the kind of person who would rob her or abduct her. She sensed it was something... darker than that. Something more primal.

Something *old*.

The woman walked right up to Georgie Popplewick. There was a chill around her, like winter. It cut Georgie to the bone in her skimpy summer dress.

The woman smiled. Her mouth was broad, red, glossy. Like a clown's, Georgie thought. She hated clowns.

'Do you know who I am?' said the woman. Her voice was pure, cold, hard. It was old, unyielding like stone. It was like the crashing of icy waterfalls in a deep cave.

Georgie, too terrified to speak, shook her head.

'Good,' said the woman.

Georgie saw the horseman, now, keeping a tight rein on the dark horse, both of them almost invisible, black, as if they *absorbed* the moonlight. And… was there someone else? A third figure, standing just to one side of the horse? Tall, dark, upright… she couldn't tell if it was a man or a woman.

Arms folded. Watching.

The woman's cold, white face moved across Georgie's vision. Georgie shivered. The woman's skin was so pale it was as if she was wearing chalk-white make-up, and yet she wasn't – it was her flesh, white as an Arctic iceberg. Her eyes were pools of blackness, her mouth blood-red.

'There are some things I need to know,' said the woman.

'Wr-wrong time of year, babe,' said Georgie, trying not to stammer in terror. 'Hallowe'en's not for a while yet.'

'I live in all seasons. All times.'

'That's… really nice for you. Look… I… I dunno who you guys are but I've had a *really* rubbish night. I just wanna get home, have a cup of tea and fall asleep to Netflix… OK?… So… could you move out of the way, please?'

'All in good time,' said the woman.

She reached out a bony, spindly finger, touched Georgie Popplewick between the eyes before she could move.

'Tell me what I need to know,' said the woman, smiling.

Georgie Popplewick froze. Unable to move.

Everything went cold, and then everything went dark.

In Rose Cottage, only the dim light of the anglepoise lamp illuminated the lounge.

A half-finished cup of tea sat on the floor beside the sofa, alongside several books with pages marked by yellow Post-It notes. Handwritten pages were strewn across the floor, as were several audio-cassettes and their boxes.

On the sofa, Aunt Gabi was snoring contentedly, one earphone of her iPod still fixed in place and the other dangling down across her shoulder.

The quietest of clicks sounded in the hall as Jess secured the front door behind her. A floorboard creaked as, holding her shoes in her hand, Jess tiptoed through the hall, keeping one eye on her slumbering aunt at all times. She put her shoes down in the hall, slipped out of Ben's jacket – which she had still been wearing – and made her way upstairs, one creaky step at a time. Gabi stirred once, muttering something, but did not wake.

A few minutes later, the back door opened and shut again. Richie turned the key and fixed the bolt in place, and crept in similar fashion past the lounge door. He peered in, glanced quickly at the sleeping Gabi, and nimbly made his way upstairs to bed.

Emerald Greene stood in the darkness under a row of chestnut trees, watching Rose Cottage. Her bicycle was beside her, with Anoushka sitting in the basket.

Emerald saw the last bedroom light go out in the cottage, and nodded in satisfaction.

'You have not told them the whole truth, yet, I take it?' purred Anoushka, as he jumped on to Emerald's shoulder and nuzzled her face.

Emerald scratched Anoushka's ears. 'Oh, my dear Anoushka,' she murmured, 'I can keep nothing from you.'

'The images you saw inside Livvy Parks' subconscious,' said the cat. 'Imprints of our enemy. I think you saw more than just the dark riders?'

'Yes,' said Emerald Greene softly.

'What else did you see?' Anoushka whispered in Emerald's ear.

'A carriage,' she replied. 'A dark, ebony-black carriage pulled by four black horses. It was riding through the ford on a misty night, lit by red lightning.'

'How very *dramatic*,' purred Anoushka. 'And was that all?'

'No.'

'What else?'

'I saw the figure inside.'

Anoushka slunk round behind Emerald's neck and stretched out, wrapping himself around her shoulders like a scarf. 'And...?'

Emerald did not look at Anoushka. She lowered her head, keeping her eyes fixed on the soft, dim light behind the curtains of Rose Cottage – the only illumination anywhere around them.

She focused on that light, keeping her eyes open, unblinking, for as long as she possibly could, as if trying to look through the light, to see more, to see *something* just beyond the reach of reality.

At last, she blinked. Her eyes glistened.

'A woman,' she said. 'It was a woman.'

Anoushka hissed.

'There is treachery in this village, Anoushka,' said Emerald softly. 'Not everyone in Little Brockwell is who, or what, they appear to be.'

'You think,' the cat purred, 'that someone is working with the Enemy?'

'I fear so. Come, we must investigate further. Nobody else will do so.'

And then, the girl and her cat retreated further into the shadows beneath the trees, and there was the lightest, softest sound of a bicycle wheel turning on the ground.

In the shadows by the dark hedges, something stirred. There was the tap, tap, tap of a walking-cane on the ground. A tall, gaunt figure in a long coat emerged for a second into the moonlight. He had a thin face under a broad-brimmed hat, and sharp, restless eyes.

Mr Alfred Bidmead, proprietor of the Antiques Emporium, stood watching Emerald Greene and Anoushka as they made their way back up to the farm.

His nostrils flared and he lifted his chin very slightly, as if something he suspected had been confirmed. Then, he retreated into the shadows again.

A moment later, there was nothing to be seen but the trees, dark and silent against the night sky.

6
Morning Light

Jess woke early, her mouth dry and her head aching.

In the bathroom, she rinsed with mouthwash, spat forcefully at the enamel and groaned at the hollow-eyed face in the mirror. Then she swallowed a couple of paracetamol.

She was beginning to wonder about her body-clock – according to her watch, it was only five-thirty. Pale light was just beginning to filter through the net curtains, and the frantic sound of the dawn chorus cut into the silence.

'Can't sleep now,' she thought. She had a quick wash, combed her hair and clipped it up. She grabbed the first clothes that came to hand: a black top, tights, some denim shorts. *So last year*, she said in her head, mimicking the sneering tones of Georgie Popplewick. Well, she had shown *her*!

Downstairs, she made a plunger-cup of Gabi's fair-trade coffee. It was bitter, not like Emerald's smooth, strong brew, but it did the job of kicking her senses into action.

Jess looked out of the kitchen window into the deserted street. Nobody around. Saturday, she remembered, so there weren't the usual crowds getting up for work, although she imagined the farmers were up and about.

She'd go to the farm shop up the road, she decided. 'Fresh eggs for everyone's breakfast!' she said to herself cheerfully. 'That'll be a nice surprise.'

She caught sight of Ben's jacket hanging on the back of the door. She wondered where Ben was. Asleep, still, of course. But what did he do on a Saturday? Help at the shop, but what else? She realised she was desperate to know.

'A good Friday night, Jess,' she murmured. 'Best so far.' She thought she probably wouldn't try cider again for a while, though. Maybe a few years.

Jess pulled the jacket on, enjoying its warm, feral aroma. A boy, she thought, and leaned against the door, hugging herself in the jacket, not quite able to believe it. Me, and a *boy*. An older one, too. With a *motorbike*.

She giggled. This could be very bad, but very good.

She liked not knowing.

She laced up her boots, then grabbed some change from the tin on the mantelpiece and slipped quietly out of Rose Cottage.

It took her a few minutes to walk to the farm shop. It was a wooden kiosk outside a farmhouse at the edge of the village, just beyond the Village Hall at the boundary-marker. Already this morning there were cooking apples on display, and eggs in a box of straw, but she couldn't see anyone around to take the money.

Jess counted out the right change and left it there beside the box, then carefully lifted three of the warm, fresh eggs. They were smaller and browner than those in the supermarkets, and they had a speckled pattern on the shell.

As she moved off, the toe of her boot nudged something on the ground. Jess peered down, saw something glinting in the early morning sunlight. Bending to pick it up, she saw that it was a small gold cigarette-lighter, with the initials 'S.B.' engraved on it. Someone will be missing that, she thought, and slipped it into the pocket of Ben's jacket. She would give it to Kate Trippett at the earliest opportunity. She'd be bound to know whose it was.

As she straightened up, she thought she saw someone standing there for a second. Right up against the gate, by the edge of the lane. A woman with dark hair, in a dark cloak with a hood.

Watching her.

Jess jumped, almost dropping the eggs. But then the shadowy shape was gone.

Breathing hard, she looked up and down the lane, across the fields. There was nobody.

She could feel her heart hammering. It hadn't even been a glimpse, she realised – the impression of the figure had barely lasted long enough to register as more than just an idea. The thought that there might be someone there.

She shook her head. The morning light was strange, unearthly. It had a cold glow, a translucent grey quality to it which sometimes deceived the eye.

Cradling the eggs carefully, Jess hurried back into the village.

In the Place of Shadows, the black globe floated down from the vaulted stone ceiling again.

The Queen extended her bony fingers and let the globe rest there for an instant. Then, she leaned forward, her eyes burning like two hot pokers.

'Show me,' she said.

The ball was old, but the image it now contained was pin-sharp, three-dimensional. The girl in the dark jacket, making her way through the grey cemetery at dawn. She was treading carefully, holding something close to her body as if afraid of dropping it.

'Ahhh…' The Queen drew back, and a long hiss of contentment issued from her withered lips. 'So… the little one dares to venture alone… Let us test her resolve.'

She waved a hand, and the image on the ball began to zoom in. It went closer and closer, until the face of the girl filled the whole space…

*

The silence was eerie, and Jessica glanced over her shoulder as she took a short-cut through the churchyard. She had never been anywhere this quiet, nor had she ever been up so early.

She emerged through an arch under a weatherboarded cottage, and realised she had come too far – she was back in the main street, with the church behind her and the Green ahead on the left. Just across the street was Mr Bidmead's antique shop, its polished windows dark and gleaming. She could see a few parked cars, but no sign of any activity. Jess checked her watch. Well, it was not even six o'clock yet.

And, just as she thought this, the tingling started.

Jess gasped out loud. Her right hand, the indicator of danger, was cold and prickling again, as if icy needles were piercing her skin.

She felt an eerie, creeping sensation in her back and her neck, too. Something made her turn round. The street behind her was still deserted. Jess scanned it intently, narrowing her eyes. She knew, now, the way to look properly.

A second later, the window of Mr Bidmead's antiques shop shimmered like the surface of a dark pool of water. Then, as Jess watched, a shape passed across the surface of the glass, soaking up the pale morning sunlight as it moved.

It was a vast shadow, three metres high or even more.

Shaking, Jess watched. Her mind was telling her to run, but her feet were unable to respond.

The shop window *bulged*.

With a hissing sound like a thousand angry serpents, the shape of a dark horse and its rider slid out of the glass, two dimensions becoming three, the shadow taking on form and substance.

The horseman brought his steed round with a sharp twist of the reins, and suddenly she realised that the creature and the rider were *there*, vast and black and solid, as real as Jess herself, facing her down the street at a distance of less than thirty metres. Silver spurs glinted in the sun, and jets of steam hissed from the flaring nostrils of the horse as it lowered its head. Two pairs of eyes glinted like rubies, behind the horse's armoured mask and beneath the black cowl of the rider.

Unable to take her eyes off the shape, she felt terror and wonder paralysing her.

Her mouth formed a silent, awestruck O. She was dimly aware of the eggs spinning from her fingers as if in slow-motion, bursting like three tiny bombs on the street. The debris – shell, white, yolk – scattered and splattered across the tarmac.

The horse reared up. The rider levelled his lance at Jess, pointing at her as if accusing her of some terrible crime, and the scarlet pennants fluttered in the morning breeze.

Jessica braced herself to run. A cold, rushing wind emanated from the darkness, ruffling her hair. There was a smell, too, a dank, horrible stench like the foul air in a long-sealed room.

The rider's shadow stretched across the street.

The horse's front hooves slammed down, sparking as they hit the sun-baked tarmac. And then it was moving, charging, coming at her like a storm.

Tenebrae, said Emerald Greene in her head, *that's what they call themselves…*

A living darkness, given form and shape and sentience…

And she felt her feet tearing themselves away from the road. Now, with what seemed like a vast effort of will, she twisted herself round, away from it.

Jess ran.

She ran, desperate and afraid, down the middle of the road, tarmac thumping beneath her feet, boots like lead weights as if this was all some terrible dream after all.

She ran, and the houses and shops rushed past, silent and empty in the morning light. There was nothing, nobody on the street but Jess and the terrible thing chasing her.

It was not a dream, it could never be, for she could hear its thundering hooves, see its uncanny darkness, smell its cold mustiness, almost feel the cold wet steam of the animal upon the back of her neck –

...we are dealing with a force more malevolent, more terrible than the people of this village can imagine...

She had reached the edge of the Green, but she did not stop, did not allow herself to get on to open ground. She ran on, heading for the humpbacked bridge.

The horse was galloping fast, the dark rider low in the saddle, his cloak streaming out behind him, incongruous against the backdrop of the timbered houses and their immaculate lawns.

She made it over the bridge and a few seconds later, the charging horse followed, pounding like a juggernaut without losing pace.

Jess kept running, the breath burning in her lungs, blood rushing in her head, heart pounding like a drumbeat. She didn't dare look back again, but she could tell that the creature was gaining on her, closing the gap with each gallop, the echo of its hooves filling the street, thundering in her head.

On and on, Jess sprinted like she never had before. She pushed herself to the limit and then further, ignoring the pain. She was running alongside the Meadows now, a low wooden fence on her left, and she suddenly saw the red-brick schoolhouse, distantly in view, just a couple of hundred metres away. If she could make it there, surely it couldn't follow her inside!

When she glanced briefly over her shoulder, all she could see was the darkness of the horse and rider, blotting out the sun, wreathed in steam and outlined in burning red, the gap narrowing now to about twenty metres.

Ahead of her, the road led off to a housing estate. And when she saw what was there, she slowed, staggered, spun around and then back again, unbelieving.

There it was, waiting, silent and still in the entrance to this road.

Another rider on another dark horse.

Jess spun round, facing first one rider, then the other. The first was approaching at a thunderous pace, the second moving out of the junction at a canter.

She was trapped.

There was nowhere left to run.

Richie awoke from unsettling dreams.

He sat up sharply, feeling uneasy and wondering why. It was light outside, but he could hear nothing but his own heavy breathing. Richie blinked, fumbled for the glasses he needed for anything to be more than a blur, and slipped them on over his tired eyes.

He then noticed something which made him turn cold. At the bottom of the bed, the quilt was bulging alarmingly, as if something were concealed beneath it. Quaking, Richie drew his legs up, trying not to disturb whatever it was and wondering if he'd make it to the door before it moved.

The bump shifted position.

Richie yelped – and then a familiar black, furry face poked out from under his quilt and turned to look at him with piercing green eyes.

'Most comfortable,' said Anoushka. 'Thank you for your hospitality!'

'Moggy!' said Richie with a sigh of relief. 'You gave me a start.'

Anoushka slipped out from under the quilt and padded across to him. 'A little reverence would not go amiss. The Ancient Egyptians worshipped cats as gods, you know.'

'Yeah, and I bet you've never forgotten that, have you?' riposted Richie.

Anoushka gave him a hard stare, before turning away in a superior manner. 'I don't suppose you could furnish me with any milk?'

'It's a bit early,' Richie protested. 'I don't do mornings... Oh, all right. You've woken me up now, anyway.' He scooped Anoushka up in his arms and headed out on to the landing. 'But please, make yourself scarce if we see Aunt Gabi. You know she has a problem around cats.'

'Most kind,' purred Anoushka, as they headed downstairs.

At the kitchen door, Richie let Anoushka go. 'Might as well make a cup of tea, then.' He picked up the kettle and went over to the sink to fill it. Then he frowned. 'That's odd,' he said, touching the smooth plastic surface of the kettle again with his fingertips. 'It's warm.'

'Of course it is,' said a familiar voice behind him.

Richie jumped. He swung round from the sink, almost dropping the kettle on his foot.

Emerald Greene was sitting in the kitchen. Her velvet coat was draped over a chair and she was sitting with her bare feet up on the table. She managed to be doing three things at once – eating a croissant, reading the newspaper and painting her toenails electric-blue – and she looked completely at home.

Now, Richie noticed the warm aromas of fresh coffee and French pastries, the pungent pear-drop smell of nail varnish, and the sound of the percolator gurgling in the corner.

'Good morning, Richard,' she said. 'An early riser, I see. Excellent!'

Anoushka hopped up on to the table and went straight to the bowl of milk which Emerald had placed there.

Richie blinked at Emerald. He wondered if he should ask why he hadn't seen her when he came in, but then decided he would not get a sensible answer.

'Sleep well?' asked Emerald Greene – and, peering over

her glasses like someone much older, she made the question full of ominous portent.

'Er… yes,' said Richie, sitting down at the table in something of a daze. He looked at the door, then back at Emerald. 'How did you…'

'Do not concern yourself.' She held up a hand to forestall any argument. 'Any dreams?' she added, delicately applying blue varnish to her big toenail.

Richie felt himself go cold. Thoughts zoomed through his head of gypsy sleepwalkers, phantom horses on photographs. And yes, he had dreamed – he remembered riding his bike along a carpeted road and being dive-bombed by giant black shapes.

'No,' he said levelly. 'Nothing.'

Despite everything, there was still an unsettling side to Emerald Greene – Richie had always thought so. And he didn't trust her enough to tell her about his dreams. Not yet.

'Good. Now then, the early worm gets eaten by the bird. So drink this.' She slid a cup of black coffee along the table towards him.

He peered into its pitch-black depths. 'It's a bit strong. Looks like treacle!'

'The strength is intentional,' said Emerald sternly. 'No,' she snapped, as he reached for the milk, 'drink it black!'

Richie frowned, took a cautious sip. The coffee was hot and strong, but had a rich smoothness which was very pleasant. 'All right,' he said, lifting his glasses and rubbing his eyes. 'Give me a chance.'

'Anoushka,' said Emerald, leaning over to the cat, 'will you please go and wake Jessica? We need to have a meeting.'

Anoushka hopped obediently off the table and scurried out, heading for the stairs.

*

Jess whirled around, spinning her arms as if she could use them as weapons. She looked frantically from one rider to the other.

Her first pursuer, coming at her in a dead straight line, was almost upon her. The second rider brought his horse across the road in front of her, blocking her way, then spurred his horse with one firm, angry movement. The second horse reared up, eyes blazing.

Jess left it until the last possible moment. And then – when the rhythm of the thunderous hooves was shaking her body and the shadows of the riders met in the middle and touched her, and the burning eyes were brighter than the sun – she dropped to the ground.

Two lances clashed with a violent crack, piercing the sky with red lightning.

Jess ducked between the horses. She threw herself at the wooden fence of the Meadows and leapt over.

Her foot caught the top of the fence, overbalancing her on to the field. She rolled – once, twice – and scrambled to her feet, glancing back at the dark horsemen on the other side of the fence.

Dew and mud had splashed her shorts, her tights and Ben's jacket. She'd lost her hair-slide and her hair streamed loose, tangling across her face. But she'd made it.

She banged a fist into the air, laughing in hysterical relief. '*Yesss!*' she yelled. 'Stick *that* in your nosebags!'

The two riders cantered in a tight circle, then split off, gathering speed again as they turned and came back round to face the Meadows. Jess's sense of triumph turned rapidly to unease, as the riders charged their horses at full speed towards the fence.

They leapt it together, landing with hooves skittering on the mud. Both horses came into the ground at an angle, then were swiftly jerked upright as the riders urged them on.

Two dark cloaks billowed out against the grey sky of the morning, as the horsemen headed towards Jess. They spread out, widening the gap between them, pinning her down in a pincer movement across the Meadows.

Jess, uncertain, swivelled one way and another as the riders bore down on her.

'Odd, is it not,' said Emerald, as she swung her feet down off the table, 'how so much of our language is filled with *sleep*?'

'Is it?' said Richie.

Emerald put down her newspaper and leaned forward, folding her hands in front of her. 'We talk about the sleep of the just. Of sleeping soundly in your bed at night. If someone is rich and successful, she lives in a house with fifty bedrooms. And then there are expressions you might use in sarcasm, such as "in your dreams" and "dream on". Have you ever wondered why this should be?'

Richie knew this had to be leading somewhere.

'What do you know,' Emerald asked, 'about REM?'

'Errr… I think my dad's got all their albums.'

Emerald looked puzzled. 'Rapid Eye Movement sleep.'

'Oh, I see.' He took another sip of the smooth coffee. It seemed to be going straight to his nerves, kicking him awake by the second. 'I've heard of it,' he said. 'It's what happens when you're dreaming, isn't it?'

'That is right. And contrary to popular belief, dreams do not occur in short flashes. They can last twenty, thirty minutes or even more.'

'Right,' said Richie uncertainly.

'And the interesting thing about that,' said Emerald Greene softly, 'is that brain wave activity, breathing, heart rate and blood pressure all rise during that lengthy period of REM sleep. But at the same time, muscle tone dramatically *reduces*.'

'Muscle tone?' echoed Richie.

'The muscles of the body... almost seize up. The body is temporarily paralysed. Effectively,' said Emerald Greene, her eyes bright and excited, 'it is as if our bodies act to prevent us from carrying out our dreams.' She paused.

'Or our nightmares,' said Richie, and immediately wished he hadn't.

'Indeed. But what if there was something else... something in the subconscious, straining to break free and not constrained by the human body? *What if nightmares could find form?*'

Richie swallowed hard. 'You're scaring me. I won't want to go to sleep again.'

'For the moment, that may be just as well.' She beamed delightedly at him. 'Do you like my nails?' she added, swinging her feet up for inspection.

'Um – yes,' said Richie, warily. 'Very nice.'

Before he could ask any more, Anoushka came bounding back into the kitchen and on to the table, scurrying back and forth in obvious agitation.

'Miss Mathieson is not in her bed!' the cat exclaimed.

Richie felt himself turning pale, and Emerald Greene narrowed her eyes at her feline companion. 'You are sure?'

'You wish to check for yourself?' snarled the cat.

'No. I am sorry, Anoushka.'

Emerald put her forefingers to her temples and seemed to stare hard at the wood-grain of the table. Richie watched, curious, as she opened her eyes wider and wider, staring *through* the table, it seemed, as if she could see something he could not. Emerald's face wore an expression of concentration so intense that it resembled pain.

'Where's Jess?' he asked in agitation, looking from Emerald to Anoushka and back again. 'Is she in trouble? Do you know?'

He was sure Emerald's eyes glowed for a second, cold

and green like two lights in the darkness – and then the impression was gone, like a ghost, and she looked sharply up at him.

'The village green,' she snapped. 'Come on! My van is outside.'

'But – ' Richie began.

'No time, Richard! Come on!'

Jess froze. She spat the harsh syllable of the worst word she knew. Blind panic overtook her. *Where could she run?* She couldn't double back towards the schoolhouse as the riders were blocking that direction off.

As they pounded towards her, she took the only option available – to run in a diagonal line towards the playground and the tennis court.

She summoned new reserves of energy, sprinting faster and faster, not daring to look behind now as her pursuers gained ground, hooves thundering on the grass with astonishing speed.

What was ahead of her? Grass, giving on to the fenced-off playground with a slide and swings. Beside it stood the village tennis court, surrounded on four sides by a wire-mesh fence about five metres high.

They were almost upon her as she reached the tennis court. She flung herself at the wire fence, disorientating the first rider to reach her – his lance sliced through the air, missing her by centimetres. The horse needed to turn, giving the agile Jess valuable seconds. She reached the corner of the fence where the metal gate was, kicked it open with one booted foot and hurled herself inside the tennis court, slamming and bolting the gate behind her.

She backed up into the centre of the court, aware of cramp gripping her legs and perspiration pouring from her body. She pushed back her damp, sticky hair and watched the riders conferring.

They rode, slowly, around the perimeter fence, in opposite directions. They were cantering, now, watching her. Feeling like a caged animal, she backed right up to the net and spun in a tight circle, always trying to keep both horsemen in view. They were trying to disorientate her, surely?

Now that she was on the other side, there was no way they could get over into the tennis court, and the bolted gate was barely high enough to admit a person. They had passed through solid glass earlier, but showed no sign of being able to charge through the solid mesh of the fence. Even in her fear, she found that interesting. So, once they were corporeal, they could not just transmute at will…?

And then, with a sickening feeling, she realised that the horsemen had slowed their pace for one very good reason.

They had no way in – but she had no way out.

And then she heard the distant sound of an engine.

Narrowing her eyes to focus, she saw it, chugging across the Meadows from the direction of the river, clattering and clanking like an old washing-machine. It was Emerald's old, battered, olive-green Volkswagen Dormobile.

'Typical! Doesn't show up till it gets interesting.' And she ran to the edge of the tennis court, pressing her face up against the chain-link fence.

The horsemen reined in their steeds, turning uncertainly towards this new arrival. Jess's heart lifted as she saw the Dormobile was heading at full tilt towards the tennis court, not slowing for an instant.

The horses whinnied, their riders struggling to keep them under control. The Dormobile, its wheels cutting deep tracks into the grass, came closer. Jess edged towards the gate.

The Dormobile swerved now, facing one of the riders head-on.

The horse reared up.

Its eyes were flashing bright crimson.

Jess was sure she could see the shimmering outlines of bones within its body, white and luminous…

Richie saw her kick the gate open. As the Volkswagen swerved past the tennis court, he reached, grabbed her, hauled her in through the passenger door.

Emerald swung the steering-wheel, swerving to avoid the rider. With the rickety van careering across the grass, Jess scrambled on to the front passenger seat and strapped herself in. She exchanged a triumphant, breathless look with them both.

It didn't escape Richie that Jess was wearing a battered, muddy leather motorcycle jacket, and he didn't need three guesses to work out who it belonged to.

'Having fun?' said Emerald grimly, as the Volkswagen accelerated across the ground with the galloping horsemen in pursuit. 'I cannot leave you alone for a moment, it seems.'

'Em…' Jess gasped, getting her breath back. 'Just… appeared… out of nowhere!'

'Yes, yes. I am aware. Although,' Emerald added, glancing in her rear-view mirror, 'I doubt it was *nowhere*. Probably an interstitial fracture of some sort. A clever piece of dimensional transfer engineering.'

Richie saw Jess look helplessly at him. 'Don't ask me,' he said. 'I'm not properly awake yet.'

'Are you trying to explain it to me, Em, or just showing off?' Jess asked.

'Just showing off,' Emerald admitted as she changed gear. She swung the Dormobile sharply around the cricket pavilion, heading for the field beyond. She glanced briefly at them. 'Block your ears.'

'What?'

'*Block your ears!*'

Jess and Richie put their hands over their ears, as Emerald flipped the dashboard over to reveal a gleaming, chrome panel covered with multi-coloured switches and dials. She steered the juddering camper-van with one hand while her other hand flickered over the controls. A second later, a shrill warble echoed across the Meadows, spreading outwards from the van.

Richie looked out of the back window and saw both of the dark riders, who had been pursuing them closely, suddenly rein in their horses. The animals reared up, and he could hear their fearful whinnying – in his head, he thought.

As they watched, pulling away as fast as they could in the van, the dark horses seemed to flicker in and out of reality. They crackled with a kind of pixellated energy.

They faded from jet-black to dark grey, then a cloudy, wispy off-white, until they were no more than two ghostly smears in the morning sunlight – and then, nothing.

The noise cut out.

Emerald slammed the brakes on and the camper-van came to a sudden, jerking stop. There was a strong odour of engine oil, burnt rubber and scorched grass. Richie could hear the harsh sound of their breath filling the enclosed space, and he and Jess exchanged nervous glances. He hardly dared speak.

'Have they gone?' Jess whispered.

Emerald Greene hopped out of the cab and strode back across the Meadows, tapping on her palm-top keyboard. Jess and Richie jumped down to hurry after her.

'Emerald?' Richie snapped, grabbing her shoulder and spinning her round. 'We asked you a question! Have they gone?' He knew he was probably out of line grabbing her like that, but fear perhaps made him bold, and angry to know what was happening.

Emerald Greene rounded on him, her expression one of subtle yet intense anger. Embarrassed and unsettled, Richie took a step backwards, clearing his throat and shifting nervously from one foot to the other. He lowered his hand.

'Yes,' said Emerald coldly, 'they have gone for now.'

'What did you do?' Jess asked, bemused.

'Sound modulation. They are manifesting themselves by psychic transfer geometrics. I was able to apply a signal on a frequency equal to that of the Enemy. It took some doing, but…' She gave one of her unexpected, dazzling smiles. 'Forgive me. You are unharmed?'

'Well… yes,' Jessica said, aware that she had a bruise on her arm and that Ben's jacket sported a broad streak of mud. 'A bit shaken up.'

'Good,' said Emerald briskly. 'You have just escaped the fate, I think, which befell Tyler, Casey and Will.'

'Will?' said Jess in puzzlement.

'Yes, Will. There is a third child involved.'

'A traveller!' said Richie excitedly, polishing his glasses. 'And he used to sleepwalk!'

Emerald said, 'Richie and I were investigating last night, while you, ah… were out, Jessica.' Jess looked away. 'Yes, all this time, and still nobody else in Little Brockwell knows that a third child was… Well, Richie will fill you in later.'

'Um, right… Look, how did you know I was in trouble?' Jess asked.

'I did not. It was a lucky guess.' Emerald squatted down on the grass, right where the two horsemen had disappeared. 'What was the source of the emission, I wonder?' she added quietly, as if speaking to herself.

'You mean where did it come from?' Jess folded her arms and looked smug. 'I can tell you exactly where. The antiques shop.'

'Mr Bidmead!' Richie felt his spine tingling. 'So he's mixed up in it?'

'Allies in the village!' Jess went on, excited now. 'You said it all along, Em. You think Mr Bidmead's shop might be where it's all been happening?'

Richie frowned. A worry was nagging at him. 'Hang on, I thought the Whispering Tree was the centre of it all?'

Emerald straightened up, holding up both hands to forestall any more questioning. She peered at them each in turn over her glasses. 'I would hesitate to jump to any conclusions as yet. But tell me more, Jessica. I want you to tell me exactly what happened, from the moment you left the house...'

Grandma Trippett slept.

Her mind carried her across Little Brockwell, in the days before the housing estates and the youth club.

Again.

Just as before.

Young Emily Trippett was floating, flying, her white dress billowing out behind her. She could feel the cold wind on her face, her heart pounding in her chest. Her arms were spread wide as she soared above the church tower, above the miniature houses, above the little white toy-like figures of the cricket players far below.

And then, suddenly, with no in-between, she was at ground level, on the deserted village street. Blue sky above her, hedgerows either side. Sunlight flickered up ahead on the water of the Brock Ford.

And there was something coming towards her.

From the other side of the ford.

She swallowed hard, unable to move, her legs suddenly huge and heavy and leaden. She turned, jerky and flickering like someone in an old film.

It was galloping, galloping down the street, the dark cloak spreading out behind it as Emily ran, breath burning in her lungs. At the Brock Ford, the horse's hooves sent up sprays of white as the beast pounded full-tilt through the water, not slowing for a second.

Emily ran, ran, ran, with the horse getting closer and closer. The creature's hoofbeats were thundering in her head, and the hot steam of its breath was heating the air right behind her neck.

'You can cheat Death, Emily Trippett,' said the woman's voice in her head. 'You only have to do as we ask. A plan seventy years in the making.'

Emily, gasping, slammed up against the gates of the farm.

Nowhere to run.

Her dress splashed with mud, her hair awry, Emily Trippett turned to face the darkness.

She awoke with a gasp.

Breathing hard, in her chair.

The back room of the shop aligned itself around her. She felt sunlight, heard the sounds of dogs barking and the till beeping, of Kate bustling around as she served customers.

Grandma Trippett opened her mouth to call Kate, then thought better of it. She got to her feet, surprisingly agile, and at the sideboard she poured herself a generous tot of whisky from the stone, glass-topped bottle she kept there. It burned her throat, warmed her inside and calmed her shaking hands.

She shook her head solemnly.

'Never again,' she said. 'Never again.'

The Queen of Shadow waved a bony hand, and the globe disappeared into the darkness of the vaults once more.

She rose to her feet, her robes of blood-red and night-black trailing behind her as she descended the ebony steps. A dark knight stood there, his hands grasping his lance, his face invisible behind his black visor. He was awaiting her orders.

'Prepare my carriage,' she said. 'I believe we have found the one we seek. But I must visit the place myself.'

The knight turned to go.

The Queen held up a hand. 'Wait. One more thing.'

She walked a little further forward. There was a raised table in the corner of the throne room – at least, in the dark, cobwebbed shadows where the corner seemed to be. On its polished surface were three smaller black globes, each perhaps the size of a football. Inside each one, a reddish glow gently flickered.

As if each of them contained something alive.

'I have no further need for the human… shells of the children,' she murmured to herself. 'But do not destroy them. Let us… have some entertainment. It will be… interesting.'

The knight clicked his heels together, bowed once, and left to do her bidding.

Jess took a deep gulp from the hot, sweet coffee which Emerald had made her. 'That's better,' she said.

In the kitchen, Aunt Gabi was unpacking some biscuits on to a plate. She hadn't seemed surprised to see Emerald Greene again – she had just looked her up and down and said, 'Oh, *you're* back, are you? I might have known.' Gabi always seemed to take things in her stride. She brought the biscuits through on a tray and offered them round to Jessica, Emerald and Richie – and also to Ben Hemingway, who, much to Richie's evident distaste, had popped round. Aunt Gabi knew to make herself scarce, then, and retreated to the study with her work.

Ben leaned forward. 'So,' he said with a winning smile, 'you're this famous Emerald Greene who Jess goes on about.'

It was odd, Jess thought, Ben being 'normal'. Just being someone else in a group of people, and not being special with her. What was she supposed to do? Was she his girlfriend, now? Hardly, after one snogging session. But she surely counted as more than just one more person in the room. He had hardly acknowledged her. God, this stuff was weird. It would take some getting used to.

'I may,' said Emerald, munching her chocolate hobnob and brushing crumbs from her velvet coat, 'and I may not. I am forming a theory, and I intend to present it at the meeting.'

'The meeting!' Richie looked up with a start. 'The village gathering at the pub – I'd forgotten!'

'Well, it all sounds crazy to me,' said Ben. 'I mean, three kids vanishing, dark horses appearing out of nowhere… it's like something out of the Brothers Grimm!' He put a hand on Jess's knee. 'Not saying you're making it up, or anything, Jess… it's just that, well, there's bound to be a sensible explanation.'

Jess blushed. 'Yeah, but what?' Okay, she thought. Hand on the knee is good, if a little patronising. 'I mean, what else could they be?'

'Well, I dunno… could they have been some sort of historical re-enactment types?' Ben suggested. 'Like, what are they called – the Sealed Knot?'

Jess tutted. 'Come on, Ben, these guys weren't doing a weekend hobby. They meant business! They chased me down the High Street and were trying to kill me!'

'Okay, okay,' Ben held up his hands. 'I'm just saying we've got to find explanations.'

'Indeed we have,' said Emerald Greene softly, leaning forward with her chin poised on one delicate finger and her bright green eyes fixing on Ben's worried face. 'Ben is only trying to be rational. I think that is very sensible.'

'Oh, right!' Ben leaned back, sprawling on the sofa. Jess shot an admiring look at him. 'Well, that's good.'

Richie glowered at Emerald, but she ignored him.

'And you mentioned fairytales, Ben,' Emerald went on, 'which is the closest anyone has yet come, I think. You did not see them, but I think you may have made a very important point.'

'What's that, then?' Ben asked.

'Fairytale wickedness is based on mythical archetypes, race memories of darkness and evil,' said Emerald. 'These are images that recur in nightmares – goblins, witches, demons –

but they are also often tied to specific places. Now, this village was a way-station, an important place on the route from London to the North... a *crossroads*. Not only is it associated with the riding of horses, it also symbolises the passing from one stage to another. Little Brockwell is a place of transition. And that enables the psychic transfer geometrics.'

'And the Whispering Tree? What's that all about?' Richie put in.

'Yeah, that thing always gave me the creeps when I was little,' Ben agreed, trying to exchange a friendly look with Richie. The younger boy just folded his arms and scowled.

'A link, a gateway,' said Emerald, her eyes pin-sharp and feverishly bright. 'Some kind of bridge for the collective psychic energy of the village, I am sure.' She leapt to her feet. 'I must locate Anoushka, and I have one or two things to do before the meeting... I will see you there, no doubt.' She strode to the door.

'But what – ' Jess began, frustrated as ever by Emerald Greene's half-explanations.

'Do thank your aunt for the biscuits, Jessica. They were most pleasant!' And with a cheery wave, she swept out of the room.

As Emerald left, Richie grabbed his coat as well. 'Yeah, I think I'll... go for a walk,' he said pointedly. 'Grab some fresh air.' He followed Emerald out, almost – but not quite – slamming the door.

Jess, folding her arms self-consciously on the sofa, gave Ben a sheepish look. 'Hey there.'

'Hi again,' he said, but he broke the eye-contact she was trying to make.

'It's only ten o'clock. Can you believe it? On a normal Saturday I'd just be sticking my head above the duvet and fumbling for my phone.'

'I suppose I would, too.'

'I've… still got your jacket,' she ventured shyly.

'Oh, hang on to it for now… Listen, Jess, I'm not doubting you saw something, you know. It's just…' Ben placed his coffee-mug gently on the table in front of him. 'Look, there were kids at school who vanished, then turned up safe and well at Victoria coach station and places like that. It's not that weird, running away.'

'I know,' said Jess, 'but people are worried. It's unusual, in a little place like this.'

'Yeah, I know,' said Ben. 'Three kids from the same area go weird in a few days… you can see why people worry.' He checked his watch. 'Look, that meeting starts soon. If we go down to the Dark Horse now, we can get a good seat.'

'Okay, but I'm not drinking again. Ever.'

'Oh, really? Why's that?'

She lifted her eyes defiantly. 'It does weird things to me. Makes me shoot my mouth off, and… well… snog unsuitable boys, and stuff.'

'Really?' Ben raised his eyebrows. 'You've been snogging unsuitable boys, Jess Mathieson?'

'Only one or two.'

'Well, didn't you have a busy night?' His eyes twinkled.

'Just a bit. Was nice, though.'

'That's a coincidence. My night was nice, too. I snogged an unsuitable girl.'

They smiled at each other in complicity.

'Anyway, I'm sure they'll do you something less potent,' Ben said. 'Come on. Let's go.' He turned to get up, and caught his cup with his elbow, sending coffee slopping across the table and dripping on to the carpet. 'Oh, hell!'

'It's okay, no problem,' Jess laughed, hurrying to the kitchen to fetch a wet cloth.

As she mopped up the spillage, Ben seemed agitated, glancing at his watch again. 'Look, um, I've just remembered

I've got something to do, actually… can I meet you there instead?'

'Sure. Whatever.'

'Okay. Bye for now.'

He waved, and hurried out, leaving a slightly puzzled Jess wringing diluted coffee into the sink and wondering if it was something she had said.

7
The Awakening

It didn't take long for the Dark Horse to fill up. Men, women and children crowded into the central bar area under Harry's watchful eye. When the meeting got underway, the debate was furious and heated.

There was an ugly mood in the room, Richie realised, especially among some of the more hot-headed young men, who were in favour of descending *en masse* on the traveller camp.

'It just ain't good enough,' said Mick Parks, to a general murmur of agreement. 'The police ain't done nothing, and all we got is scare stories.'

Right beside Richie was Emerald, tall and pale and impassive in her long coat. She seemed to be biding her time, he thought. In the corner was Jess, wondering where Ben Hemingway had got to. Nearby, Kate Trippett was occasionally casting concerned glances over at Jess, talking intently to Aunt Gabi.

'What else can we do?' the Rector demanded, standing on her chair and appealing with both hands spread out in front of her, as she did in her pulpit every Sunday.

Mick put an arm round the shoulders of his daughter Livvy, who was sitting beside him, looking pale but otherwise well. 'Someone, or something, Rector, frightened the life out of my daughter, and she don't remember what it were. I ain't prepared to put up with that.'

Again, there was a rumble of angry agreement from the young men.

'May I say a word?' asked Emerald Greene.

Oh, no, thought Richie.

Heads turned, looking towards the unfamiliar voice, as Emerald raised a hand. To Richie's dismay, she even hopped up on to a bar-stool and then on to the bar itself, parading above the assembled company like an actress on a stage.

'It seems to me,' said Emerald Greene carefully, walking along the bar with her hands clasped behind her back, 'that we are missing the essential point here.'

'Where you from?' asked Mick Parks aggressively. 'Who are you?'

'Oh, forgive me.' Emerald Greene looked around the room, making sure she had everyone's attention. 'My name is Emerald Greene, and I have been observing events in the village for some time. I am from… well, everywhere and nowhere, you might say.'

Richie covered his eyes in despair. Please, Emerald, he thought. Stop digging that hole, right now.

'In fact,' Emerald went on, 'I always find it far less interesting to talk about where people are from than about where they are *going*.'

There were real rumbles of discontent, now, and one or two derisive laughs from the young men. Richie's stomach flipped and he started to calculate the number of people blocking the way between him and the door. It was a large number, and so he stopped counting.

'What makes you think you've got all the answers?' shouted another young man in the crowd.

'I do not,' said Emerald Greene. 'I just ask the right *questions*.' She paused for effect. 'Let us, for example, ask a question about the children.' She sat cross-legged on the bar. 'Where do we imagine they went to – mm?'

The Rector bustled forward, puffing and panting and trying to put her glasses on straight. 'Young lady,' said the

Rector, 'I appreciate your enthusiasm, but I really feel that this is better left to the adults.'

'Hear the girl out!'

There was a silence in the bar. Richie, like everyone else, was looking around to see who had spoken in such a clear, commanding voice – a voice which was used to being obeyed without question.

People became aware that the door to the saloon bar had quietly opened, and as the people by the entrance stepped back to allow the new arrival some space, Richie realised in delight that it was Grandma Trippett.

Her electric wheelchair made a gentle whining sound as she manoeuvred herself into the centre of the bar and did a full turn, nodding silently, the half-blind eyes behind her dark glasses presumably registering what she could see of people. Then, she lifted a proud chin and seemed to fix her gaze on Emerald Greene.

'Hear the girl out,' she repeated.

Leaves skittered softly over the school playground.

One member of the village had chosen, for his own reasons, not to attend the meeting in the Dark Horse. The tall, bony figure of Mr Bidmead leaned on his cane, narrowed his eyes and focused on the tarmac.

And at that moment, something odd happened to the noonday light. It was as if three clouds passed fleetingly over the schoolyard, leaving three shadows.

As Mr Bidmead squinted into the sunlight, he saw that three children stood there – two boys and a girl. They were all casually dressed, with their arms at their sides and with strangely content, knowing looks on their faces. They were silent and still, too, their eyes unblinking.

He recognised them. Of that, he was certain.

The taller boy, dark-haired and brown-eyed, was the lad

called William Carver, the one who had temporarily vanished from the travellers' entourage. The other boy was Tyler Uttley, and the girl was Casey Burgess.

The returned children.

The children looked at one another, as if agreeing on something, then started to walk in unison across the schoolyard.

Towards Mr Bidmead.

Grandma Trippett's arrival in the pub had got everybody talking at once, Richie noticed. It was quite funny. Now, Kate pushed her way forward to the front of the crowd.

'Gran, you shouldn't be here!' she exclaimed. 'You ought to be at home!'

'Give over, girl!' said Grandma Trippett, who was obviously enjoying all the attention. 'Had too much of people telling me what I should and shouldn't do. My time of life, I ought to be deciding that for meself!' She lifted her stick from its holder on the side of her chair, pointing it towards Emerald Greene. '*She* may be half-crazed, and not from round here – but I know there's *something* about her. For good or ill, we should listen to what she has to say. Listen!'

There were uncertain glances now, and murmurs of a more surprised and interested kind. People were looking at one another as if for confirmation. Richie could tell what they were thinking – Emerald Greene, a strange outsider, was one thing, but Grandma Trippett commanded respect in the village. And Grandma Trippett had no time for fools and charlatans.

Emerald Greene, who had been watching with her usual composure, smiled at Grandma Trippett. 'Thank you,' she said, getting to her feet again. Emerald paused, her eyes gleaming. The silence in the bar was incredible, and all Richie could hear was the blood rushing in his own head. 'Those of you who know me,' said Emerald, with a glance at Richie, Jess and Aunt Gabi, 'will know that I do not like to talk about the *impossible*. But we are faced with a solution which, although it will seem impossible to the majority of people here, is indeed the only conceivable answer.'

Emerald looked around the faces in the crowd, her eyes shining with the light of conviction. Richie held his breath.

'The children,' Emerald said softly, 'never left Little Brockwell.'

Richie wasn't sure what he had been expecting, but it certainly wasn't that. He swallowed hard in the moment's silence that followed Emerald Greene's extraordinary claim, and then he became aware of a babble of voices all around.

'What?'

'*Preposterous!*'

'Girl hasn't a clue!'

'What's she *talking* about?'

Richie looked over at Grandma Trippett to see her reaction. The old lady raised an eyebrow knowingly.

Now the Rector stepped forward again, taking charge and quelling the babble with a gentle wave of her hand. 'Emerald,' she said, 'you must understand... this just won't do! It doesn't make *sense!*'

'Of course it does. All I am saying is - in terms of their position in *space* – they never left the village.' Emerald Greene spread her hands, as if the solution were easy.

And now, Richie realised he knew what she was going to say – just a millisecond before she said it.

'The children,' said Emerald Greene softly, 'were taken out of Time.'

Mr Bidmead hurried over to stand firmly in the path of the three children. He planted his walking-cane on the tarmac and held it firmly, his bone-white hands gripping the handle as if it were some kind of talisman.

'And where exactly are you going, may I ask?' he said sternly.

Casey Burgess folded her arms, tilted her head on one side and looked at him with a sneer, the same sneer which had irked one teacher after another, first in Little Brockwell and then in Westmeadow High School. Then the boys, either side of her, did the same.

Mr Bidmead looked into the children's mocking eyes, and drew a sharp breath.

The whites of their eyes shone unnaturally, brilliant like gloss paint, while the irises were polished, as black as spheres of jet. It was as if the dark holes of each of their pupils had expanded, blotting out the iris, creating six windows on black, hollow emptiness.

Mr Bidmead shuddered involuntarily. Leaning on his cane, he lowered himself to look at the children's eyes more slowly. His sharp, lean face was full of foreboding, and the creases around his own eyes were etched with the shadows of fear.

'You *are* the children,' he whispered. 'And yet – not…'

'We are,' said Casey Burgess. Her voice was calm, confident. 'Same as we was, ain't we? Except there's nobody to tell us what to do.'

She lifted her hand, and Mr Bidmead saw that she was holding a stone – a large, flat pebble. Tyler and Will lifted their arms too, and they, too, held stones between their fingers.

The children lifted their arms and drew them back, ready to launch their stones into the air.

'No!' Mr Bidmead exclaimed.

At the last minute, the three children swivelled round as one, so that they faced the schoolhouse. They hurled their stones. The projectiles sailed through the air, arcing perfectly, and hit the windows of the schoolhouse with a resounding smash. Broken glass fell both inside and outside.

Mr Bidmead advanced, brandishing his cane. 'I am warning you. I know what is afoot here, and I represent an authority, one whose force you cannot imagine!'

'I don't care who you are,' said Casey, and she turned and spat on the ground in front of him. She nodded, first to Will and then to Tyler.

Mr Bidmead straightened up. 'You are, without doubt, the same children, and yet...' he murmured. 'You – you have no...'

'Yes?' said Casey in mock encouragement, and the boys exchanged a knowing look. 'What ain't we got, then? Go on. You might get it – if you think about it.'

Mr Bidmead reached for something inside his coat. It was a hand-held radio, sleek and smooth like an ultra-modern smartphone. He thumbed a button and put the handset up to his ear. 'Bidmead,' he said. 'Condition Black. All units – go.'

Will threw something to Casey. The girl lifted her hand again, and this time it was holding a long wooden match. She was holding it up to the rough brick wall of the schoolhouse.

Casey gave a cruel, lingering smile. Mr Bidmead, listening to the voice jabbering in his ear from his link, took an involuntary step back and lowered the device, not listening now to the words being spoken at the other end.

Casey's hand flicked once against the wall. A spark flashed, and a flame snicked up from the head of the match.

A flame of pure, glowing crimson.

Jess bit her lip as derisive laughter echoed around the bar.

'Taken out of *time*!' said Mick Parks contemptuously. 'Girl needs her head examining. Been watching too much telly, ain't she?' There was a murmur of agreement.

'And furthermore,' said Emerald Greene, undeterred, 'our enemy is not working alone. This kind of force needs a focus, a bridge.' She paused dramatically, her eyes sweeping across the crowded bar. 'Someone in this village, ladies and gentlemen, is working with them.'

There was a shocked silence, then an uneasy murmuring in the room. People didn't quite know what to make of Emerald Greene.

Jess felt goosebumps, and drew breath sharply. Emerald was right, of course. She had said it several times, now, and it made sense. But these adults with their fixed ideas – they were going to have a hard time swallowing it, she could tell.

It did not help her concentration that, since before the meeting began, she had been unsettled by a nagging feeling of something that *wasn't quite right*. She couldn't place the thought – it was almost a mental equivalent of that warning tingle in her hand, as if something deep in her brain was trying to tell her that a piece, somewhere, didn't fit. Something someone had *said…*? Jess looked around the room at the villagers.

The Rector, Grandma Trippett, Mick Parks, Kate…

Kate.

The tingling in Jess's mind grew briefly stronger, then faded again.

Zoe Parks, sitting with the subdued Livvy, was watching Emerald uncertainly. 'I don't know,' Zoe murmured. 'She seemed to know what was going on with Liv… seemed to be able to speak to her. I think we oughta trust her.'

'Thank you, Mrs Parks,' said Emerald graciously, and bowed.

'And Shona said you spoke to her too,' Zoe went on. 'Casey's mum. She said you helped her. That you seemed to understand, more than anyone.'

Well, that's two supporters, thought Jess – but they seemed to be getting nowhere fast, all the same. She wondered why Richie was glowering at her.

'Oh, c'mon, Zo,' Mick growled, leaning back in his chair. 'She's a nutter. Probably on drugs… It's them gypsies! Everyone knows it is!'

There was a worrying rumble of assent from some of the other young men in the pub.

'I've had enough of this!' Mick Parks said suddenly, striding over to the door. 'I'm goin' over to that gippo site right now, and I'm gonna find out what they know. Who's with me?'

A group of the older lads and young men, scowling ferociously, joined him at the pub door. One or two of them were thumping fists into their palms as if in preparation for a fight.

Jess, fearful, exchanged glances with Aunt Gabi and Kate. 'They're going to do something stupid,' she said. 'We can't let them go!'

'Come on,' Gabi said, appealing for calm, 'let's talk about this.'

'We're all in this together!' Kate agreed.

Grandma Trippett barged her way forward in her chair. She poked Mick Parks in the shins with her walking-stick. 'You was always a bit daft, Michael Parks. Just like your father, God rest his soul! But this is just *ridiculous*.'

'Listen, Grandma – ' Mick began, waving a finger.

'I ain't your Grandma, son!' bellowed Grandma Trippett. She brandished her stick at Mick Parks, who took a sudden step back in surprise. 'Show a bit of respect. It's Mrs Trippett to you, or you'll get a clip round the ear!'

Mick Parks clenched his fists, torn between seething anger and his respect for the old lady. 'I'm… sorry, Mrs Trippett,' he said eventually. 'But we're angry, see? Gotta do something.'

Grandma Trippett made a dismissive sound and shook her head. 'Always the same,' she said. 'Men. Fighting, battles, wars. Always the same. I can't stop you. All I can do is talk sense, but I can't stop you, Michael Parks.'

Jess glanced nervously out of the window, looking down the village street. Then, she did a double take, not quite believing what she could see.

A pall of black smoke was rising into the sky from somewhere beyond the humpback bridge, down towards the end of the Meadows.

Jess leapt to her feet. 'Outside! Look!'

Kate, following her gaze, put a hand to her mouth in horror. 'The schoolhouse!'

And now, one by one, people stopped talking and looked.

Mick Parks turned from Grandma Trippett, and Grandma dropped her stick as she stared open-mouthed out of the window. Richie folded his arms and scowled. The Rector joined them, crossed herself and began murmuring a prayer.

With fearful glances, people were hurrying over to the door and the windows to look at where Jess was pointing. Even Harry put down the glass he was polishing and came round the bar to join the others at the windows. The eyes of Little Brockwell gazed down the street into the heart of their village, and they saw it together.

An angry, infernal roar was echoing down the street. And billows of thick, black smoke lifted into the sky, borne on the flickering orange flames from the roof of the village school.

'You're listening to County Radio.

Police are investigating the huge fire which yesterday destroyed a primary school in the village of Little Brockwell, near Westmeadow.

'The inferno completely gutted the hundred-year-old main building and its modern extension. The school was empty at the time and nobody was hurt in the blaze.

However, the flames destroyed all seven classrooms as well as the school hall, cloakrooms and offices, together with years of pupils' records and valuable project work.

'It is believed that the fire was started deliberately, but police are refusing to comment on speculation about a link with three children who had been missing from the village, all of whom returned safely to Little Brockwell just before the fire began...'

'Well,' said Jess glumly, stirring another cup of coffee, 'is it all over?'

'It is far from over!' snapped Emerald Greene.

They sat at the kitchen table in Rose Cottage. An eerie stillness hung over the whole of Little Brockwell – even the birdsong had stopped, and no church bells had woken them this morning. It was, Jess thought, as if a giant bowl had been placed over the village, shutting it off from the outside world.

The school was a shell. The stone walls remained, blackened by smoke, but everything inside had been consumed by the fire. Those who had tried to fight the blaze had spoken of strange, angry red flames, like demons, larger and fiercer than anything they had seen before. Kate Trippett had told Jess this, her face pale and tear-stained.

Incredibly, nobody had been hurt – but it was as if the heart of the village had been torn out. Fragments of ash had drifted over the trees, and black dust had, in the hours after the fire, settled on the village. Everywhere, the acrid smell of burning pervaded people's houses and gardens, and the sky itself seemed to have turned a dull grey.

Jess remembered the villagers racing down the street to fight the fire. There had been a babble of confusion, with nobody seeming to be in charge. A group headed out into the street, led by the Rector and Harry – Jess could picture Grandma Trippett, too, bringing up the rear in her motorised wheelchair. There were shouts of 'Call the fire brigade!' and 'Fetch water, we can put it out!' All the men who had been about to head off to the gypsy camp had run as fast as they could down the village street, towards the giant black exclamation-mark of smoke which dominated the skyline.

And as for Emerald Greene, Jess recalled that she had jumped down from the bar and strolled slowly over to the nearest window, as if she was completely unfazed by it all. Jess was sure she had muttered something like 'Retribution…'

People had tried their best to fight the fire, of course, but it had taken hold quickly. A fire-engine from Westmeadow had arrived eventually, but by then it was too late.

At about half past four that afternoon, when the school was still smouldering, three black cars had drawn up in the village street outside Bidmead's Antiques Emporium – watched by a curious, muttering crowd of villagers, including Jess and Ben.

A young man in a dark coat, accompanied by two WPCs, had brought Casey Burgess, Tyler Uttley and Will Carver out of the antiques shop. The children did not look distressed, hurt or even vaguely concerned. They wore calm, serene expressions and allowed themselves to be led away unresistingly.

And then everything went quiet.

In the aftermath, rumour began to spread even faster than the fire.

First, the rumour said that Mr Bidmead had kidnapped the children all along and had been holding them in his cellar. Then another version said that Mr Bidmead was dead, and that the children had killed him. Before long, it had become impossible for anyone in Little Brockwell – even Harry the landlord – to separate fact from fiction.

Jess and Richie knew, even without having to ask, where the dark cars and the young man were from. Back in Meresbury a few months ago, they had encountered the shady Government department known as the Special Measures Division, and they knew enough to be able to recognise their operatives. In fact, Jess reflected, it was a surprise that they hadn't got involved before now.

The children, Jess imagined, would be taken away to separate rooms to be quizzed – politely, but searchingly – about where they had been, and the Special Measures Division would begin to piece together most of what Emerald Greene had already worked out.

Which left one nagging question.

Where – and, indeed, who – was Mr Bidmead?

It made Jess shiver, now, as she thought about it.

'Please keep drinking the coffee,' said Emerald Greene, topping up Jess's mug from a large coffee-pot.

'Mine's gone cold,' Richie said, over by the microwave. The machine hummed softly as it warmed his cup. 'Hey, d'you think that if you make instant coffee in a microwave, it sends you back in time?' he pondered aloud.

'Don't be silly, Rich… Please, Em, what is this coffee stuff about? You've been making us drink the stuff constantly. It's giving me the jitters – look!' She held up a trembling hand. 'I can't taste anything else, and it's making my mouth go dry.'

'Me, too!' said Richie, scowling as he gulped from his newly-warmed mug. 'I couldn't sleep at all. I was walking up and down, listening to some rubbish phone-in.'

'Excellent!' said Emerald Greene, with a mischievous glint in her eye. She pulled two oblong, gold-foil sachets from her pockets and placed them on the table. 'More supplies of the finest, pure coffee,' she said, as they gawped at her. 'From Miss Trippett's shop. You must stay awake until this business is over.'

'You're joking,' Jess said. She exchanged glances with Richie. 'Tell me she's joking!'

'I am perfectly serious,' said Emerald. 'I, too, am following the regime – although I am relying on certain mental disciplines I have learned, rather than on stimulants.'

'Em, we can't!' Jess exclaimed. 'Look, all this coffee isn't good for my blood pressure! Or my complexion…'

'And sleep deprivation's really dangerous,' Richie added. 'I've read about it – you can start seeing things.'

'I am afraid there is no other choice,' Emerald told them sternly. She leaned forward, pressing her fingers together, and they could see now that she looked pale and drawn, her eyes outlined with dark rings. 'If you fall asleep,' Emerald murmured, 'you run the risk of dreaming. Your brain will begin to reverberate with delta-waves and the Enemy will home in on them.'

'I'm getting sick of this,' said Richie. 'Can't we just leave and go back to Meresbury? After all, everyone else seems to be getting out!'

Little Brockwell had been echoing to the sound of doors being locked, car engines revving and gravel crunching. It had started with the Parks family, who were seen bundling suitcases into Mick's van around lunchtime – Zoe had been heard to shout something about going to her mother's in Westmeadow. After that it had been their neighbours, the Apsleys, with their two boys, and then the young couple on the other side had the same idea.

Stories spread through the village. Someone said the Popplewicks had left their farmhouse and gone to an aunt's house by the sea – stopping at the hospital to pick up Georgie, who, it seemed, was now perfectly fine, if a little unnerved and with no memory of her walk home from the village the previous night, or of falling asleep in a ditch by a country lane.

And over the course of a few hours, the idea of escaping Little Brockwell seemed to take hold and to spread like wildfire – until, by the evening, the village was silent and practically deserted. People had gone to family, to friends. Tyler and Casey had been returned to their families, Will to the travellers.

As far as Jess, Richie and Emerald knew, only a handful of people now remained in the village at all. Even Harry the landlord was gone – Gabi had encountered him locking up the Dark Horse as he headed off, muttering something about his caravan on the coast.

Jess folded her arms and squared up to Emerald. 'Well, answer him! Why can't we go?' She knew, though – it was all too obvious.

'Please understand,' said Emerald urgently. 'The Darkness knows the texture of your dreams. If you return home now, it will hunt you down – and in your deepest nightmares, it will find you. We must see this business through – even if the rest of the village deserts us.'

Jess and Richie exchanged concerned glances.

'So… let me get this right,' said Jess. She tried to look brave, but Emerald's words had shaken her. 'We can't go to sleep? *At all*?'

'Do not doubt it, either of you. The Enemy has come for Jessica once. It could return for either of you, if you allow yourselves to dream again…'

'But Livvy Parks was fine,' argued Jess.

'And so was Georgie Popplewick,' said Emerald.

Jess raised her eyebrows. 'Don't tell me. You've been hacking into hospital records again?'

'Oh, yes, Georgie.' Emerald shrugged. 'Amnesia, chill, a sense of dislocation – I gather she is fine, but we have to conclude that she met the darkness somewhere on the road, and something happened.'

Jess shuddered. She didn't like Georgie, but it was awful to think of the girl encountering some dark force and having a traumatic experience. 'So some people are okay,' she pointed out.

'Some people, yes, but we cannot *assume*!'

'They were right,' said a languid voice from the kitchen

doorway. 'You do seem to know an awful lot about what's going on here.'

'Ben!' Jess exclaimed, and leapt up to give him a hug.

Ben Hemingway, swinging his motorbike helmet from one hand, smiled uncertainly as he untangled himself from Jess. 'Your aunt said to go straight in,' he added, sitting down with them at the table and pushing back his floppy hair. He was wearing an expensive-looking pair of black jeans and a T-shirt saying 'Motorcycle Emptiness'.

'Sit down,' she said. She could tell he was worried – still mistrustful, perhaps, of Emerald Greene, as everybody seemed to be at first. 'Have some coffee!' she added.

'No, thanks, I won't… They've all gone mad out there,' Ben said, indicating the village with a wave of his thumb. 'All leaving.'

'Where have you been?' Jess asked softly. She was curious, but also realised she had been missing him.

'Out and about. Errands… Seriously, have you *seen*? First a few people start talking about leaving, next thing everyone's getting out! Families piling into cars like it's a Bank Holiday!'

'We know,' said Richie glumly. 'So what's our next move, Emerald?'

Emerald Greene sat bolt upright and looked at them all in turn. 'Richie – you and I are going to pay a visit to Mr Bidmead,' she said.

'We are?' he answered, surprised.

'Yes, indeed. And Jess?'

'Yes, Em?' she said.

'This picture,' said Emerald Greene, and she passed over a printout of Grandma Trippett's old photo of herself on May Day as a little girl. It was the enhanced version, with the shadow of the black horse and rider clearly visible in the background.

Jess shivered. 'I know, Richie showed me. What about it?'

'Go back to the old lady and find out *exactly* what she knows. She trusts you. She will confide readily in you, I am sure.' Emerald glanced briefly at Ben, as if he was of no consequence. 'You may take your... friend with you, if you so wish.'

'Thanks,' said Ben acidly, frowning at Emerald. 'She's my gran, remember. I'll go and see her if I want.' He pulled the picture over and stared at it himself, raising his eyebrows momentarily.

Jess decided she had better do as Emerald said – even if, as she thought, Ben was suspicious of Emerald's motives. She hoped he would come round. After all, they were both important to her, so she wanted them to get on.

'All right,' Jessica said. 'I s'pose it'll help me keep awake, won't it?'

'There is another matter, too,' said Emerald, leaning forward and folding her hands together on the table. 'One which we have, in the excitement, allowed ourselves to forget – a village mystery which may yet hold the key to the whole thing.' She looked round, making sure that she had eye contact with everyone. 'I would draw your attention,' she said, 'to the curious incident of the disappearance of Miss Davisham.'

Ben looked up. 'The schoolteacher?' he said, puzzled. 'But I thought she just left, quietly?'

'Yes,' said Emerald Greene. 'That is the curious incident.'

And she refused, for now, to be drawn any further.

Richie followed Emerald through the almost-deserted village, struggling once again to keep up with her long strides. He caught sight of the Whispering Tree, looking like a dark creature poised to spring, and he shuddered. He was sure that the Tree had grown even darker and more evil-looking in the last few hours, and he made sure to give it a wide berth.

Emerald – with the loyal Anoushka once again trotting at

her heels – just kept in a straight line, marching purposefully towards the dark shop-window.

'So you think he's mixed up in this?' Richie asked, as they walked up the steps to the shop door.

'Mr Bidmead has been withholding information,' said Emerald Greene. 'For his own ends, naturally. I do not necessarily blame him for that.'

Richie looked up at the shop sign. Written in an unfussy gold script on a black background, it read: ALFRED H. BIDMEAD, ANTIQUES EMPORIUM. Richie supposed an 'emporium' was just a posh name for a shop. He also wondered, briefly, what the H stood for.

Emerald lifted the knocker and rapped firmly on the door. *Rat-a-tat-tat*! The sound echoed through the empty village.

Richie rubbed his eyes. 'It's all a lot to take in,' he murmured, gazing down the street to where the crumbled ruins of the school could just be seen in the distance. 'I'm getting tired again. Can I just have a little lie down? I won't go to sleep, I promise.'

'Absolutely not,' said Emerald firmly, and pinched his arm.

'Ow!' Richie yelped.

'Stop complaining. Lesson for the day, Richie – you do not learn much while your mouth is moving.'

'Oh, thanks,' he said sardonically. 'I'll try and remember that.'

Emerald went round to the darkened plate-glass window, shaded her eyes with cupped hands and peered inside. 'Hmmm. Anoushka, I think a mode transference is called for.'

The cat lifted himself up on his hind legs, his fur bristling. 'If you are sure, Miss Greene.'

'Absolutely,' said Emerald, standing back. 'Please go ahead.'

Richie knew what was going to happen. He had seen the

cat do this at the Cathedral in Meresbury, months ago in their first encounter with Emerald. He hadn't quite believed it then, and he wasn't quite ready for it now.

Anoushka hissed, clawing at the ground. Then, he hurled himself forwards, snarling and spitting as he headed straight for the window of the Antiques Emporium.

Without disturbing the shape of the glass, he seemed to pass straight through it, and disappeared inside with a fizzing, popping sound.

'I still think that breaks the laws of physics,' Richie said.

Emerald ignored him, and checked her stopwatch. 'In five seconds precisely, he will let us in through the front door.'

'Oh, come on,' said Richie. 'Even *you* can't – '

The catch clicked, and the door to the Antiques Emporium creaked slowly open.

'After you,' said Emerald Greene with a smile.

In the room behind the Post Office, Grandma Trippett looked from Jess Mathieson to Ben Hemingway and back again. The long-case clock went *tick-tock-tick*, and seemed to make the moments last even longer. Behind them in the shop, they could hear Kate bustling around, rearranging shelves.

Grandma Trippett's lips pursed. 'Sit down,' she said.

They sat.

'Emerald wanted me to show you this,' said Jess, unrolling a printout copy of the enhanced photograph. 'It's that picture, from when you were a little girl – but it shows what was really on it.'

Grandma Trippett's gnarled old hands took the photograph and she held it close to her shaded eyes.

'You knew all along that the Tenebrae were in Little Brockwell, didn't you, Grandma Trippett?' said Jess gently. 'Because that little girl on the picture – you, little Emily – she's not looking at the camera.'

217

Grandma Trippett didn't react.

'At first, when Richie showed me it, I thought you were just being shy,' Jess went on, confidently. 'But then I took a closer look and realised where your eyes were. *You're looking at the horse.*'

Grandma Trippett said nothing.

'You saw it,' Jess went on. 'Emily saw it that day.'

'Gran?' said Ben, astonished, and he pushed his fringe back from his eyes. 'Is that true?'

'Just a glimpse,' Grandma Trippett answered, and there was a note of fear in her voice for the first time. 'Only for a few seconds at most. I'd seen it afore, in me dreams.'

'Just like the children,' murmured Jess.

'Didn't dare look up properly,' Grandma went on, 'as I knew folk would never believe me. Little girl, vivid imagination and all that? They'd think I was like those two lasses, them as said they'd found fairies down the garden.' She lowered her voice to a whisper, and they had to lean forward to hear her properly. 'I were frightened. So frightened. That were the first time, you know. Just after Winnie and Tommy disappeared.'

'Winnie and Tommy?' asked Jess, puzzled.

'Winifred Gilmore and Tommy Taylor. Two children in my class at school who went missing. They never did find them. Never. Over the years, the village forgot about them, didn't we?' Grandma Trippett drew a sharp breath. 'And then there were that funny business with the schoolmistress.'

'Miss Davisham,' said Kate, who had appeared in the doorway.

Ben and Jess turned round, startled.

Kate came in, wiping her hands on her apron. 'Yes, I was there in the pub when one or two of the locals were talking about her. Miss Davisham was the new schoolteacher here, a few months ago. She left, quite abruptly – nobody knew why.

Even Debbie Chaney, the new teacher, doesn't seem to know anything about it. Personal reasons, people said.'

'No, no!' Grandma Trippett was shaking her head, thumping the arms of her chair in frustration. 'I'm not talking about *her*! The other teacher, I'm talking about!'

'The... *other*...?' Jess frowned. 'Sorry, I'm confused.'

'Yes, from years back! Miss *Pemberton* were our teacher. Mine, and Tommy and Winifred's, and Bert Parks, and Hetty Burgess... Mmm, and those names are still in the village. Names stay in a village like this. People stay.'

'Never mind that now,' said Jess, flapping her fingers in agitation. 'What happened to her, Mrs Trippett?'

'Who?'

'Miss Pemberton?' Ben prompted hopefully.

'Oh, her!' Grandma Trippett snorted. 'Nothing *happened* to her, as such. It were just that she appeared out of nowhere, one day. Nobody seemed to know her, and she weren't from the village. She were an odd 'un, like your friend Emerald. Always seemed to know things she shouldn't... Folk said she had the second sight. And I should know, hmm!'

'Psychic powers, you mean?' Jess asked excitedly.

'It were all just talk!' Grandma replied determinedly. 'People are like that in villages. They prattle. Afore you know it, something's gospel truth, when you only made it up yourself yesterday evening!'

'Right,' said Jess uncertainly. Her head was spinning, and she knew she had to get this information back to Emerald.

Grandma Trippett's clock broke the silence, the mechanism clicking and whirring and four long, loud *bongs* echoing from its wooden depths.

Ben, checking his watch, jumped up, grabbing his motorcycle helmet. 'Sorry! I've got to go and see Dad,' he apologised.

'Give James my love, boy,' murmured Grandma, as Ben

gave her a kiss goodbye.

'And mine,' said Kate, 'and take care! Don't you go vanishing like the rest of Little Brockwell.'

'I'm coming back,' he said. 'Don't worry!'

He hurried out, touching Jessica's cheek gently as he went. She felt the blood roaring into her cheeks, and she couldn't look at Grandma or Kate as they heard Ben's motorbike revving up outside.

'Sweet on you, ain't he?' said Grandma, amused. Jess had to look away, smiling in embarrassment.

'Anyone home?' Richie called out.

The silence inside the Emporium made Richie shiver. The place was crammed full. Every available piece of floor-space was covered with rocking chairs, lacquered Victorian writing-desks, elegant pine hat-stands and velvet-trimmed footstools.

The shelves were packed with trinkets and oddments right up to the shadows in the rafters. There were ornamental boxes and engraved thimbles, sets of coins and carved bookends, porcelain vases and china plates. Oil paintings in heavy gilded frames covered the wall behind the counter, and there was a stuffed macaw mounted in a glass case above the door. Nothing, though, was worn or dusty – all of the antiques seemed exceptionally well cared for, and a strong smell of polish pervaded the place.

Anoushka, mewling in agitation, prowled the shadows while Emerald Greene walked around, idly tracing her finger over one or two items. Here and there, she paused with a pensive frown.

'He's not here,' Richie said. 'Let's go. Come on.'

He didn't like the thought that they might, right now, be in the lair of the villain behind all this. He wanted to expose Mr Bidmead's machinations as much as Emerald did, but he didn't especially want to do it by walking straight into the lion's den.

'Just a moment,' Emerald Greene held up a finger.

'What is it?' Richie ambled over, sighing with boredom, and peered over Emerald's shoulder.

She was examining a polished wooden musical-box. 'Walnut wood, I believe,' she murmured, sniffing it, and lifted the lid.

A plink-plonky tune started to play, and Richie peered into the box. To his astonishment, he saw a tiny, sculpted ballerina in a pink skirt, no more than three centimetres high, like a sugar-icing figure on a cake.

The ballerina moved in time to the music, circling inside the box – on a turntable, Richie saw – with her arms swooping up and down in a surprisingly realistic motion. They watched until the musical-box wound itself down.

'Cute,' said Richie with a sigh. 'So can we go now? *Please*?'

'Hmmm,' said Emerald Greene. 'Charming, I am sure, but what is its function?'

'Entertainment, Miss Greene,' Anoushka purred, his ears twitching. 'For Victorian children.'

'Of course.' Emerald put the box close to her nose again. 'It is in quite excellent condition,' she murmured, staring into space. 'Just like *everything* else here.'

'Yes, quality stuff, I s'pose, for your discerning buyers. I expect he sells loads of it online. Em, can we please...' He stopped, seeing that she was wearing her 'look' – wide-eyed, triumphant, knowing. 'Em?' Richie asked, sensing the prickle of excitement again. 'Emerald, what is it? Have you got something?'

'Good afternoon, Mr Bidmead,' said Emerald Greene, without turning, and Richie jumped as she slammed the lid of the musical-box shut.

As one, they spun around. Richie swore he hadn't heard the old man sneak up on them, and yet there he was, behind the counter.

'Now, then,' said Mr Alfred H. Bidmead, leaning on his cane and looking at them hawkishly over his half-moon spectacles. 'Before I call the police, perhaps you young people could explain *exactly* what you are doing in my shop?'

8
Cat's-paw

The sun was low in the sky as the motorbike wound its way along the high road. Its rider, clad in black T-shirt and jeans, guided the bike steadily, unhurriedly.

At the top of the hill, high above the village, he stopped, cut the engine and listened. Sitting on his faithful bike, he slowly and cautiously removed his crash-helmet.

Looking all around, Ben could see nothing unusual – just the hills, fields and chalk escarpments of the countryside.

He let his gaze wander down into the valley, across the river, back to the Green and from there to the Whispering Tree, its darkness like a cancerous growth at the core of the village. That tree had always made him shiver, even as a little boy.

Nervous, now, he looked over his shoulder, stared down the lane, back the way he had come. Nothing to be seen.

He turned back round.

And it was there in the road in front of him.

Silent and still on the ridge – barring his path back into Little Brockwell – was a stark, ebony-black carriage pulled by four magnificent black horses, their red eyes like flaming coals and their breath steaming in the early evening air. A coachman held the reins, his face hidden by a cloak and hood.

Ben swallowed hard. His heart was thumping. He turned the ignition key of his bike, letting the engine purr, and gently revved a couple of times. The horses remained impassive.

And then, the door of the carriage swung open. Ben watched, unmoving, as an elegant figure in a long, black dress stepped down. A high-booted foot stepped on to the tarmac. The carriage door closed behind her, and she turned and approached him.

He wasn't frightened. He had seen the figure before.

He had seen her – and spoken to her – in his dreams.

He got off his motorbike, removed his crash-helmet, and started to walk towards the woman.

Jess, back in Rose Cottage, was restless and fidgety.

Sipping at another mug of bitter, black coffee – and she was sick of drinking the stuff – she felt her whole body geared up for something and yet unable to respond. It was as if she needed to fight or to run, but had nobody to fight and nowhere to run to.

She slammed her mug down on the table beside the computer, which was still humming quietly in the corner of the dining-room.

Jess slumped sulkily into the padded chair and glanced at her watch, wondering what time Ben would be back. She couldn't begrudge him his time with his dad, she knew that. She wondered for a second if she would ever get to meet Ben's father, before…

She remembered something she wanted to look up. 'No time like the present,' she said to herself. She opened the search engine and typed 'Klemmer's Syndrome' into the dialogue box.

A long list of websites was revealed. Jess's eyebrows shot up in surprise – she had never even heard of the disease before Ben mentioned it, after all. She clicked on the first site, which appeared to be one offering general information.

Text flowed on to the screen, yellow characters on a restful green background. An old site. Hideous. She leaned forward, squinting a little at the small typeface, and began to read.

Most of it was fairly straightforward and didn't appear to add much to what Ben had told her. A debilitating condition of the blood, Klemmer's Syndrome could lie dormant in a healthy adult for several years before it manifested itself. *'The illness has no effect on fertility,'* she read, *'and adult males with the syndrome can go on to father children. However –'*

She read the next few part of the sentence aloud, was not sure she had read it correctly, and read it again, taking in every word one by one.

She saw his face, laughing with her in the silvery moonlight.

She remembered feeling safe up there with him, the two of them enveloped by the chalk horse. Alone, high above the village, she had tasted the strange, spicy, fruity warmth of the drink, and then she had moved her mouth to cover his, felt the soft firmness of his lips on hers, allowed his arm to steal around her waist and pull her close to him. Closer, physically, than she had ever been to anyone.

Something else came into her mind, now, throwing itself high above the rest of her memories like a salmon leaping from water. A sharp image of Ben, here in the dining-room at Rose Cottage just the day before, knocking a cup of coffee flying with his elbow. One he'd barely touched.

Dad was fine for years, he'd said, up there on the chalk horse. *The first thing was when he got clumsy – knocking things over, dropping stuff – then his co-ordination totally went.*

Then she finally got it, as the last piece clicked into place with clinical precision. The thing which had been nagging at her all weekend, ever since before the fire, since before the village meeting – since, in fact, that conversation with Ben about the three children.

It hadn't been something about Kate that was bothering

her, after all. Or Grandma Trippett.

It had been about Ben.

And now, the words on the computer screen were dissolving in front of Jessica as the hot, angry tears welled up in her eyes.

Ben stopped in the road, folded his arms and waited as the dark figure approached.

The woman was tall, slim, elegant. She cast no shadow across the ground, but perhaps this was because she herself was a living shadow.

She wore a dark suit with a broad-brimmed black hat, black gloves and creaking black leather boots. Over this, she had a red-and-black cape with a high collar. In her hand she carried a black fan inlaid with intricate spider-web designs in crimson thread, which she gently fluttered as she approached.

But the most frightening thing about the woman was her face.

As she looked up, the shadow of the hat lifted to reveal a bone-white complexion, perfect red lips and pinched nostrils. Her cheekbones were high and prominent, as if cut with a knife from the white clay of her face. And her eyes were black, but not just the pupils – in each of the sockets, there was nothing but a deep, cold darkness, empty like the void of Space.

Ben faced her, unflinching.

At a distance of just a few paces, the woman stopped.

Then, she stretched out a black-gloved hand. And then she smiled, and that was the most chilling thing of all. It was a broad smile, but it was like the vivid red stripe on a clown's face, the mouth closed, devoid of any true feeling.

'A bargain of necessity,' she said, and her red lips hardly moved as she spoke. Her voice rustled, like a cold wind in the leaves of aspen trees. 'Is that not what we called it?'

'If you like,' said Ben, and his face was expressionless.

He reached out – and shook the woman's hand.

'I am here, as promised,' said the Queen of Shadow. 'This is my manifestation in your domain… Pleasant, is it not?' And she gave her cold, glittering smile again, and her black eye-sockets burned for a moment with the palest of crimson flames.

Ben shuddered and looked away. 'Let's just get on with this.'

The Queen tilted her head on one side and looked him up and down. 'Human life,' she whispered. 'Such a fragile thing. You are born naked, wet and hungry… and from that moment on, it is a struggle. You rely on others to feed you, clothe you, warm you. Before long, you are old enough to perform the tasks yourself, and you are trapped in the circle of life.'

'Is this the long version? Only I've got stuff to do.'

'You produce offspring whom you must feed, clothe, keep warm. Life is a constant cycle of work and scavenging, of desperation to stave off the inevitable. For what is life but the slow, steady means towards the end… the ultimate end… death itself?' The Queen's mouth twitched. 'Unless, of course, you can say that you have cheated death.'

'Yeah, and life cheated *me*,' said Ben, and his face burned with anger now. 'I'm seventeen years old. Seventeen, and I know I can't hope to live much beyond forty. I know that if I ever have a son, he'll be the same. Can you imagine what that *does* to someone?'

The Queen drew herself up to her full height. 'So, then, think of it, Ben Hemingway. All normality will be restored to the village in twenty-four hours, and you will have your victory over death – if you keep your side of our bargain.'

Ben's nostrils flared, and he looked away.

'What is this?' said the Queen of Shadow – and her voice hardened, like water freezing to ice. 'Second thoughts? You will not fail me now. We had an agreement.'

He looked up, but he couldn't look into her eyes.

'You came to me in a dream,' he said. 'I didn't think you were real. I couldn't be sure. But then… with Jess, up on the hill.'

She inclined her head. 'One of my many watchers. You sensed us, did you not? And you knew.'

He looked down at the ground. 'Yes. You're real enough.'

'You have feelings for the girl.' The Queen stated it emotionlessly.

'Yeah,' he said, so quietly it was almost inaudible. 'So?'

'In twelve hours,' said the Queen, 'our agreement dies. And you, Ben Hemingway, are destined, ultimately, to die with it – unless you bring me the chosen one. The girl we now know to be the Perfect Soul.'

Only now did Ben look into the echoing chasms of those terrible eyes, and he shuddered at the Queen of Shadow's next words.

'So you had better make up your mind.'

Mr Bidmead moved to sit down in a nearby armchair. 'I can't imagine that you children have acquired a taste for antiques,' he murmured, folding his hands on his walking-cane.

Richie shot an agonised look at Emerald Greene. How were they going to talk themselves out of this one?

'In my experience,' continued Mr Bidmead, 'young people are obsessed by the new. In fact,' he added, waggling his bushy eyebrows, 'they're seldom interested in anything which doesn't make a shocking noise or flash lights at them!'

'Um – ' Richie began.

'So, I must conclude that you are here on another mission. Espionage, perhaps!' Mr Bidmead rolled the word around his mouth, seeming to savour it. 'Indeed, I was under the distinct impression that I'd left the door locked.'

Richie felt guilty. 'Oh, yes,' he said, 'I'm sorry about that. It was – ' He glanced down at Anoushka, and the cat twitched his ears and bared his teeth. Richie bit his lip. 'Em?' he finished helplessly.

'Richie,' she muttered, 'never put both feet in your mouth at once, or you will not have a leg to stand on.' She stepped forward, smiling, spreading her hands wide. 'Mr Bidmead. Fascinating shop you have here. Quite an amazing collection!'

Mr Bidmead inclined his head gracefully. 'One of the best,' he agreed.

'Yes,' said Emerald, hefting a leather-bound book from a nearby shelf. 'I can see that.' She thumbed the flyleaf. 'Goodness me, *Alice Through The Looking-Glass*. A handsome edition!' She scanned the first couple of pages. 'Hmm, well, *that* is different for a start... and that.'

'It's an exclusive imprint,' said Mr Bidmead, leaning forward and looking at her very seriously, 'signed, you'll note, by the Reverend Charles Lutwidge Dodgson himself.'

'So it is,' said Emerald, raising her eyebrows. 'The real name of the author, Lewis Carroll, of course,' she added for Richie's benefit. 'Mr Bidmead, this book must be priceless!'

'It is,' agreed Mr Bidmead quietly. 'Put it down,' he added – and a more threatening tone entered his voice for the first time.

Emerald replaced the book and picked up a silver carriage-clock. 'Oh, now, this is splendid.' She hefted it in both hands. 'I am no expert, but...' She clicked her tongue. 'Edwardian? Ooooh, I say. How about that, Richie? A late Edwardian carriage-clock,' she tipped it upside-down, 'and hallmarked, yes... My goodness, a Brandt! Quite a find.'

Mr Bidmead tapped his cane on the floor, making Richie jump. 'Young lady, I'm a patient man, but I'm also busy. I suggest that, if you have a point, you get to it swiftly!'

'All right,' said Emerald Greene. 'All these antiques,' she swept an arm out in a broad arc, 'are from around the same period, about seventy to a hundred years ago, and they are all

– as far as I can see – in tip-top condition.' Emerald narrowed her eyes. 'Now what are the chances of *that*, Mr Bidmead? Hmm?'

Richie had not really been following the verbal jousting, but he tried his best to seize on what he could. 'Are you saying these aren't real antiques, Em? Just clever forgeries?'

'Oh, no, every piece is genuine,' said Emerald. 'And very valuable, I would guess. But they are not *antiques* in that they have not aged. These items all appear to have been bought in the last few months.' She raised her eyebrows. 'Am I right, Mr Bidmead?'

Mr Bidmead smiled tolerantly.

A memory suddenly came back to Richie – of Emerald, peering interestedly at the clock in Grandma Trippett's living-room. 'Grandma Trippett's clock!' he said. 'That came from here!'

'Quite. The perfect condition of the clock is what first alerted me to the anomaly.' Emerald folded her arms. 'And you *are* an anomaly – are you not, Mr Bidmead?'

'Not personally,' he said, smiling coldly. 'But I do perhaps deal with them for a living.' He reached into his pocket and pulled out a silver business card with a strange, triangular logo on it. 'I am from what you might call the, ah, intuitive wing of the Special Measures Division. I expect you're going to tell me you've never heard of us?'

'Actually,' said Richie boldly, 'we have. I've worked with Mr Courtney. He gave me a ride in his car!' He had been hoping that his casual name-dropping would take the wind out of Mr Bidmead's sails, but he was disappointed when the antiques dealer just chuckled.

'Old blood-and-thunder Courtney, eh! Well, I never. You must have been involved in that Meresbury business last year.'

If Mr Bidmead was at all surprised, Richie thought, then he was doing a very good job of hiding it.

'So you're just posing as an antiques dealer, right?' Richie hazarded.

'Oh, indeed, no, no!' Mr Bidmead clicked his tongue. 'Young man, I *am* a very successful merchant of fine antique collectables. It's an excellent front for my work with Special Measures.'

Emerald threw the silver card aside contemptuously. 'You know what is happening here?' she snapped.

'Only too well, I'm afraid,' said Mr Bidmead.

'Um, just to be clear,' said Richie, raising a hand, 'is this the bit where you have to tie us up and say "I shall tell you my plans, seeing as you will shortly die"? And then you lock us in your back room and we have to escape through the ventilation shaft?'

Mr Bidmead chuckled again, narrowing his eyes. 'Dear me, young fellow. Cheap fiction, eh? Listen, and you may learn!'

Richie scowled and folded his arms. 'Well... all right, then.'

'When I first came here,' said Mr Bidmead, 'I had a young associate, named Adele. She was assigned to work with me undercover, on a long-term survey of strange activity in this village, Little Brockwell... '

'Things went wrong, didn't they?' Emerald asked.

'Yes,' said Mr Bidmead sadly. 'And now, Adele has become rather more closely bound up in the whole business than I would have liked. The upshot of it all is that, in investigating the holes in the continuum caused by these *Tenebrae*, she became a victim... of temporal displacement.'

Richie, deciding that he'd had enough of saying 'What?', bit his tongue and thought this one through. 'Temporal dis...' His eyebrows shot up. 'Stranded in time, you mean?'

'Indeed, yes,' said Mr Bidmead. 'When we first began our investigation, we located two nexus points, you see.' He produced a blackboard and chalk from behind his chair, and drew two small crosses. 'One in the here and now, at the start of the twenty-first century... and the other approximately seventy years ago. The last time, you will mark, that Tenebrae were seen in Little Brockwell.'

'The photo,' said Richie. 'Grandma Trippett's photo!'

'Let him go on,' said Emerald softly.

Mr Bidmead took his chalk and joined the two crosses with a line. 'The two points in time had become linked. Like two ends of a railway tunnel, if you will. The odd fragment started to slip through... Oh, you wouldn't have noticed,' he assured Richie, as the boy opened his mouth to ask. 'Some objects... plus, yes, the odd dazed traveller. Most of them ended up having a bit of therapy, settling down nicely in Gloucestershire. After a while, they weren't really bothered about living in a different time-zone.'

Richie's mind boggled at the idea of the Home Counties being full of exiled time-travellers, but it seemed to make a kind of sense. After all, there were those friends of his parents, the Stapleton-Browns – always braying on about children being seen and not heard, using funny words like *beastly* and *ghastly* and enthusing about fox-hunting. Yes, he could just imagine them being from years ago. It all made sense now.

'Well, yeah,' he said. 'That's Gloucestershire for you.'

He wondered, briefly, why Emerald was rubbing her neck and looking shifty.

'Anyway,' Mr Bidmead went on, 'with a little applied knowledge, one can manipulate such a gap – engineer objects to come through, that sort of thing. It's amazing how much some people will pay for genuine antiques in mint condition! My pension is assured.'

Cunning old devil, thought Richie. I wonder if his superiors know he's set himself up a little source of time-travelling income?

'And did anything go the *other* way?' Emerald asked – sounding, Richie thought, as if she already knew the answer.

Mr Bidmead's sharp blue eyes fixed on each of them in turn. 'Of course,' he said softly. 'Time is an equation. There must be balance.'

'Adele,' said Emerald, her eyes cold and hard.

'Yes. It was just a couple of months ago that she went through.' He reached over to a nearby shelf and took down an oval-framed, sepia photograph of a young woman with her hair in a bun, a brooch adorning her high blouse. He passed the photo to Richie. 'My associate, apprentice and friend,' he said sadly. 'Miss Susannah Pemberton – also known as Miss Adele Davisham.'

Richie almost dropped the picture. 'Miss *Davisham*!' he gasped. 'The schoolteacher!'

'Yes. She was the village schoolmistress here for five years, during which time we worked undercover. And then... then she went back, to fulfil her destiny. A destiny I knew awaited her as soon as I looked up the story of this cursed village.'

'Destiny?' said Richie. 'What do you mean, destiny?'

Mr Bidmead looked sad. 'History, my dear chap. It was a matter of record that a teacher called Susannah Pemberton appeared in the village, as if out of nowhere, offering her services at a time when the village school was in great need. And so I was forced to make the only, the inevitable conclusion. That it was she.'

Richie stared in horror at the picture. 'And you saw this photo before she went back?'

'Naturally. I knew it instantly, then. Look closely at the picture – well, maybe only an expert could tell, but little things give it away. Her complexion, her teeth, they're all wrong for the period. And there are obviously contact-lenses on her eyes.'

Emerald leaned over, glanced at the picture again.

'Goodness me. You are so right. I had missed that.'

'But... what happened?' Richie asked, aghast. 'I mean, if the Tenebrae are passing through Time, you can get Miss Davisham back through the time-gap, right?'

'No, no. Adele – Susannah, if you prefer – died peacefully, in her bed, in the year of the Queen's Silver Jubilee. That death was always a matter of historical fact. Her grave is here, in the village churchyard!'

Richie blinked. 'That's... beyond crazy,' he said eventually.

'Yes, I know,' agreed Mr Bidmead with a sigh, 'the paradoxes are evident. At the same moment, her eleven-year-old self was finishing primary school up in Scotland, starting on the route which would take her to Cambridge, to her recruitment by the Division... and her first arrival here, with me, to begin our investigation.'

There was, for a few moments, a silence in the dark clutter of the shop.

Richie blinked, swallowed hard as he struggled to take it all in.

So Mr Bidmead hadn't sent Miss Davisham back in time unwittingly. He had done so in the knowledge that she was fulfilling her destiny – to become Miss Pemberton in the past, to be what she had always been.

Perhaps – and this suddenly, chillingly occurred to him – perhaps Miss Davisham had gone of her own free will. A sacrifice, to restore the balance and harmony of Time.

'I don't know about you,' Richie said, 'but that well and truly does my head in.'

Emerald Greene had a chilly, haughty expression on her high-cheekboned face, and she was perched on the arm of one of the antique chairs, hands folded on her lap. She fixed her gaze on Mr Bidmead and did not let go.

'All right,' said Emerald coldly. 'Now tell me about the

children.'

'I'm not sure about this,' said Kate Trippett nervously, pouring two cups of tea from Grandma's thermos flask. 'Not sure at all.'

'Don't you fret, child,' said Grandma, trundling her chair up the aisle of the church. 'Best place for us to be, I'd say.'

The evening light was painting gentle stained-glass reflections on the stone floor of the nave, and they could hear pigeons cooing high in the rafters. The two women had installed themselves on one of the pews, armed with blankets and provisions. Not far away, at the altar, the Reverend Fenella Parsloe was kneeling and murmuring a short prayer.

The Rector might, in normal circumstances, have been surprised to see the Trippetts. Kate, after all, was agnostic, only setting foot in the church at Christmas, while Grandma just came to the odd Evensong and complained about the 'new-fangled' hymns and orders of service. But the Rector had welcomed them, almost as if she had expected them to make the church their refuge on this uncertain night.

'Little Brockwell's become a strange place,' Grandma went on. 'Some of the stuff going on in this village these past few weeks... You'd say it was wickedness if you didn't know better. You'd say it was devilish work!'

'*If* you didn't know better,' Kate repeated firmly, sipping her tea and watching the Rector straighten up, cross herself and bustle down the aisle towards them. 'That's the thing.'

'Those boys and girls had evil in their hearts,' Grandma Trippett murmured. 'Seen it afore, I have. As if a darkness had descended inside them, a darkness instead of their souls.'

Fenella Parsloe, hands folded across her cassock, approached them. 'You noticed it too, then? I've been worried about those poor children ever since I saw them.'

'But you believe in redemption,' said Kate. 'Don't you?'

The Rector lowered her eyes, and folded her hands. 'Of

course,' she said softly.

And Kate thought she didn't quite sound convinced.

Back at the cottage, Jess was trembling. Her face was hot and angry, her mind in turmoil.

Now, with the information she had, the image of his hand haunted her. She could see it shaking slightly as he got his penknife out to open their illicit bottle of cider. To think she had imagined he was just nervous… She cursed herself for not realising something was wrong. And the drink he spilt – that should have made her see.

'Jessica?'

She could see him saying, *What's the matter? Are you cold?* and gently placing his warm leather jacket around her. She could picture his eyes – dark, compelling, limpid in the starlight. And that smile… that beautiful smile, which she had thought – imagined – to be for her, to tell her how much she meant to him.

She felt the sobs tearing into her as if she was retching. Like an animal inside, the shudders were twisting her body, kicking and shaking it. There was nothing but this room, nothing but here and now and the hot tears which would not stop pouring from her eyes.

'Jess? Are you all right?'

She was aware, now, of figures at the doorway, but could not be sure who they were. She blundered forward – aware of the chair toppling, crashing to the floor – threw her face into a shoulder and sobbed bitterly. A soft, gentle voice murmured to her, telling her everything was going to be fine.

When she looked up, wiping her eyes and nose, she was dimly aware of Richie standing there, looking uncomfortable – and also of the dark figure of Mr Bidmead, there beside him in the hallway, watching her with a mixture of sympathy and puzzlement.

'You,' Jess managed to say, her voice thick and choked. 'What are *you* doing here?'

'Mr Bidmead is going to help us defeat the Enemy,' said the voice at her ear. And then, more softly, 'Trust me, Jess. Trust me.'

Now, only now, Jess realised that she had been hugged and comforted by her friend, her true and loyal friend, Emerald Greene.

Emerald's hands rested gently on Jess's forearms. 'She has had a shock,' she said, over her shoulder. 'Richie, would you pour her some tea, please?'

Tea, thought Jess wildly as she found herself slumping into an armchair. Typical English remedy for everything. Emerald's fitting in….

She felt perfectly lucid, and yet she was suddenly, horribly unable to do anything for herself. Beside her, as if mocking her, the computer still hummed, the screen showing the words she had almost been unable to read.

Emerald Greene leaned down and gently, calmly righted the fallen chair to its proper place in front of the computer.

With her eyes red and raw, Jess looked up. 'Tell them, Emerald,' Jess said, somehow managing to focus on her friend. 'Tell them what you know.'

Emerald, tight-lipped and jittery, flitted over to the computer screen. She read the information, taking it in quickly. 'As I suspected,' she said quietly. 'I would not have wanted Jess to find out this way.' She turned and read from the screen. *'Adult males with the syndrome* – that is Klemmer's Syndrome, of which Ben Hemingway's father is dying – can go on to father children. *However, the gene causing the disease is hereditary on the father's side.'*

'Hereditary?' Richie seized on the word as he poured the tea. 'You mean handed down the generations?' His jaw dropped. 'Oh, my…'

'The bottom line,' said Emerald, 'is that Ben Hemingway is bound to inherit the syndrome which his father has. He is under sentence of death.'

Richie brought Jess her mug, and she folded her shaking hands around its warmth.

'Jess,' he said, 'I'm so sorry…'

She looked up, pushing back her dishevelled hair. 'You said, Emerald… that the Tenebrae could have power over… life and death. So if the person working with the Enemy was someone…' Her voice cracked. She shut her eyes tightly for a moment, swallowed and went on. 'Someone who was afraid of the course of Time… *Afraid of death…*'

Emerald could not look her in the eye. 'Yes. It is … probable.'

'If only I'd thought!' Jess wailed. 'If only I'd been more logical!' She lowered her face to the warmth of her tea, feeling a cold, creeping sensation spreading over her, feeling her world twisting into something unimaginable, strange and horrid. She suddenly felt less than human – like a cog in a machine, someone who had had no say in her destiny. 'He's used me,' she whispered.

Richie tutted. 'Traitor… I never did like that guy.' He put a comforting hand on Jess's shoulder.

Emerald said, 'I would estimate that they will move tonight. All the conditions are set. We have approximately four hours to deal with this menace.'

'But what do they want now?' Richie asked, confused. 'The kids are back, everyone's gone…?'

'Mr Bidmead?' Emerald prompted.

The old man sat down at the dining-room table and folded his hands across the handle of his cane, his expression very serious. 'Those poor children…' He shuddered. 'They're in the safe hands of our trained counsellors now, thank goodness, but… I have never seen anything like it. I knew there was something wrong from the moment I set eyes upon them.'

'Had they been hurt?' Jess asked, looking up, her voice croaking.

'Emerald was quite right in what she surmised,' replied Mr Bidmead. 'The children had been taken out of the normal timeline. They were held in an interstice – a kind of no-man's-land, in the middle of the tunnel I told you about.'

'But why?' Richie asked. 'That's what I never could understand. What were they taken away *for*? And then just brought back like that?'

'Ah, well. When they returned, I could tell straight away that they lacked something. At first I couldn't put my finger on it, but, yes, now I see what it was… An essence – a conscience!' He paused, looking at each of them very gravely. 'I imagine that some people might like to call it the *soul*.' He was leaning back and forth, staring at a space just above the table. 'Yes, yes… the more I think about it, the more appropriate that seems. The soul. They enter the consciousness through dreams, you see. Dreams are a window on the soul.'

'The Tenebrae steal souls?' Richie breathed. 'Creepy or what?'

'Potentially lethal,' said Mr Bidmead with a frown. 'Unless these children are properly re-balanced, they risk never being properly human again.'

'So they want something in return,' Jess said softly.

Everyone turned to look at her.

'Well, it's obvious, isn't it?' she said, spreading her hands. She realised she had known all along, but could only now put it into words. 'They want something they can't just come and steal, and so they're using the dreams as bargaining power.'

'I think you may be right,' said Mr Bidmead. 'The question is… what do they want? And why? I have been asking myself this ever since I first detected the presence of the Tenebrae in this village.' He shook his head sadly, gazing into space. 'And I fear finding the answer…'

'Gather coats and food,' said Emerald Greene, who appeared to have come to a decision. 'There is one place which may yet be safe. We must head there immediately.'

'Where?' asked Richie, puzzled.

Emerald Greene smiled. 'The church, of course!'

'Emerald,' said Richie, shaking his head. 'You're not telling me you suddenly believe in God?'

'Not at all,' she said. 'But it may help to act as if we do.'

In the cool, vaulted space of St Leonard's Church, the silence was heavy. Kate Trippett glanced nervously at her phone. 'What time do you make it, Rector?'

Fenella Parsloe checked her old pocket-watch. 'About… six-thirty.'

'Me too.' Kate shivered. 'The sun's gone down,' she said, looking up at the windows, where a darkening sky could be seen over the village. 'Ben's not back… Do you think something's happened?'

Grandma Trippett lifted her head, as if her shaded, near-sightless eyes had suddenly seen something. 'Ben…' she murmured.

'Gran?' Kate said, hurrying over to her.

'The boy,' she said softly. 'Is he… all right?'

Kate bit her lip, looked away. She had never discussed this with Grandma, and had wondered for some time if, perhaps, she knew. 'I… don't know what you mean,' she lied.

Grandma's face became pinched, angry. She reached out with one bony hand and clamped Kate's wrist in a surprisingly firm grip. 'You do know what I mean, Kate! We don't have secrets, not us! There was something Annie said, a while back. Just made me wonder, that's all.' She leaned back, and released her grip on Kate.

The younger woman winced, rubbed her wrist where it

was red and marked. 'You don't know your own strength, Gran,' she murmured.

'First sign's the coordination, ain't it?' said Grandma. 'It's why the boy's clumsy. And he was so relieved to have got his motorbike test out of the way, but don't want to drive a car. Little things like that, they make you wonder.'

Kate bit her lip. 'Yes,' she murmured, 'Ben has the gene. So, yes – we have to assume the symptoms will gradually worsen over the next ten, twenty years. With medical help, he could live, at most, to the age of forty-five.'

The Rector had been listening, with mounting concern. 'I'd no idea,' she said softly.

Kate lifted her eyes, and for a second they reflected the dwindling light from the stained-glass windows, two tiny curves of luminescence in her irises. 'I thought he didn't know himself. But he does. Somehow, he does.'

Taking the road slowly and carefully, Ben rode back into the village, the engine of his bike purring, a solitary, dark, lean figure in black. He wore no crash-helmet now, as if recklessly inviting death. A pair of slim, jet-black wraparound shades sat across his eyes.

On the humpbacked bridge, he slowed the bike to a crawl and let it stop. The gentle evening breeze ruffled his hair, and he allowed himself a slow, sad smile.

Around him and above him, the sky above the village was turning velvety-blue. Shadows – deep, ancient shadows – were creeping from the between the ivy-clad cottages, from the cracks in the road, from the stone walls beside the Meadow. He directed his gaze down the street to the Green, saw clearly what he needed to see.

The Whispering Tree.

It was twice the size it had been several days ago. Huge and swollen, the bark creeping and creaking as if it was alive, growing. Branches spread outwards. They arched over like bowlers' arms, touched the Green and embedded themselves, making pools of shadow which yellowed and killed the grass. Further across the Green, the same branches popped out in showers of earth, emerging like vicious, angry moles from the depths, the snaking, crackling black twigs turning this way and that as if seeking prey.

As he watched, the trunk seemed to take on a deeper, richer black than it had ever been before; a black of the night, of the interstellar void.

And then the blackness acquired form.

Bulging out from the tree, the shadow of a horse's head emerged, taking on details as if being magically moulded in black clay – an eye, the strands of a mane, the flash of white teeth.

The dark rider, casting shadow in an aura around him, took up his place, silent and still, on the Green, as another elongated head started to emerge from the black bark of the Whispering Tree.

He felt a pang, for a second, as a memory of the night before passed through his mind. The touch of her lips and the soft feel of her hair. The big, dark, trusting eyes in her young face.

Then he shook his head.

He kick-started his bike again, revved the engine twice. With his bike churning up a cloud of dust behind him, he sped towards the centre of the village.

This was about to be finished.

9
A Bargain of Necessity

Jess, Emerald and Richie hurried across the street from Rose Cottage to St Leonard's church – with a sprightly Mr Bidmead following close behind, and Anoushka trotting at Emerald's heels. Jess felt her hand tingling again as she looked up and down the deserted street.

'Is this going to do any good?' Richie demanded as they reached the lych-gate. 'The Tenebrae aren't just going to say, "Oh, a church – better not go in," are they?'

'The power of a symbol is great, Richie,' said Emerald, who was busy checking readings on her hand-held detector. 'The Darkness may not respect the hallowed ground – but it will fear what it stands for, and may hesitate. Maybe not for long, but it could be long enough for me to do something. Old traditions die hard.'

'Anything, Em?' Jess asked breathlessly. She almost knew the answer already.

'Yes,' Emerald said. She held up a hand, her finger in the air as if testing for the presence of a wind. Then, she slowly lowered her finger through ninety degrees until it was horizontal, pointing down the street.

Jess and Richie followed the line of her finger, and Jess's heart skipped a beat as she saw what Emerald had seen.

A sleek, black motorbike sat in the middle of the street. Astride it was a tall figure in a black T-shirt and jeans, his hair fluttering gently in the evening breeze, his eyes covered by black sunglasses. The shadow of the bike and rider stretched across the sun-baked ground, colouring it with an inky darkness.

At Jess's feet, Anoushka arched his back, dug his claws into the ground and hissed. 'Be still, Anoushka,' murmured Emerald, and bent down to touch the cat's bristling fur.

Then, Jess felt the cold, almost comforting tingle – the unearthly pins-and-needles in her right hand, the hand which had felt the touch of the otherworld all those months ago. And she knew that something big was going to happen.

'Get inside,' Jess murmured, narrowing her eyes.

Mr Bidmead placed a hand on her shoulder. 'I really think, child – '

'I don't *care* what you think,' Jess snapped, shrugging off his hand. 'I can deal with this. Get inside, all of you.' She folded her arms. 'Who knows? He might just want his jacket back.'

'Do as she says,' murmured Emerald Greene to Richie and Mr Bidmead. 'I shall stay.'

As Mr Bidmead bustled a protesting Richie up the path to the church, Jess started to walk forward, her eyes fixed on the unmoving figure of Ben. She glanced over her shoulder and was aware that Emerald Greene was there beside her, like her shadow.

'Em, let me do this myself,' she hissed.

'I am afraid not,' said Emerald firmly.

Jess steeled herself again and kept walking. Through the shadows of oaks and aspens she walked, past the latticed windows of cottages as they reflected the waning sunlight. She could smell the exhaust and oil of the motorbike – she could taste it in the air.

She stopped, about ten metres away from Ben, and folded her arms.

Behind her, Emerald hung back. 'I am here, should you

need me,' she murmured.

He looked pale, Jess saw, and tired. His hair seemed blacker than ever and his cheekbones even sharper – as if this was not Ben, but some constructed version of him. She could see the street and the church reflected twice over in his wraparound shades.

'Jess,' he said, and tilted his head on one side. 'Jess, it's me! What's the matter?' His voice sounded strained, croaky.

'You didn't tell me,' she said. 'You didn't tell me that you knew.'

'Knew?' His face took on an expression of puzzled amusement.

'That you're dying!' she snapped. 'I know all about it now.'

'Oh.' He lowered his face for a second. 'That.' He grinned, suddenly, bone-white in the gloom. 'Well, I'm a dark horse.'

'Oh, very funny. So, what was it? I wasn't important enough to tell?' She swallowed hard, bunched her fists. 'I told you all about my mum and dad. Showed you the photo. I opened up to you, I took a risk!'

She could feel her eyes and her throat burning, and knew that she had to hold back the tears – had to seem strong, or everything was lost. Everything was betrayed.

'I don't take risks, Ben,' she went on. 'I don't let people... care for me, because people who do... they... disappear. But I risked it, I went with the feeling. I... thought you liked me.'

'Jess,' he said sadly. 'Oh, Jess! Look, the evening was... nice, okay? I didn't know you were going to read so much into it.'

In a second, she felt as if a dozen crushing blows had descended on her from all sides at once, kicking and punching her while she was down. She felt... she felt so many things. Hurt. Angry. Used. So that was it? She'd been *nice* – a bit of fun for one crazy evening?

'I suppose you thought all your birthdays had come at once,' she said coolly. 'Saying all the right things, coming over as Mr Sensitive, and then before you know it, you've got yourself a weekend snog. Yeah, something to tell the lads about. *Hey, I pulled this stupid fourteen-year-old! You'd never believe it. Threw herself at me, she did.*'

'Jess –'

'Pretty cheap date, wasn't I? Two Cokes and a bottle of budget scrumpy – bargain! You'd never have got your tongue down Georgie Popplewick's throat for *that*.'

'Jess, come on! Everyone knows the game.'

'The *game*!' She stared at him open-mouthed. 'So it's all a game, is it? Well, I'm sorry, but I'm new to this game. I'm brand new. Didn't anyone tell you?' She couldn't help it, now – the bitterness and anger pervaded every syllable. 'I'm the newest kid on the block, Ben. And nobody told me the rules, right? So I…'

'You wanted it,' he said. 'You let yourself get close to me. In a way, you actually asked for this.'

She felt the most terrible, dark anger rising in her, something twisted and righteous, the kind of anger she had never felt in all her time on Earth. Nobody had ever treated her like this. Nobody. She struggled to speak.

'Don't you dare…' she croaked. 'Don't you *dare* say that!'

'Which bit in particular?'

It was like he was no longer Ben. It was like he was some evil, twisted creation who used to be Ben, some version of him controlled by someone or something else. Something which looked like Ben, but was no longer fully him.

'That… that *horrible* expression,' she gasped. 'Like you're one of those awful boys who…' Her voice tailed off. She was barely able to speak, trying hard to swallow down the lump in her throat. 'I thought I'd found someone who actually cared about me.'

He smiled. It wasn't a warm smile. 'Babe,' he said. 'We all make mistakes.'

She physically took a step back, stung by the double blow. A shocking, prickly anger engulfed her, something which felt red and hot and evil. It made her think she could actually strike out and kill Ben Hemingway right there.

'You bloody *scumbag*,' she whispered.

'Okay.' Ben spread his hands. 'I deserve that. Just out of interest, how did you find out?'

'That you were ill,' she asked, not looking at him, 'or that you were working for *them*?'

'Try me with both. One led to the other, after all.'

'Long story. Used my head, didn't I? But all weekend I've felt there was a *wrong* thing, a piece that didn't fit. Nagging like an ache in my head, all through the meeting in the pub and all today.'

He spread his hands for a moment. 'Go on. You'll have to tell me.'

'In the lounge at Rose Cottage, when we were talking about how people sometimes run away from home, right, but how it was unusual in a place like this? And you said yes, it was unusual for *three children* to disappear.' Jess swallowed hard, trying to ignore the trembling in her knees. 'Three. Not two. You knew about Will, the traveller boy, and yet nobody else in the village did. Emerald and Richie only found out the night before – they'd only told me that morning, and they'd not told you.'

'Ah. Very good.' Ben gave her an ironic, slow hand-clap which echoed eerily off the surrounding buildings. Jess, angered at being mocked, took an instinctive step forward, but she felt Emerald's softly restraining hand on her elbow. 'What can I say?' Ben went on. 'Well done. But the fact remains that I have a deal with them. A deal which might give me a chance of life.'

'You *can't*!' she shouted, clenching her fists so hard that her fingernails cut into her palms. 'You can't make deals with the darkness, Ben! It uses you, it eats you up and spits you out!'

'I'm sorry, Jess. They want *you*. I dunno why, but they do. And if I give you them, I get to live… As bargains go, it's pretty good.'

Jess's face filled with horror. 'As bargains go, it's pretty horrible!' She realised properly what Ben had said. 'They want *me*? What do you mean, they want *me*?'

'The Whispering Tree,' Ben said, 'represents the power of all the minds of the village – or, more precisely, the dark side of that power. And it needs to be controlled.'

'It is true,' whispered Emerald, leaning towards Jess. 'Just as I suspected. Little Brockwell, as well as being located right on the fissure of a time interstice, benefits from the presence of an excessively strong psychic field – generated by the inhabitants of the village themselves. Strong minds, strong wills, passed down through generations. It's an incredible power.'

'And that force needs to be held in check,' said Ben softly. 'By a strong force – an *independent* mind – ideally, someone from outside the village. Little Brockwell needs a Perfect Soul, one to hold the Whispering Tree with the power of imagination alone. You could be that one, Jess! Think of the power you would command!'

'I – well, I – ' Jessica was lost for words. She ran a hand through her head and wondered if she could possibly be dreaming this whole crazy situation, or if she was imagining all of this because she hadn't slept properly for several days. Hadn't Richie said something about *seeing things*?

She shut her eyes tightly, felt herself rock back on her heels for a moment, then righted herself and forced her eyes to open once more. She was still there, facing Ben on his motorbike, under a velvety-blue sky.

And now, there was another.

A fragment of shade had detached itself from the nearby wall. As they watched, it lengthened into the shape of a tall, pale woman, clad in a black cloak and boots. She was dark-haired, deathly pale; her eyes were pools of black and her mouth a broad, cruel stripe of red. She opened her hands in a welcoming gesture, then moved, almost glided, to stand next to the motorbike. She had no shadow herself, but was like a pillar of darkness, topped with a sculpted, bone-white face.

The woman smiled, and Jess felt her whole body gripped by terrible shivers. Next to her, even Emerald Greene tensed with fear.

'Well?' whispered the Queen of Shadow, and her voice was like a winter wind skittering across the rooftops. 'Do you accept willingly – or must we make you?'

In the church, a cool silence reigned, shutting out the world. Richie shivered, leaning against the font, and Mr Bidmead came over to join him.

'I fear the poor child may have been hurt too badly to forgive,' said Mr Bidmead. He shook his head. 'Love is a cruel mistress… I was hurt myself, once.'

'Were you married?' asked Richie tentatively.

'No, young Richard,' he said with a heavy sigh. 'But I could have been. Yes, I could have been.' He clapped Richie on the shoulder, bent down to look him in the eye. 'Listen, Richie. Man-to-man,' he said. 'When you find a pretty young lady who is good and kind to you, who makes you laugh and makes your heart sing – never let her go. Follow her to the other side of the world if you have to. Follow her through hell, high water and bizarre temporal anomalies – but never, *ever* let her go.'

'Um… okay,' said Richie, not sure what to say.

'Trust me,' said Mr Bidmead, and tapped the side of his nose. 'Experience. It's something you don't usually get until just after you need it.'

The stand-off in the street was growing more tense.

'Well?' the Queen demanded. 'Your answer, girl!'

'Um… it's kind of inconvenient.' Jess somehow knew she had to babble to save herself. 'I mean, I've got my GCSEs to do… and then there's the hockey team, who'd probably get relegated without me.'

'I told you she was stubborn,' Ben said.

The Queen tilted her head on one side. 'Jessica?' she whispered.

'What?' she said nervously.

'Feeling… sleepy?'

'No,' she snapped back, even though she was… terribly, achingly tired. She wanted to close her eyes, go to sleep and let it all be just a bad dream.

'I think you are,' murmured the Queen of Shadow. 'You can feel terrible when deprived of sleep, you know… Your core body temperature starts to drop. You shake, tremble like a leaf in the wind. Your brain loses the chemicals it needs. You find yourself subject to… suggestions.'

'Ignore her, Jess,' muttered Emerald, placing a hand gently on her arm. 'You are not feeling tired. You are on a caffeine high. You have never been more awake. *Awake!*'

Jess blinked uncertainly. In the evening sunlight, the dark figures looked hazy and blurred, now, like something out of –

Something out of a dream.

'No!' she snarled, and clenched her fist, digging her fingernails into the palms of her hands. 'If I fall asleep, the Tenebrae get in my subconscious. And if that happens, you've won! I know that!'

'Feeling cold yet, Jessica?' persisted the Queen of Shadow. 'Or is there, perhaps, a prickling in your skin? Like hundreds of ants crawling all over you?'

And she was sure that she *was* feeling cold, here on this summer evening... and that her skin was starting to itch uncomfortably. Almost without realising it, she had started to scratch her arm.

'Just close your eyes,' Ben murmured, 'and it'll all go away.'

'Jess, do not listen to them!' Emerald begged. 'It is auto-suggestion! They are trying to make you fall asleep!'

'Ignore this girl,' hissed the Queen of Shadow. 'She is the one who has been trying to keep you awake artificially, tormenting you. She fills your body with stimulants, makes you ill! Surely you do not believe that can be good, Jessica?'

Jess gritted her teeth. She *knew* the Queen of Shadow was trying to entice her, and yet what she said seemed to make perfect sense. The coffee had been bitter, it had been strong... it had grabbed her sleepy body and shaken it, made her stay awake longer than was natural.

Why had Emerald done that to her?

Why had her friend... *poisoned* her?

'You are doing yourself great harm, girl,' said the Queen of Shadow, and she spread her bony hands wide. 'End it. Come to the arms of sleep. Dream with us, Jessica.'

Dream with us.

Her heavy eyelids sank. She felt herself rocking on her heels.

'Do not listen to her, Jess,' warned Emerald urgently. 'She is evil!'

'A dream, Jessica,' murmured the Queen of Shadow. 'Dream of the wind in your hair... and of your feet running, running so fast on the ground... of the hoofbeats echoing like thunder in the mountains! Dream, dream of the speed and the power... of riding through Eternity!'

And there *was* something.

Shocked, she heard it now in the back of her mind.

First, it did sound just like thunder in the hills. Then, straining to hear, Jess realised that it was a continuous rumble, almost a regular beat. It was growing steadily louder and louder, and now she could hear that it was made up of individual, drumming noises.

Hoofbeats. The sound of an army.

'Jess.' It was Emerald's voice behind her – soft, yet more urgent now.

She turned angrily on her friend. 'Look, you said you'd let me deal with this!'

'Yes, but I… merely feel I should draw your attention to something,' Emerald said. 'Look!'

And there, on the brow of the hill, she saw an approaching tide of darkness, as if the night itself was rolling in across the fields, leaving the land behind in shadow. The sky darkened, too, overlaid with dark masses like storm-clouds, and a cold, rushing wind sped in from the North, slicing through the village.

She gasped, turned to run – but now, Emerald Greene tightened her hold, held her arm in a vice-like grip.

A crazy, helpless thought zipped through her head: *You too?*

Her friend's eyes burned, green and feline in the gathering gloom, and she held Jess firmly in place. 'Do not run,' she hissed. 'They *want* you to run!'

Trust me. Jess seemed to hear Emerald again, in her head this time. *Trust me, Jess.*

Knifed by the wind, her hair streaming, Jess gripped Emerald in fear; but they stood firm. They stood firm and waited as the Tenebrae approached.

Like tiny coals in the darkness, a line of flickering red lights had appeared at the edge of the village. They formed a great, sweeping curve, spreading from the ruins of the schoolhouse round to the ford at the eastern end of Little

Brockwell. Jess, squinting into the darkness, could see now that the lights were the flames of torches. Each was held by a hooded rider, and that each rider was atop a huge, shimmering, magnificent black horse with glowing eyes and the faint, ghostly hint of a skull in its face.

The wave of darkness closed in on the village.

Ben, smiling sadly, revved the engine of his motorbike. Jess could see herself, pale and fearful, reflected twice as a tiny figure in his black shades.

The engine growled once, twice, and a cloud of smoke billowed from its exhaust as it began to accelerate down the street towards them.

'All right,' said Emerald Greene, softly. '*Now* we run.'

They turned and fled.

And the Tenebrae followed.

Jess, Emerald and Anoushka ducked into cover in the dark passageway between two of the stone cottages.

Pressing her back up against the hard, cold wall, Jess hugged the motorbike jacket to her like a comfort blanket, hardly daring to breathe as the huge, snorting shapes thundered past.

Hundreds and hundreds of them, it seemed. The riders' burning torches cast an unearthly glow on the lane, and sparks flew up from the cobblestones. A wave of darkness washed through the village, leaving lingering shadows in its wake. A cold, angry stench filled the air, a smell like decay and death.

'They'll find us,' Jessica hissed.

'Of course,' said Emerald Greene.

'It seems inevitable,' agreed Anoushka drily.

'The thing is,' Emerald went on, 'to be prepared when they do.' Jess realised that Emerald was holding up a small, matt-black tube. 'Cadmium explosive,' she said. 'I keep it for a rainy day.'

'Cool!' Before Emerald could stop her, Jess had grabbed the cylinder admiringly.

'Careful! It is highly unstable! You could set it off merely by spitting on it!'

'Oh.' Jess felt herself turning pale. 'Right.' Gingerly, she handed the stick of explosive back to Emerald Greene. 'Wh – what are we going to do with it?'

'If we can explode a section of the Tree,' said Emerald, holding the stick of cadmium explosive up to the light, 'it should create a localised *implosion* in the psychic field. And this should be enough to weaken its control on the village. And fracture the bonds of the psychic transfer geometrics. I hope.'

'And the Tenebrae?' Jess asked.

'They will… no longer have a purpose,' said Emerald grimly.

'What do you mean, no longer have a purpose?'

'Jessica, the Tenebrae were manifested as a response to the power contained within the Whispering Tree. They have been monitoring it for centuries, keeping its ebb and flow under control. They should be its guardians… instead, they have become its controllers, its perverters.'

'Fine,' Jess said, shuddering. 'If the choice is having my soul going off to do time with them, then I'm open to suggestions.'

'There is one small problem, though,' admitted Emerald. 'I do not possess any suitable detonators.'

'I don't suppose we could just spit on it?' Jess suggested archly.

Emerald gave a her a withering look. 'Jessica, there is a time and a place for flippancy,' she said sternly. 'Mainly on popular radio stations, during breakfast.'

'Okay, okay… so what do you need?'

'Something to create a spark,' said Emerald, 'and a method of activating it remotely.'

'Hang on,' said Jess with a grin, and she rummaged in the pockets of Ben's jacket. 'I'd forgotten about this, but...' She pulled out the gold cigarette-lighter which she'd found by the farm-shop – was it really only yesterday? – and handed it triumphantly to Emerald.

'I see. In addition to intoxicants and foul language, you have acquired another anti-social habit?' Emerald Greene muttered.

'God, no! I found it. I was going to give it in to Kate.'

'How very fortuitous...' Emerald snicked the lighter a couple of times experimentally, watching the spark appear and the flame leap up. 'Hmm, simple ignition and a gas propellant... butane? What an odd invention. However, this may be ideal.' She glanced at the letters on the side. 'S.B. Ah, this must belong to Shona Burgess.'

'Ideal for what?' Jess said, absently stroking the smooth sleeve of Ben's jacket.

'Yes,' said Emerald – which was not an answer, of course, but Jess did not press her. Rummaging in her pockets, Emerald produced a roll of parcel tape, a slim silver phone and a handful of what looked like odd bits of a transistor radio. She sat cross-legged in the passageway with the various oddments spread in front of her. 'Do you have one of these?' Emerald asked, holding up the phone.

'Well, yes, of course, but –'

'But nothing. Give it to me.' Emerald held out her hand in an impatient, snatching gesture. 'Come on, Jessica, I will buy you a more expensive replacement.'

'Well... okay,' she said doubtfully, and threw her phone to Emerald. 'Why do you need two?'

'Simplest way of setting up a remote signal.' Aware that Jess was staring at in fascination at the bits and bobs laid out in front of her, Emerald waved her away. 'I can take care of this. You keep watch. Anoushka will assist you.'

'Yeah. Whatever.'

Emerald looked up, then did a double take as she saw Jess still hugging the jacket. 'Jessica,' she said sternly, 'you have to let him go, you know. He has passed over to the dark side. The Ben you knew is not… never was the true person.'

'I know,' she said softly. 'I hate myself. Why did I fall for him?'

'Well,' said Emerald, 'he is a good-looking young man.' She met Jess's surprised gaze. 'I expect,' she added levelly.

'I'll keep watch,' Jess said, and slipped to the end of the passage as Emerald began tearing off strips of parcel tape.

'Gettin' fearful dark, it is,' said Grandma, from the far side of the nave.

Three heads swivelled towards her as one, then looked out of the window to the bending trees and the darkening, storm-lashed sky, and back to Grandma again.

'How do you *know*, Gran?' asked Kate in astonishment.

Grandma Trippett slowly swivelled her electric wheelchair round, so that she was facing them all, her old face wearing a thin, superior smile. She lifted her pale hands to her face and, in a decisive movement, took her dark glasses off.

Her eyes, Richie saw, had pale, powder-blue irises set in yellowing whites, inlaid with the pinkish-red of bloodshot capillaries.

'I'm seein' it,' she murmured. 'I can't say as I can see much else, but I can always see the Darkness.' She shuddered. 'Seen it afore, ain't I? Seen it that day back in May when I were just a little girl, and in my dream when it chased me to the Ford.'

'The Darkness came for you,' Richie murmured, leaning down to the old lady. 'It came for you!'

Grandma Trippett was still staring straight ahead, as if oblivious to Richie. 'Didn't get me, though, not little Emily. Didn't want me, I expect. Too strong for it, see? Seventh daughter of the house, I was, young Richie – you remember the photograph?'

'Yes,' he said. 'I remember.'

'You know what they sometimes say about the seventh daughter. Got the special sight, that's what they believed! Too strong for it. Too strong.'

'The Tenebrae tried to take your soul?' Richie breathed. 'And you resisted?'

Grandma Trippett gave a grim, triumphant smile. 'Yes, Richie. I did.'

Kate was looking around the church in puzzlement. 'Have you seen the Rector?' she asked Richie and Mr Bidmead. 'She was here a second ago.'

They looked around, frantically. The Reverend Parsloe was nowhere to be seen.

'No sign of her,' muttered Mr Bidmead. 'Damnation. These clerics… you never know what they are going to attempt.'

'I'll go and look for her,' Richie said.

Mr Bidmead placed a gentle hand on his arm. 'Best not, lad, eh? Safest in here.'

'But I feel like I'm stuck here doing nothing!' Richie snapped. 'Besides, Jess and Emerald are my friends – and I want to know what's happening!'

There was suddenly a great noise echoing through the church – a rumbling, creaking sound which seemed to be coming from beneath their feet. Richie, Mr Bidmead and Kate looked at one another in alarm, while Grandma gripped the arms of her chair and leaned forward slightly, as if seeing something with her powerful mind.

'What on earth is that?' Kate whispered, looking fearfully around the church.

The noise grew in intensity, echoing off every pew and pillar, and then there was a loud, cavernous BOOM, followed by silence.

'Well, don't just stand there,' said a voice they knew well. It seemed to come from under their feet and from somewhere behind the font. 'Is one of you coming with me or not?'

Richie swallowed and took a step forward, peering round the edge of the font.

There was an opening in the floor which hadn't been there before. It was about two metres square and it led down to a flight of worn-looking stone steps. Standing on the steps, impatiently bobbing her electric torch up and down, was the Reverend Fenella Parsloe.

'How did you…? What…' Richie began incoherently.

'Oh, honestly. It's merely an access hatch to a network of secret tunnels. Most villages have them, you know!' The Rector's chubby face wore a knowing look. 'How do you think I manage to come and go in a place like Little Brockwell without being constantly stopped and asked to do things?'

'Secret passage,' said Richie. 'Wow, that's great!'

'I'd never have got any work done without it, you know,' said the Rector, rubbing her nose awkwardly. 'The link from here to the Green and the Rectory, well, that's been especially useful.'

'The Green! Of course!' Richie remembered their first meeting with the Rector, and how she had seemed to disappear out of sight with remarkable speed.

'Well?' The Rector gave an encouraging smile. 'Are you coming?'

The Tree was whispering.

It could have been human voices that echoed off the nearby houses as the Tree gained a hold on the Green, or it could have been the scraping of the tar-black branches as they tore the earth, ripped up the grass.

They made a *skitter-skatter* noise like restless mice, and a *pop-pop-pop* like breaking glass, and a *scrrritch-scrrratch-scrrritch* like fingers on a coffin-lid.

Tendrils of bark and leaves embraced the telephone box, pressing against the glass. First one pane shattered, then another and another. The metal frame itself of the box began to buckle, creaking under the pressure of the Tree's spindly fingers.

Emerald, running on to the Green, kept her distance. In one hand she held her home-made explosive device, while the other was sweeping a small object, like a microphone, in front of her. Anoushka clung to her shoulder like a witch's familiar.

Jess picked her way across the pitted Green too, making sure to keep in Emerald's footsteps. Her stomach flipped at the sight of the living Tree, thrashing and snaking now, like a caged animal desperate to escape. She tried not to listen to the scratching noises – those sounds which could so easily have been whispering human voices, just at the edge of audibility.

'What's happening?' Jess breathed in horror.

'Psychic reanimation,' said Emerald grimly. 'The Tree is the repository of all the dead minds of the village. It's coming back to life as the Tenebrae's control over it slips.' Emerald swung her microphone-device in a wide arc around them, and the crackling branches seemed to recede as if sprayed with hot steam, waving agitatedly in the air.

'What's that thing you've got there?' Jess asked.

'A simple sound modulator. A version of the device in the van which I used to repel the horsemen – you remember? The correct frequency can help to keep it at bay. For a while.'

'Does it know we're here?' Jess breathed, horrified.

'Oh, yes,' said Emerald cheerfully. 'But luckily, it does not perceive us as a dangerous threat. Not yet, anyway. Which is why we may have a chance…'

'You cannot escape, you know,' said a soft, insidious voice from behind them.

Jess whirled around. There, at the edge of the Green, an ebony-black carriage had appeared, making no sound.

The four horses which pulled it were huge, magnificent beasts, their burnished pelts shining like tar, their nostrils shooting steam into the darkness. Beside them stood the Queen of Shadow. Jess felt her heart drop into her stomach – a primal fear, the terror of recognition, as if she knew this person already.

And there, behind the woman, Jess saw the unmistakable shape of Ben's motorbike. He was a menacing figure astride the saddle, his face hidden now by his dark crash-helmet – just as it had been, Jess remembered, when she had first seen him here in Little Brockwell.

'You may run from us in the physical world,' whispered the Queen of Shadow. 'You may even evade us for some time. But sooner or later, you will need to sleep, and *you will dream*. And when you dream, we will take you.'

Emerald ducked down behind the Tree and began frantically fixing the components of her home-made bomb to the trunk, using a small screwdriver and a length of string. It appeared that the Queen of Shadow had not seen her.

'What do I do?' Jessica hissed.

'Keep her talking! Talk rubbish!' Emerald ordered.

Behind the Queen, the motorbike revved its engine, its flashlight bathing the scene in a strange orange-red hue rather than the usual white. Jess swallowed hard, tried to forget the fear, the betrayal. Tried to forget everything but focusing her courage on now, on this moment which could change everything.

'Okay – so what do you want with me?' Jessica growled, backing up, kicking a loose, snapping tendril of the Tree aside.

'You know what I want. My emissary told you.'

'Yeah, well, your emissary's a lying git, so I'm not too bothered about anything he said,' Jess retorted, aiming her comments at the motorbike. She glanced nervously over her shoulder. Emerald, still fiddling with the screwdriver, gestured frantically to her to continue. 'I mean, it's not on, you know. All that smooth talk. I'm not a stupid little girl any more.'

The woman held up a hand. 'Enough!'

'I've looked fear in the eye,' she said boldly, as the woman raised one gloved hand and her red eyes began to burn with a fierce intensity. 'I've looked it in the eye and told it to f – *nnyaaaghhh!*'

Jess's face contorted as something slid into her brain, something big and dark and cold sliding into her mind like a tentacle. *Trying to take hold.* Her legs suddenly felt unable to support her – and as they gave way, she sank on her knees to the muddy Green.

'Your soul is strong,' said the Queen of Shadow dispassionately. 'And deep… oh, there is pain deep inside! How that pain needs to be taken away.' The glow of her eyes intensified. 'So, I could not make you sleep, though I could extract your beautiful soul from this body, if I wished. But then… no.' She snapped her fingers. The cold slithering in Jess's head receded and the burning in her legs ebbed away. 'It would be weakened. Far better for you to control it yourself, use it willingly… you will be stronger that way.'

Jess staggered to her feet and tried to focus on the dark figure. 'Hey, I like the threads, but maybe black isn't your colour? Goth is *seriously* out this year. Have you thought about getting yourself a nice little green number? It'd look great with your complexion.'

'Silence!'

'Honestly, the things you people say. It's like you get it all out of some villainous handbook or something. You can never say "Change the record!" or "Give it a rest!"… I suppose it's just to shake people up a bit – *nnnyaaaagh!*'

Jess clutched her head and fell to her knees once more. The probing coldness had entered her mind again, and the Queen of Shadow took another step closer across the crumbling, bubbling Green.

'You,' said the Queen of Shadow softly, 'are a deceiver. Your mouth may prattle the inanities of a simple schoolgirl, but in your eyes, in your mind, I see a fierce, dangerous intelligence.'

'Flattery... will get... you everywhere!' Jess gasped, struggling to stay upright on her knees.

The Queen hissed in anger.

Jess closed her eyes, tried to focus her thoughts, summoning all the strength she had. It was like arm-wrestling, only inside her head – the Queen's power pushing her there, straining against her own mind, trying to force her down in submission.

And then it stopped.

Jess, blinking back a throbbing headache, opened her eyes and saw the Queen of Shadow turn and focus her gaze on the crackling bark of the Whispering Tree.

'Who else is there?' the Queen snarled.

Emerald stepped out of the shadows, holding her phone aloft, her thumb over the call-button. Anoushka jumped down and stood beside her, fur bristling.

'Ah, good evening,' said Emerald. 'I expect I should explain a few things.'

'You are irrelevant,' said the Queen of Shadow, her nostrils pinched in disdain. She twirled her cloak with a theatrical flourish. Behind her, the horses snorted menacingly and pawed the earth, their hooves sending flashes of red up into the darkness.

'Well, strictly speaking, I am not,' said Emerald. 'You see, although I hate to resort to these crude methods, I should point out that there is a small explosive device currently attached to the foot of the Whispering Tree. It is primitive, I grant you. But it would be effective if I were to press this button.'

The Queen of Shadow hissed and took a step forward, her eyes glowing with anger.

'You see,' Emerald went on, 'that would send a coded signal to the other phone, causing a small diode to break, and this in turn would strike the flint of the lighter. The resulting spark, next to a quantity of cadmium explosive, would cause quite a large implosion, effectively destroying the Whispering Tree's link to the real world.'

The Queen of Shadow looked from Emerald Greene to the Whispering Tree and back again. Her eyes burned crimson and for a second, Jess felt her mouth turning dry, convinced that Emerald had pushed her too far now.

'What do you want?' hissed the Queen of Shadow.

Richie was following the Rector through a dark, stone passage. She hurried ahead of him, holding her flashlight up and occasionally turning round to shine it at Richie's feet so that he could see where he was going.

'Slow down a bit, Reverend Parsloe!' Richie called, puffing and panting. He stopped to lean against the wall, but the Rector grabbed his arm and pulled him along.

'We cannot stop! The Darkness won't rest, so why should we?'

Richie adjusted his glasses and looked into the Rector's chubby, determined face. 'You really mean that, don't you?'

'Richie, I've spent hours poring over the Church records. The Darkness, the Tenebrae, call it what you will – its power is inextricably linked to this village. It's undeniable!'

'All right, all right… Keep shining the torch back. If I'm walking in darkness,' he added wryly, 'then I want to see a great light…'

*

Jess was trembling. She had been given Emerald's phone to hold. It was hot and clammy in her palm, and her thumb rested nervously on the all-important call-button.

She was holding it while Emerald negotiated.

Negotiated the future with the Queen of Shadow.

Just a few metres away in the reddish-lit gloom, Emerald Greene was talking urgently with the impassive Queen, while Anoushka stalked around them both in an anti-clockwise circle. *Widdershins*, thought Jess with a shiver, not quite remembering how she knew the old word. She felt her teeth chattering, didn't dare look at Ben or at the horses.

Beneath her feet, the branches and twigs of the Whispering Tree churned the earth, meshed with each other and entwined themselves around the smashed shell of the phone-box. Occasionally, a tendril snaked towards Jess, but brandishing the phone in its direction seemed to make it withdraw, snapping and crackling.

One of the dark, hooded riders had stepped forward and was getting something from the coach. It was a big, black wooden box, riveted with iron and firmly padlocked. As Jess watched, the Queen of Shadow gestured to the knight and he took a key from his belt. He unlocked the padlock and opened the chest.

Jess watched as Emerald leaned over the chest, and saw her face suffused for a moment with a dull, reddish glow. Emerald appeared satisfied with what she saw. The dark rider slammed the lid shut, padlocked the box again and handed it to Emerald.

Staggering slightly under the weight of the chest, Emerald placed it on the bench at the edge of the Green. Then she patted the box gently on the lid – as if something was alive inside – and strode back over to Jess, her face grim and pale.

'We have an agreement,' she said.

'We do? What agreement?'

Face to face, the two girls looked one another up and down. Friends, but again with a kind of barrier between them. Jess knew what it was – her reluctance, yet again, to trust this strange, unearthly person who had introduced her to so many new experiences.

'Answer my question,' Jessica said, and she tried her hardest to put a tone of steely menace in her voice. She wasn't quite sure that it worked, because Emerald just gave her a grim, strained smile in response. Jess felt her face glowing with anger.

'I cannot tell you the... exact terms of the agreement.' Emerald glanced over her shoulder, and there – just for a moment – Jess swore she saw her looking frightened.

'What do you want me to do?' Jess whispered in fear.

'Stay here. I am going with *them*.' Emerald gestured at the Queen, the riders and Ben.

'No!'

'It is decided,' she said loudly. Then she lowered her voice to a whisper. 'Watch this portal, Jessica. The second anything comes out of it – detonate.'

'Em... Em, wait!' Jess wailed.

Emerald Greene, striding away, stopped and looked over her shoulder. In the deep, blood-red light, her velvet coat framing her slim form, she looked somehow grown-up, knowing, wise. On her shoulder, Anoushka's green eyes gleamed for a second as if trying to tell Jess something, but Jess did not know what.

Emerald's eyes opened wide for a second or two, and then she shut one eye in a slow, deliberate wink.

Jess felt her heart skip. What was going on here? Why couldn't Emerald tell her?

Emerald stood before the deep, enveloping darkness of the Whispering Tree.

The trunk, now, resembled a pillar of blackness, darker

than the night, darker than tar or pitch, a gateway into a void. The agents of the Darkness gathered themselves there, too: the Queen of Shadow, her expression cold and betraying nothing; the carriage and the horses; Ben, on his motorbike.

For a second, nothing happened. Then, as Jess watched in fear, she saw a shadow fall across Emerald Greene's pale face, darkening her skin to a sullen grey and her hair to a rich purple. The shadow reached out like tendrils – like a hand. Pulling them in.

Jess stepped forward with a gasp.

A second later, the reddish light from around the Green flared as brightly as a bolt of lightning, and Jess, dazzled, put a hand up to her eyes. When she blinked, and looked again, the Green was dark. Beneath her feet, the hissing and the crackling had subsided, as if the tendrils of the Tree were waiting, anticipating something.

Emerald, Ben and the Tenebrae had vanished.

Now, there was a shadow stirring at the base of the Tree. With her heart pounding and her hands sticky with fear, Jess crept forward, not letting go of the phone. The shadow resolved itself into a shape. Legs, a small head. Whiskers.

Anoushka!

'Miss Jessica,' said the cat, as Jess relaxed a little, and he trotted – slightly unsteadily – towards her.

'Anoushka, what's happening? Where have they gone?'

There was a commotion behind them, and Jess turned to see Richie running towards them, with the Rector, puffing and panting, a short distance back.

A roll of thunder echoed across the valley, and Jess looked up at the dark sky, suddenly fearful again.

'I wonder if that means anything,' she said to herself.

The thunder shook the walls of the church, and Mr Bidmead spun round in the nave, glowering up at the pillars. 'Ah, the elements conspire too. How very apt.'

'Mr Bidmead,' said Kate Trippett uneasily, folding her arms and looking him up and down, 'am I to understand that you're not really an antiques dealer after all?'

Mr Bidmead rubbed his eyes. 'Oh, my dear, how very tiresome. Must I go through this again? Yes, I am an antiques dealer, but you don't seriously imagine that is my entire life, do you? I am an agent of a Government department which does not officially exist.'

'Oh, no,' said Kate with a groan, 'you mean like in *The X-Files*?'

'Heaven preserve us,' said Mr Bidmead softly, leaning on his cane and glancing briefly up into the rafters. 'Yes, if you like,' he said with heavy sarcasm.

Grandma Trippett banged her stick on the stone floor of the church, and the others turned to look at her in surprise. 'Stop prattling, the pair o'you!' snapped Grandma, holding up her hand. 'I can feel something.'

'Gran?' Kate suddenly felt cold, and pulled her cardigan tightly around her. She ran over to Grandma, squatted down beside the old lady's wheelchair and took her hand. 'Gran, what are you saying?'

'Something's changed,' said Grandma Trippett softly. 'Something's not right. It's just a sense... one of your young friends...'

Kate felt herself turning pale in horror. 'Oh, no. No.' She put a hand over her mouth and started to back away. 'What do you mean?'

'Calm yourself,' said Mr Bidmead, taking Kate's arm. 'It may mean nothing. We have no idea of what is happening out there.' He fished his slimline radio out of his pocket, pressed a couple of buttons, tutting in frustration. 'And this thing doesn't appear to be working, dammit! I could have called for Special Measures reinforcements, got this business sorted out hours ago.'

'That wouldn't work,' said Grandma contemptuously. 'No… you have to meet the Darkness on its own terms. Give it what it wants.'

'And what's that?' said Kate, shuddering.

Grandma Trippett took off her glasses, stared sightlessly into the gloom, as if realising some deep, universal truth.

'A soul,' she whispered. 'They've taken a soul.'

The thunder intensified. Jess glanced nervously from Richie and the Rector to the Whispering Tree and back again. Anoushka prowled around the Tree, sniffing and mewling.

'He knows something,' said Richie at last. 'Moggy! What is it?'

And Jessica stared into the black, unyielding heart of the Tree. It was a tunnel of blackness now, a tunnel with light at the end of it.

Jess had a glimpse of tall stone towers and of red lightning flickering around steely, black mountains, and then the impression was gone. Now there was a wind, a cold wind, howling out of the Tree and into Little Brockwell, into their world.

Something was coming out.

'Back away!' Jess shouted, retreating to the edge of the Green.

'What is it?' Richie asked. 'What is it?'

The Rector, who had been standing and watching in incomprehension, peered over her glasses. Her jaw dropped and she clutched at her crucifix with her spare hand. 'I think we should pray,' she said firmly.

'Whatever works for you, Rector,' Jess muttered. 'Me, I'm always up for the practical solution.' She lifted the phone in both hands, pointing it high in the air like a starting-pistol, her thumb over the call-button. With her feet planted firmly apart,

Jess braced herself.

'What are you doing, girl?' The Rector grabbed at Jessica's sleeve, trying to pull her back to safety. 'Get away from there!'

Jess squared up to the Tree, narrowed her eyes, ignoring the fierce, snapping tendrils of bark which were trying to entwine themselves around her legs.

The rushing wind grew in intensity, now, and Jess was dimly aware of the Rector and Richie behind her, staggering back. She felt the cold, harsh needling on her skin, she felt the evil chill reaching out for her with clammy fingers, and yet she remained firmly rooted to the spot, holding the phone like a talisman.

Like a screech of anguish across the emptiness of space, like the screams of the dying, like a hurricane it howled. A pinprick of white was there against the darkness, like a single, icy star. And it was growing. Growing. It became the size of a coin, then the size of a hand.

Jess lifted the phone high above her head – keeping her eyes fixed not on the thing emerging from the tunnel but on the makeshift device which Emerald Greene had fixed to the bottom of the tree-trunk.

Now she could see the thing hurtling towards her, she could make out the wheels, the handlebars, the dazzling light of the motorbike. The visored helmet of the rider.

Jess swallowed hard.

The darkness seemed to shimmer and break for a moment, and the motorbike smashed its way out, tearing the fabric of reality, leaving a trail of smoke and bark and burnt grass in its wake. It screeched to a halt on the Green, the wheels carving up a trench in the earth and slicing through tendrils of bark as the bike came to a stop.

With the darkness all around and the headlamp of the bike dazzling her, the rider was not quite visible to Jess. It was like a living shadow.

'You get back,' Jess said, and her voice trembled. 'Back, now!'

The rider reached up and unclipped the crash-helmet.

Jess's finger tightened on the call-button.

The rider lifted the crash-helmet off, and suddenly Jessica saw a wisp of red hair unfurling, and then another. And as the helmet came off, she saw tomato-red locks tumbling over a pale, intelligent face, and she looked into the eyes of Emerald Greene.

And then the Tree blurred and shimmered again, and another figure leapt from it – young and male and dark-haired. Ben hit the ground with thud, doing a commando-style roll on to his shoulder, knocking Emerald flying from the bike.

Jess didn't even look at him.

'Now!' hissed Anoushka, hopping on to Jess's shoulder. 'Do it now!'

She paused, hardly daring.

'Quickly!' hissed Anoushka. 'They are coming, and they will be angered at the deception! We *must* seal the gateway for ever!'

Jess narrowed her eyes.

Deep within the blackness, what looked like a hundred angry horsemen thundered towards her, eyes blazing. She briefly took in the skull-faces of the ghostly horses, the glinting of their lances, the red sparks flashing up as if struck by a hammer from an anvil, and, there, among them all – more of a sense, an impression in her mind – the Queen of Shadow in her chariot, her dark eyes full of rage.

She saw it all in a second.

She looked into the eyes of the Queen of Shadow.

Shaking, she swung her arms down in an arc until they were extended in front of her. Oblivious to everything around her, ignoring the shouts of Richie and the Reverend Parsloe, she held the phone out in both hands, pointing it like a weapon at the heart of the Whispering Tree.

'You *are* the weakest link,' she said softly. '*Goodbye.*'

She pressed the button.

The phone beeped.

There was a dull *ooomph*, then flame and smoke gushed from the foot of the Whispering Tree, as if someone had set fire to it. Jess was thrown to the ground by a hot, powerful rush of air which rolled her over and over in the earth.

Shards of blazing bark shot outwards, scattering across the Green, some of them zig-zagging across the grass with alarming force.

Then, the fire and smoke seemed to turn in on itself, to be sucked into the void with a great, bellowing roar. And Jess was sure she heard a scream of pain inside her mind.

She had a brief vision of a tall, black column like a whirlwind where the Whispering Tree had stood, and then that, too, dwindled, as if pulled deep beneath the ground. There was a great sucking noise and then a *pop*, as if something had just vanished from existence.

Jess felt the phone dropping from her numbed fingers. She lay on the muddy ground, exhausted, and was aware of the others rushing forward to see the smoking crater where the Whispering Tree had stood.

Anoushka slowly lowered his head, as if saddened by something. He sat on the grass and scratched his ear, then he sidled up to Jess and nuzzled her.

'Hey, moggy,' she whispered, sitting up, not quite sure now what was real and what was illusion. 'Either I'm hyper-awake, or dreaming, or you're actually being affectionate for once.'

Anoushka purred softly. 'No,' he said, in his usual clipped tones. 'I've just realised something, that is all.'

'What?'

Anoushka sat down and scratched an ear with his back

paw. 'It's a little embarrassing,' he admitted, 'but I think I am down to just two lives now.'

10
Aftershocks

'I cannot force this on you,' said Emerald Greene, as dawn rose over Little Brockwell. 'You must take it of your own volition.'

They were in a dark, featureless room with brick walls and a wooden table. Three pairs of black orbs stared out from the eye-sockets of Tyler, Casey and Will.

The children made no sign of having understood her, nor even having heard her. Behind them, armed Special Measures men formed a solid and unyielding barrier, while Mr Bidmead stood to the side, watching, leaning on his cane.

Emerald Greene lifted the wooden chest on to the table – the chest which the Queen of Shadow had given to her as part of their agreement – and began to unlock it.

One of the younger Special Measures men moved forward, uneasily reaching for his gun, but a raised hand from Mr Bidmead was all it took to forestall him.

'It's all right,' said Mr Bidmead. 'I've got this.' He met Emerald's gaze and gestured to her. 'You may proceed.'

'Thank you,' said Emerald Greene as she unlocked the chest. 'I did not need your permission, but I expect it makes you feel better.'

She pulled the padlock free, swung back the hasp and, standing behind the chest, lifted the solid wooden lid. An ancient, creaking noise echoed off the walls of the small room.

Inside the chest, three football-sized black orbs pulsed

with a soft, reddish light.

'The containers themselves are irrelevant,' said Emerald to the children. 'A mere depiction in the physical world of something which it is impossible to make. What is inside them is the important thing.'

There was silence.

The children remained impassive.

Then, at last Casey Burgess stepped forward. At the edge of her black, evil eyes, something was glistening.

As they watched, a tear welled up, responded to gravity and made its glistening, wobbly way down her pale face. Her hand came up, stretched out, her fingers opening.

Emerald exchanged a triumphant look with Mr Bidmead. 'I was right,' she said. 'There is still enough humanity in them for the desire to be there...' She exhaled deeply. 'Thank goodness for that!'

'Rather restores your faith in human nature, Emerald, m'dear. Perhaps this race of ours has something to recommend it, after all.'

Emerald tilted her head on one side, as if seriously considering the question. 'No,' she said. 'I would not go as far as that.'

Mr Bidmead chuckled. Then, he said, 'A question, if I may?'

'Yes?'

'How did you obtain them?'

Emerald looked shifty for a second. 'A bargain of necessity,' she said, taking her glasses off and polishing them. 'It would not be helpful to go into the details.'

'I see.' Mr Bidmead pointed with his cane to the three pulsing globes. 'And, pray tell me – how do we make sure they each get the right one back?'

Emerald replaced her glasses on her nose. 'We are not talking about three identical pairs of trousers, Mr Bidmead, nor three identical hats. Not even three reasonably similar pencil-cases. No...' Emerald turned to look at him. 'The essence of humanity. The soul. You would know your own, would you not? It is like looking into your own face.'

Mr Bidmead looked Emerald Greene up and down for a second. Then he gave a reluctant, thin-lipped smile.

'I under-estimated you, Miss Greene,' he said, and stepped back, tapping on the floor with his cane. 'Proceed!'

The children stepped forward.

She was waiting for him when he emerged from Kate's house.

She stood there, arms folded, coldly watching him as he shrugged on his motorcycle-jacket, walked with that casual, calm air down the garden path. She made sure to be wearing sunglasses, so he could not see the redness of her eyes.

Jess could see Kate watching them from the window. She was trying to hide behind the curtains, to make herself inconspicuous. It wasn't working.

The distance between them narrowed to ten metres, five, three. Jess held up a hand.

'That's far enough,' she said.

Ben spread his hands, smiled. 'I suppose I deserve that.'

'Yeah. I suppose you do.'

There was a silence. Then he gestured towards her. 'Kate said you needed to speak to me.'

She nodded. 'Are you feeling okay now?'

'A bit light-headed. I still...' He rubbed his eyes awkwardly. 'I still don't remember a lot of what happened back there, you know.'

For a second, she felt her heart give a little leap. Was that possible? That he really... But no. She had made a decision. This could not go any further.

'How long have I been asleep?' he asked.

'About twenty-four hours.'

'Wow. Like a really bad hangover.'

'You could say that.' She did not allow herself to smile. 'The doctor's looked you over, Kate told me. You'll live. For now.'

'Well, that's a bit cruel, Jess.'

'Yeah. Maybe you deserve it.'

He folded his arms. 'Have you invited me out here just to insult me?'

'No.' She steeled herself. 'I need to know…'

'Yes?' He raised his eyebrows expectantly.

'How much of it was real, Ben?'

That was it. The question was out there. The question she had kept bottled up inside her for a day, hardly daring to think it. She had realised that she would burst if she did not ask it, even if she feared the reply.

'What do you mean?' he asked. He sounded pleasant, casual. As if they were having a conversation about the weather. His face gave nothing away.

'How much of it was *real*?' she repeated. 'The time we spent together… the… You know. In the beer-garden, up on the hillside…'

'Oh.' He thrust his hands in his pockets, looked away nonchalantly. There was even the ghost of a smile on his face now. 'That.'

'Yes, that. Was I just some stupid girl you had to snare as part of the plan? For that… creature? Or did I ever actually mean anything to you?'

He looked at her, now. Looked at her properly. His dark, moody eyes compelled her to look directly at him, and she felt herself, despite everything, excited and scared again.

'I don't know,' he said eventually. 'I… I'm fond of you. I guess.'

'Fond.' She repeated the word in a disgusted tone. '*Fond*? You make it sound like I'm… I'm… a cat. Or a dog.'

'Sorry. Maybe that's the wrong word.'

'Yeah, maybe it is.'

She was astonished that she was controlling her rage. But it suddenly felt right. The anger gave her control, it gave her direction. It made her all the more certain that this conversation was going to be final, and it filled her with a kind of strength. It was a strength which flooded her body like a rush of adrenaline, making her realise it would hurt later. But she had it now, when she needed it.

'I just need to hear something from you, Ben. Something that says... that it may have been... important. That you weren't under her control. I know... I know there were... dreams and stuff, and... and it's hard to remember what you were doing, but...'

'Look, Jess,' he said awkwardly. 'It's maybe for the best. You're a bit... well... You're younger than me, y'know? You're still... working stuff out. I've been through all this.'

'Oh, great. Thanks for the work experience. I appreciate it.'

'I didn't mean it like that.'

She opened her mouth to give him a caustic response, then thought better of it. She tried something else. 'In the pub garden,' she said. 'Just... that moment. When you said you were with me, and put Georgie Popplewick in her place. You remember?'

He nodded. 'Yeah. I remember.' He half-smiled now. 'That was quite funny.'

'It wasn't just funny, Ben. It was... It was the first time, you know? That someone's...' She was struggling, and hoped he would know, hoped he would join the dots here. 'I know loads of Georgies. Dozens of girls like her. Slim, cool, confident, effortless. And guys like you swarm around them like flies round...'

'Honey?' he suggested.

'I was going to say something else. But if you like... But you... You didn't. You made it clear I was important. That I *mattered*.'

He spread his hands. 'Glad to be of service.'

'But, you know what? Thinking about it since... Why did that matter so much to me? Why do I care? Am I really so vacuous, so worthless, that I need the validation of people like you and Georgie Popplewick?'

'I dunno, Jess.' He frowned. 'You tell me.'

She shook her head, looked away. 'I'll come back when I've got an answer,' she said. 'I'm still working stuff out, remember?'

Silence hung in the air, now. It seemed they had finally run out of things to say to one another.

'Are you staying in the village?' she asked eventually.

'No, I... I've got a few plans. Things I can do before college.'

'Right... Well, I'm off soon. Back to Meresbury.'

'Yeah. Okay.'

'Maybe we'll text each other, or... Snapchat or something.'

'Sure. Write something witty.' He nodded to her, and turned to go back into the house.

'Ben.' In just the one syllable of his name, her voice cracked, and she hated herself for that.

'Yeah?' He stopped, looked over his shoulder.

'Have a good life.'

He looked puzzled for a moment, then smiled. 'Oh, yeah. That. Yeah, I mean to. Don't worry.'

He turned back towards the house, walked back up the path, opened the door.

Inside, she was screaming to call him back. Her body was aching to run to him and hug him, despite everything, one last time.

But she stayed where she was, her sunglasses hiding her face, and he closed the door and went inside, and it was as if a shutter had come down. A barrier had closed on a part of her life, and a light had come on, allowing her to move on.

The afternoon sun was warm as Tyler Uttley, aged ten-and-three-quarters, strode down the gentle hill from his parents' farmhouse to the village.

There was a cricket match on the Meadows today. White figures flitted on the sunlit grass, their movements graceful as they fought a very English battle. Tyler, swishing a stick through the hedge as he walked, wondered if he would meet up with his friends later. They might watch the game, he thought, as they ate ice-creams bought from the van which parked by the Green on Saturdays.

In the Post Office, he smiled shyly at Miss Trippett. She looked at him in concern – like he was ill or something, Tyler thought.

'Hello, Tyler,' she said. 'What's it to be today?'

'Wine gums, please,' he said, and held out a handful of change. 'I'm… not sure I've got enough.'

'Tell you what,' said Miss Trippett kindly. 'Have these on me.'

And, before Tyler's wide eyes, she got the jar down, shovelled a generous helping of wine gums into a paper bag and held them out to him.

'Are you sure?' he asked.

'Of course,' she said. 'Go on.'

'Thanks!'

'And, Tyler?'

'Yeah?'

'Are you… feeling all right now?'

He stopped at the door to the Post Office and General Stores, frowned.

A picture had come into his mind, just then. Something about *not being all right* before. A bad dream.

Something about a dark horse, and a girl... A weird, red-haired girl holding a black ball, like a bowling-ball, to his head... And the ball containing all of his memories, and all of his personality, and everything that... everything that made him Tyler Uttley.

What a weird dream.

When had he had it? Probably when he was ill, he thought. He knew he'd been ill, and that he was better now.

Tyler popped a wine gum into his mouth and looked up at Miss Trippett's concerned face.

'I'm fine, thanks, Miss Trippett,' he said, chewing happily. 'Just fine.'

At the edge of the Green stood an ornate, wooden caravan, led by two horses. Not dark, terrifying horses like the Tenebrae, Richie Fanshawe was relieved to see – these were elegant creatures, with pelts of a shimmering, creamy brown and manes of snowy white. They looked ruminative, patient and wise.

Kim, the travellers' leader, patted each of the horses on the nose and, Richie was sure, spoke a brief word to each of them before striding across the sunlit Green to shake hands.

'You did a good job, you and your friends,' he said softly.

Richie puffed his cheeks out and exhaled. 'It... looked a bit dodgy for a while,' he confessed.

'Will's found a new friend,' Kim added, pointing over to the caravan.

Will Carver and Casey Burgess were sitting side by side on the end of the caravan, swinging their legs, laughing and chatting. Richie decided he'd better not interrupt.

'You never know,' Kim added, 'perhaps the people of Little Brockwell might even be a bit friendlier next time we're passing through…'

'Anything's possible,' Richie said. 'Although some people are never going to change. That Mick Parks bloke, for one. Not the biggest fan of your community.'

'Ah, yes…' Kim folded his arms. 'Livvy's father.' He looked down at the ground for a second, deep in thought. 'Livvy, you know, seems to have gone through quite a trauma. Some of the women in our group, they have… experience in these things. They know certain ways to help. I know your friend Emerald repaired some of the damage, but…' Kim shook his head. 'Who knows how else she may have been affected?'

'Well,' said Richie thoughtfully, 'I suppose you can only offer.'

They both looked over at Casey and Will again. They had been joined, now, by young Tyler Uttley, who was laughing and sharing a packet of sweets with them.

'As for *them*,' Richie murmured, 'I'm still not quite sure what happened there…'

'I think they're fine,' Kim said. 'Better than ever. After all – it's not every day you get your soul back.'

Jessica Mathieson stood in the middle of a gently-sloping field of rippling corn, gazing blankly – or so it seemed – into space.

Her eyes were red-rimmed and her face showed the strain and stress of the past few days. Anyone watching her would have remarked that she suddenly looked older, wiser than her fourteen years.

A figure appeared on the brow of the hill behind her. Red hair blazed in the evening sun, and blue glasses caught the sunset and reflected it twice over. Emerald Greene was a tall, imposing silhouette, her velvet coat a dark stripe against the evening blue.

'No sleep?' she asked.

Jess did not need to turn round.

'Well?' Emerald said.

Jess closed her eyes for a second or two, then opened them again. 'Some,' she said. 'It won't come naturally. I'm… scared to.'

'You must,' said Emerald. 'You must try, now. You can even dream. They will not come for you, you know. They have gone. Truly, they have.'

Jess did not answer. She just kept staring straight ahead, over the waving ears of corn to the field beyond, down into the valley at the sinking, orange orb of the sun.

'I need hardly remind you,' Emerald said softly. 'Sleep is as essential as food. Without it, your serotonin and dopamine levels begin to fall. Your core temperature will drop. You will begin to shake, to have no control over the trembling in your body. Your neural receptors start to dull, and you find yourself responsive to auto-suggestion.'

'I know all that,' she snapped crossly.

Emerald opened her mouth to add something, then seemed to think better of it. She thrust her hands deep into the pockets of her velvet coat.

'Is Anoushka okay?' Jess asked, still not turning round.

'He is well,' Emerald replied.

'Good. Just wondered. After all… it's not every day you lose a life.'

'True,' said Emerald, 'very true. I had hoped to save his seventh life… right up to the last minute. I truly did. But… it proved impossible.'

'It was very good of him,' said Jess softly. 'Sacrificing one like that.'

'You understand,' said Emerald Greene, 'that it was his own decision? I could not possibly have made Anoushka do that. The idea of exchanging his soul for the children, of maintaining the deception that it would be mine. It came from him.'

'Yes. I thought so.'

'However,' Emerald went on, 'I am pleased to say that your swift action with the explosive device will have sealed the gateway for ever... Anoushka's reign will have been a mercifully swift one.'

'And I left a bloody great hole in the middle of Little Brockwell's village green, too! I don't know how Special Measures are going to explain *that* one away to the guys at the tourist board.'

'Oh, they will think of something,' said Emerald absently. 'They always do...' She checked her watch, looking almost embarrassed. 'Are you... coming back to the house?'

'In a bit,' said Jess. 'I want to watch the sun go down.'

'Oh. Very well.'

Emerald turned to go.

'All this is going to go,' said Jess softly, making Emerald pause, turn back.

'I'm sorry?' Emerald said.

'All this corn. It's going to be harvested. In just a few weeks.'

'Well, yes. That, I believe, is the nature of agriculture,' agreed Emerald Greene, tilting her head on one side in that inquisitive, feline way of hers.

'Change,' Jess said. 'That's what I mean. The end of summer. It's kind of... symbolic.'

'Ah. I see.'

'No, I don't think so,' Jess murmured.

'I think I do. You... cared for someone. He was false. He has moved on. Nobody seems to know where... You learnt a valuable lesson, and now it is time for you to move on as well.'

'Yeah.' She blinked, a long slow blink. 'Whatever.'

'Things change, Jessica,' said Emerald Greene. 'People come and go in our lives. These things build us, these things make us strong.'

Jess gave a short, scornful laugh. 'Sure.'

'You doubt that?' Emerald asked, concerned.

'It's just… I'm sorry if I don't buy it, but… Anyway, what would you know, Emerald? After all, you've never been in love.'

Emerald Greene raised her eyebrows, opened her mouth to speak, then closed it again. A curious, intense expression passed across her high-cheekboned face, one which Jessica, still facing the sunset, would never see – a mixture of surprise, hurt and passionate anger.

Then, like a cloud across the sun, it passed on, faded away and was gone for ever.

'No,' said Emerald softly. 'Perhaps not.'

And she turned on the ridge and strode down towards the village, not looking back.

Jess stayed for a while.

She folded her arms across her body, hugged herself, told herself that there was to be no crying this time, that she was strong. A young woman, not a little girl any more. In just a few weeks, she would be fifteen. There was no going back.

Her destiny was sealed. She just wished she knew what the hell it was.

These things build us, these things make us strong. Emerald was right, of course. She knew that. Emerald Greene, damn her, was always right. Always there with all the answers, yet none of the answers at all.

This was the first evening upon which Jess stayed and watched, just long enough to see the sun vanish, the orange-edged sky turning a deep blue, almost black, as around her the murmur and clink and rustle of late evening turned into the more unfamiliar sounds of the night.

The first evening when she let the cool breeze wrap

around her in the darkness, and listen, and watch, and *sense* what else, beyond mere hearing and sight, might be out there, as her hand tingled with the familiar chill.

The first evening when she gazed out at the huge, undulating expanse of the dark country and realised that he was gone, that there was no going back, and that it was as if no shadow of his being was left upon the face of the Earth, now. Only the memories.

The first evening when tears ran down her face for the remembrance of things lost: a taste of apples, the sound of chiming guitars, a warm jacket, a stolen kiss upon a chalk horse high on the hill. The memory of her heart hammering wildly, and of a moment of happiness so perfect, so beautiful, it could never be recaptured in her life again.

The first evening when she would remember all this and feel empty, and lonely, and lost and incomplete.

The first, but not the last.

Not the last by far.

The hitch-hiker stood at the edge of the village.

Here, gardens gave way to open fields and rolling hills, and the lane led to the main route into the towns and cities. The landscape became empty, featureless except for a line of pylons and the winding, grey strand of the A-road.

A big, thundering juggernaut slowed and stopped in response to the upraised thumb of the hitch-hiker at the side of the road. He was a boy of maybe seventeen, in a motorcycle jacket and jeans. He had floppy black hair and a studied air of cool arrogance, and he was hefting a sizeable sports-bag.

The boy, slipping a pair of sunglasses over his eyes, hurried to the waiting lorry. The cab door opened and he climbed up.

'Where to, mate?' said the lorry-driver cheerfully.

The boy slung his bag behind the seat and settled

gratefully into the passenger seat.

'I don't know, yet,' he said. 'Away from here.'

'Not running away, are you, mate?'

'Nah,' said the boy, and he leaned back gratefully in the seat. 'Running towards something.'

'Very deep,' said the driver. 'What's your name, mate?'

'Ben,' he said.

'Righto. Well, Ben, no questions asked, mate. I can take you as far as Newport Pagnell, if that's any good?'

'Fine by me,' said Ben.

The lorry indicated, pulled out from the side of the road and accelerated away along the grey strip of the A-road.

Into the future.

'Right!' said Aunt Gabi, as she shoved the last suitcase into the boot of her car and slammed the boot shut with enough force to go right through the driveway. 'I think we're ready!'

The morning sun was weak in a cloudy, grey sky, and Gabi, Jessica and Richie had already said their goodbyes to Rose Cottage. Rhiannon was coming back tomorrow, school started again in a few days, and Gabi had pretty much finished her university work – so there was no more reason to stay around.

Beside the car, a little reception committee stood waiting – Kate Trippett, Grandma and Mr Bidmead. To Richie's obvious embarrassment, both Kate and Grandma hugged him and kissed him on both cheeks. Jess couldn't help smiling as she saw his discomfort.

'You look tired,' Kate said to Jessica. 'Have you been sleeping all right?'

'Stayed up all last night. Watching the night sky.'

'Well, that's quite cool… It's been a few years since I was a teenager, but I sort of remember that's one of the things you have to do. A rite of passage.'

'Mmm... Listen, you'll let me know?' Jess murmured. 'If you... hear from him?'

Kate frowned. 'I wouldn't have thought you'd ever want to see him again, Jess.'

Jess gave a little half-smile which could have meant anything. 'I just don't like unfinished business. That's all.'

Grandma Trippett approached, her motorised wheelchair whirring quietly, and Jess leaned down to kiss her on the cheek. The old lady took both of Jess's hands in hers and leaned to speak quietly into her ear.

'Take care, comely girl,' said Grandma Trippett. 'And let your hand guide you,' she added.

Jess was smiling as she straightened up. 'Thank you,' she said softly. 'I will.'

'What?' Richie asked, suspicious. 'What will you do?'

'I'll explain later,' Jess told him.

Mr Bidmead came bustling forward, beaming. He kissed Aunt Gabi on both cheeks – much to her surprise – and then shook Richie's hand with enough force to send the boy nearly off-balance. 'Young man! Now, remember what I said to you in the church... experience, boy!'

'Y-yes,' Richie said awkwardly.

Jess gave him a quizzical look. 'Well, that's one you can explain to me later!'

'Now, I need a quick word with young Jessica,' said Mr Bidmead, 'if you wouldn't mind.'

'We'll be in the car,' said Aunt Gabi. 'Don't be long!'

Gabi slid into the driver's seat, laughing, and Richie got in the passenger seat beside her. The engine started, and Jess saw Kate and Grandma Trippett leaning into the window, sharing some joke or other with Gabi.

Mr Bidmead gestured for Jess to follow him, and they took a few steps across to the other side of the village street. Now Jess was effectively alone with Mr Bidmead, where nobody else could hear what either of them had to say.

Mr Bidmead shook Jessica's hand. 'Well, young lady,' he said. 'You and your friends are all very interesting, I have to say… for different reasons.'

Jess scowled, folded her arms. 'What's that supposed to mean?'

Mr Bidmead leaned on his cane and looked sternly at her over his half-moon glasses. He suddenly looked even older and wiser than before to Jess, and she shivered as she felt a strange sense of the unknown, the undreamt-of.

Jessica could only guess at the strange relationship which Mr Bidmead now had with Time. She decided he wasn't at all like Mr Courtney and Mr Odell, the Special Measures men she had met last year. They had been firm, brisk, stuck in the certainties of their military attitude. Mr Bidmead was more interesting, more elusive. She had the feeling that she was going to see him again.

'I merely mean,' said Mr Bidmead, so softly that Jess had to strain to hear, 'that everyone has their part to play. A great darkness may have been cast out… a battle won… but the war against the forces of evil is never won, Jessica. It goes on. And ever since you, Richie and your enigmatic friend Miss Greene came to Little Brockwell, I've had the oddest feeling that you're going to be part of it. A big part.'

Jess folded her arms, tried to look nonchalant. 'Oh, yeah? So you can see into the future, then, can you?'

Mr Bidmead laughed. He seemed to find this genuinely funny. 'See into the future. I like that. Ha-ha.'

'Was that funny?'

'It was, yes.' Mr Bidmead's expression suddenly became stern and cold again, and he lifted his walking-cane so that it was pointing at her. Jess took an involuntary step backwards. 'The past and the future… they are merely two different words for the same thing – speak one word and some may hear the other. Or hold a mirror to one, and you may see the image of the other.'

'Do you always speak in riddles, Mr Bidmead?'

'Only on Thursdays,' he said delightedly. He raised his hat to her and gave a little bow.

Jess pondered this for a second. 'It's not Thursday,' she objected.

'Really?' Mr Bidmead twirled his cane. 'How extraordinary.' He pulled out his pocket-watch, flipped it open and peered at it. 'Time is marching on. You'd better rejoin your friends. Go back to your life in Meresbury, at St Agnes' School for Girls, and await the next moment of import. It'll come. Be sure of that, Jess, m'dear. It'll come.'

'Right,' she said uncertainly. Her hand, she noticed, was tingling.

As she walked away from Mr Bidmead, she turned, gave him a little wave.

Mr Bidmead waved back.

Jessica's mind was racing as they drove home, and she hardly exchanged a word with Richie or Gabi. It should have felt like the end of something, she thought. And it was, of course: the end of summer, the end of Ben, the end of the Tenebrae and of her time in Little Brockwell.

But she couldn't help feeling that now, in her dealings with this strange world to which her eyes and ears had been opened, the crucial moments were just around the corner.

And it suddenly didn't feel like the end any more.

Instead, it felt like the start of something even bigger.

In the village street, outside the Dark Horse, Mr Bidmead flipped open the top of his pocket-watch again.

'Poor girl,' he said. 'There's no way I could tell her, of course.'

A tall shape unfurled itself from the shadows of the nearby houses – and emerged into the light as a familiar, red-haired figure, with a black cat trotting loyally at her heels.

Emerald strolled, hands in the pockets of her long velvet coat, over to where Mr Bidmead was, and stood beside him. Anoushka, feigning indifference, decided to choose this moment to wash his paws.

'You would risk upsetting a very delicate equilibrium,' murmured Emerald Greene. 'The Darkness has been banished, for now, but the Enemy has many forms.'

'I know that,' Mr Bidmead snapped. 'And when it comes to fighting it, we've all got different ideas – haven't we, girl?'

Emerald did not answer. Instead, she indicated the open pocket-watch which Mr Bidmead still held in his hand like a talisman. 'You are no nearer to finding the answer, then?'

'What do you think?' he snapped.

Together, they looked down at the watch.

The inside cover, which was about six centimetres across, was inlaid with a colour photograph which appeared to show the translucent image of a girl in Victorian dress, standing in a modern-day cathedral precinct and clutching a posy of flowers. The girl was in her teens and looked extremely worried. Although the girl was ghostly and pale, her features were very clear – it was unmistakably Jessica Mathieson. Her hair was elegantly braided in nineteenth-century style and her nose-ring was conspicuously absent.

The picture was one which another Special Measures man, Mr Courtney, had shown at a secret presentation in a bunker beneath London several months earlier, shortly after the strange events at St Agnes' School in Meresbury. Mr Bidmead had been in the audience then – and now, even after he had met Jessica Mathieson, he was no closer to understanding the picture.

'A message from the past?' said Mr Bidmead. 'Or from

the future?'

'Who knows?' said Emerald.

'Maybe you,' said Mr Bidmead, narrowing his eyes.

'Maybe. That would be telling.'

'Don't use her,' Mr Bidmead warned softly. 'You've seen how she hates being used, that one. She's got a temper. Wonderful, when used correctly, but I wouldn't want to be on the wrong end of it.'

Emerald's face gave nothing away. Anoushka hopped on to her shoulder, digging his claws into the velvet for a firm purchase, and settled down as if to go to sleep. Emerald scratched him behind his ears. He changed his mind, though, and hopped down again, curling around her legs.

Mr Bidmead flipped the watch shut and replaced it in his pocket. For a moment, there was silence in the deserted village street.

'Well,' said Mr Bidmead, peering at the clouds which were massing above the ridge, 'I do believe there's a storm coming.'

Emerald Greene narrowed her eyes and, just for a moment, shivered.

She was looking not at the sky but at something else. Something invisible, intangible, deep within her thoughts alone.

'I know,' she said. 'I can feel it.'

Then she turned and walked away, not once looking back, Anoushka trotting loyally at her heels.

Within a minute or two, the first drops of rain began to darken the streets and roofs. But by then, the girl and her cat had disappeared completely.

Books by Daniel Blythe

For young readers

Doctor Who: Autonomy
Shadow Runners
Emerald Greene and the Witch Stones

For reluctant readers

New Dawn
Fascination
I Spy
Kill Order

For adult readers

The Cut
Losing Faith
This is the Day

Non-fiction

The Encyclopaedia of Classic 80s Pop
Dadlands: The Alternative Handbook for New Fathers
I Hate Christmas: A Manifesto for the Modern-Day Scrooge
X Marks the Box
Collecting Gadgets and Games from the 1950s-90s
Famous Robots and Cyborgs

Still available: Emerald Greene's first exciting adventure
Emerald Greene and the Witch Stones

'Severe temporal disturbance,' said Emerald casually. 'That, I am afraid, is what happens if you go poking into old places that are best left alone.'

What is the secret of the tomb which the eccentric Professor Ulverston has unearthed in an ancient stone circle? Where does the talking cat come from? And why have Mr Courtney and his Special Measures operatives arrived in town?...

With unearthly apparitions stalking the land, Jess and Richie soon realise that their mysterious new classmate might be the only one to know what's happening. But it seems Emerald Greene has her own secrets – and nobody is quite sure whose side she is really on...

Also available:
Shadow Runners

Miranda's new home is a seaside town at the edge of the world, the sort of forgotten place where nothing ever happens. Until something does. Something strange and sinister.

With her schoolteacher and her odd new classmates, who might know more than they let on, Miranda sets out to uncover the mystery. She thinks she's chasing shadows, tortured spirits from centuries past, but could true darkness lie within? With a mixture of science and magic in play, Miranda has to figure out how to break and banish the evil before it destroys her.

Daniel Blythe was born in Maidstone, Kent. He grew up an avid reader, especially of the *Doctor Who* novels, and as an adult was lucky enough to become a writer for the *Doctor Who* books himself. He is now the author of many books, both fiction and non-fiction, for adults and for younger readers. He has taught on the Creative Writing MA at Sheffield Hallam University and has led writing days in hundreds of schools. He lives in Yorkshire, with his wife and their two children.

www.danielblythe.com